FIXED POINT

A PSYCHOLOGICAL THRILLER
OF FATE AND OBSESSION

BY LYNN M. KRISTOPHER

Feline Orchid Publications, LLC
27251 Wesley Chapel Blvd
Ste B14 #760
Wesley Chapel, FL
www.lynnmkristopher.com
ISBN (eBook): 979-8-9987865-0-1
ISBN (Paperback): 979-8-9987865-1-8
ISBN (Hardcover): 979-8-9987865-2-5

Book Cover Design and Interior Formatting by 100Covers.

First edition, June 2025

TABLE OF CONTENTS

This novel is dedicated to my dad, who said he might even read it twice.

Content Warning

This book contains scenes depicting mental health struggles, including
depression, suicidal ideation, and self-harm.
Power-based exploitation and sexual assault (non-explicit)

Reader discretion is advised.

Early Praise for *Fixed Point*

"Mindblowing read!!!! This was a brilliant story that kept me guessing and invested throughout the story. I was tired, but I needed more and kept reading until I finished this. I sat in silence processing it and letting it soak in. This is the type of book I love. It felt so full of possibilities and promises that resonated with me. A must read."

— **Beverly**, reviewer via BookSirens

PROLOGUE

"Hey Maya! What are you up to today?" Olivia asked, standing outside the laboratory building amid a snowy backdrop. She was delaying her entry into the lab, trying to prepare herself for her dreaded PhD committee meeting.

"Oh, well, I'm being *sent* downtown, of course, in the middle of this snowstorm, to deal with these student surveys. You know how Karen can be." Maya tilted her head toward the building, where Olivia could see Dr. Karen Lynch, her mentor, engaged in an intense discussion with Bradley Parker, the university ombudsman.

"I saw her in there talking with Bradley just now, and she looked absolutely pissed. I'm sure you're gonna have fun at your meeting," Maya said with a wry smile, her eyes twinkling in the brisk winter air.

"Right. Thanks for the heads-up about Bradley. Just what I needed to hear before my meeting. I should say I'm surprised she's making you travel in this weather, but I'm not," Olivia said.

"Yeah, I know. I had hoped she would become a better person after she married that psychologist, but I guess that was just wishful thinking," Maya said as she climbed into her car, her engine idling.

"Drive safely," Olivia said as Maya slowly reversed out of her parking space and began her slow trip downtown.

Olivia turned her attention back to the laboratory building, her attention drawn to the picture window. She took a deep breath, steeling herself for the meeting that awaited her. She felt uneasy about this, but with determination, she walked into the building and made her way towards the conference room.

The room was emptier than expected, with only her PhD committee members, Dr. Edward Kingsley and Dr. Sean O'Brien, and the university ombudsman, Bradley Parker, in attendance. Bradley Parker, dressed in a fitted sweater and tailored charcoal-gray pants, seemed to demand attention, his horn-rimmed glasses adding to the performance. Dr. Kingsley, tall and lean, exuded smugness with his British accent and polished appearance, always donning designer suits and accessories. In contrast, Dr. O'Brien looked unkempt, his rumpled clothes and disheveled hair suggesting a lack of care, while a faint scent of alcohol hinted at his rumored habits.

Dr. Lynch's absence stood out, given her role as Olivia's mentor and her expected presence at the meeting. Her external committee member, Dr. Walker, would be joining via Zoom. Bradley Parker was not on the schedule. Although Olivia had met with him to discuss the misconduct involving her committee members, she ultimately chose not to report it. But she now suspected Bradley was just as corrupt as the rest of her committee—he hadn't kept their conversation private. It hardly mattered that she had stayed silent, focusing instead on trying to graduate in a few months.

The purpose of this committee meeting was to set a date for Olivia's upcoming dissertation defense. Her committee had assured her she was well-prepared and on track. She hadn't anticipated any major issues—until she spotted Bradley Parker through the window.

"Please, take a seat, Olivia." Dr. Kingsley's voice bore the weight of authority, embellished with his unmistakable British accent.

"Shouldn't we wait for Dr. Lynch and make sure Dr. Walker can join us on Zoom?" Olivia asked.

Dr. O'Brien, who seemed to be in his usual drunken state, let out a slight chuckle. Meanwhile, Bradley, positioned near the closed door, observed Olivia with an air of condescension through his horn-rimmed glasses.

"Olivia, Dr. Lynch has recused herself from her role as your mentor and advisor." Dr. Kingsley, maintaining his stern demeanor, broke the surprising news to Olivia.

"What? Why?" she asked, her eyes widening, her voice catching on the words.

"We've noticed that you've expressed your dissatisfaction with this lab and have raised concerns with Bradley that appear to have upset Dr. Lynch," Dr. Kingsley said.

Olivia's mouth went dry, her pulse pounding in her ears. The warning from one of the postdocs, Sofia, echoed in her ears: "Just keep your mouth shut and do what she says, or Dr. Lynch will ruin your life." Olivia's fingers tightened around the edge of her seat. She had ignored Sofia's warning, thinking she could trust Bradley Parker. Now the weight of that choice crushed her.

"We also have concerns regarding several items in your research, including study design, interpretation of results, and conclusions presented in dissertation sections," Dr. Kingsley said, "So you will need to make substantial revisions, even if we find a replacement for your advisor."

Olivia had always excelled at maintaining her mundane routine: updating computers, erasing whiteboards, and completing the straightforward dissertation tasks assigned by Dr. Lynch. Her committee had repeatedly assured her that she was on track to graduate within the next month or two. But now, after her conversation with Bradley, sudden concerns had emerged about her work.

"After careful consideration, we have placed further evaluation of your dissertation on hold. It is very clear to us that completion of your dissertation defense in the next few months is not possible given the deficiencies in your early draft and the process constraints of replacing Dr. Lynch," Dr. Kingsley concluded, delivering his final remarks with a measured tone, as if he were reciting from a prepared document.

Once more, Olivia remained in silence, her emotions teetering on the edge of tears, yet she held them at bay. The last thing she wanted was to give them the satisfaction of witnessing her distress over what felt like a farcical decision.

"We understand that this is a difficult process and want to assure you that we are here to provide support. There are also student counseling services available on campus," Dr. Kingsley said, a subtle, almost mocking smirk playing at his lips.

He ended the meeting with a decisive rise from his chair. Bradley swung the conference room door open and stepped out, setting the departure in motion. Dr. Kingsley followed, prompting Dr. O'Brien to trail behind.

Olivia rose from her chair, her limbs heavy, each step toward her car felt like trudging through thick mud. Once inside, she gripped the steering wheel, her knuckles white, her breath hitching. Minutes stretched into what felt like hours as she stared at the dashboard, a hollow ache settling in her chest. Words from her committee chair echoed in her mind. Every late night in the lab, every page she had written, every ounce of herself she had poured into this journey—gone.

Olivia had spent years turning a blind eye to the troubling instances of academic misconduct and the unsettling behavior of her lab members—though unsettling was putting it mildly. She had convinced herself that staying quiet and focused on her work was the safest path. And now, it seemed, all her efforts were for nothing.

She eased her car out of the parking spot, her grip tight on the steering wheel. The events of the meeting pressed down on her, heavy and unrelenting, as she made her way back to her apartment.

When she got home, Olivia went straight to her bedroom, where her perpetually grumpy old terrier, Mulder, greeted her with a disinterested glance. He heaved a heavy sigh, as if to convey his indifference, before returning to his slumber.

She thought about contacting a lawyer. Was it worth considering a lawsuit for retaliation? The idea crossed her mind, but she dismissed it. She couldn't afford legal fees, and the school knew it. They held all the cards, fully aware that they could act with impunity.

Once again, Olivia sank into a profound depression. For days, she remained cocooned in her bed, emerging only to shuffle to the kitchen and prepare toaster waffles for Mulder.

After a while, Olivia summoned the courage to reach out to several attorneys. But her efforts proved futile. Every lawyer she contacted refused to take her case. Their explanations stung even more—because she wasn't technically an employee, her situation was an uphill battle for whistleblower or retaliation claims. The staggering cost of five hundred dollars per hour for legal services only underscored her limited options. With each rejection, Olivia felt herself sinking even deeper into the abyss of her depression.

After nearly a month, Olivia decided to explore alternative options. She reached out to several schools, hoping to transfer into another PhD program. But she quickly encountered a harsh reality—Dr. Lynch had blacklisted her.

She branded Olivia as lazy, troublesome, a disruptor, and unable to stay focused, tarnishing her reputation by spreading unfavorable information to every physics PhD program on the East Coast. The aftermath of her smear campaign left a bitter taste, as schools refused to accept Olivia because of her damaged standing.

Dr. Lynch had ruined Olivia's life, leaving her with no discernible options in sight. She couldn't transfer to another school, and finishing the program she'd been suffering through here was impossible. Regret clung to Olivia. Why hadn't she just stayed silent? It had become painfully clear that she was powerless to alter the trajectory of her fate. Throughout her life, Olivia had repeatedly tried to improve her circumstances, yet it appeared the universe had a cruel penchant for constantly raining misfortune upon her.

Why didn't the people in her lab just disappear? Why did those who behaved reprehensibly always land on their feet? Why did the universe reward the undeserving while leaving her buried under hardship?

Olivia knew what she had to do; she had no other recourse left. Her life had unraveled to a point where it was utterly irreparable. The thought crept into her mind that perhaps everyone, including herself, might be better off if she simply ceased to exist. Her mother had died when she was young and her father abandoned her, leaving her in the shadow of his new family.

Her so-called "colleagues" in the lab didn't just undermine her—they inflicted emotional wounds, smeared her reputation, and ruthlessly sabotaged her career. Even her dog didn't really like her. It was as if the universe had conspired against her, making her believe that she truly didn't deserve a place in this world anymore.

Olivia filled the bathtub with warm water, her movements slow, almost mechanical. She sat on the edge, toying with a razor, running her thumb absentmindedly along its edge. With little thought, she placed it on the rim of the tub and slid into the bath, still fully clothed, the warmth of the water wrapping her in a strange comfort. She felt a sharp sting—a brief, intentional movement—and then the warm water felt heavier somehow, pulling her down, making her limbs feel weightless but heavy all at once.

She thought she heard something—a bark, maybe, or footsteps just beyond the door. Mulder? It was hard to tell. Her vision blurred, and she blinked, struggling to focus. As darkness crept in, she felt the faintest brush against her hand—a presence, maybe, or just her imagination.

Then, nothing.

CHAPTER 1

She dreamed about the wall again. It was always the same dream. Slow motion, misty, the roses climbing up the stone wall. She reaches through the mist to touch the flowers but never gets the chance.

It was nineteen degrees in Boston this morning, and of course, it was snowing. Olivia had always despised the snow, and each flake seemed to mock her decision to move here. Yes, she had come for the unparalleled opportunities to pursue her physics PhD—but on mornings like this, she couldn't help but question everything. She was supposed to graduate this spring—six years after she first arrived.

From her second-floor apartment window, she spotted her landlord outside. He lived below her in the two-family home and he was always good to her. As far as she knew, he didn't have any family, so he treated her like his daughter. He was always helping her carry groceries, take out the trash, and shovel her car out when it snowed. He was up early this morning, already plowing the driveway.

She made the mistake of trying to pet Mulder, the grumpy old terrier she found by the dumpster outside the Chinese restaurant. He always growled and snapped whenever she tried to pet him.

It took her months to get him close enough that she could snatch him and bring him inside. His fur was long and matted, tangled with leaves and twigs, and covered in fleas. Olivia brought him to the vet, who sedated him for an examination and cleaning. Despite being old and thin, he seemed in good shape. He grew fond of sitting next to Olivia and sleeping in her bed, but he did not allow affection.

She had been dreading this day. This morning's meeting with her PhD committee was intended to focus on scheduling her dissertation defense for the upcoming spring—everything had been on track. But now, she was almost certain they knew she had spoken to Bradley Parker, the ombudsman, about their scientific misconduct. The ombudsman was meant to address student concerns confidentially and provide guidance, but when Olivia had met with him, she wasn't so sure he would keep quiet.

Before this, she had never stood up for herself, and she had doubts about meeting him. It never occurred to her that she would actually file an official complaint. All she wanted was to tell someone—but now it was too late. They knew.

She threw on the same clothes she wore every day: baggy jeans and an old black sweatshirt from a random '90s rock band she loved. Today it was Tool. On her way to the kitchen, she couldn't stop thinking about her committee. She hated them. When she began her graduate program, she was filled with so much hope. Convinced of her abilities, she believed she could learn so much and change the world.

It felt like everything fell apart when she discovered how corrupt and cutthroat academia could be. She wished her committee members would just disappear. If they didn't exist, she could pursue the temporal theories that had led her to study physics.

She shook her head and focused on the task at hand, trying to get Mulder to eat his breakfast. Of course, he just sat on the bed, staring at her as if she were crazy for offering him a bowl of dog kibble. She sighed, giving up. Instead, she made herself a cup of coffee and a quick breakfast of toaster waffles, which she shared with Mulder.

As she was about to leave, she noticed Ethan had forgotten his keys. She realized it was odd; Ethan never forgot his keys, even though he took public transportation. A miniature hourglass keychain, its delicate glass encasing tiny flecks of sand, added a touch of charm to the otherwise mundane task of carrying keys. He spent the night but left before Olivia woke up.

Ethan was a lab technician she had started dating, but he ended up having a remarkable impact on her. He had entered her life when she was low, considering quitting her program, but he had a knack for lifting her spirits. He appeared to have genuine concern for her and supported her with the challenges in the lab. However, he also discouraged her about reporting her committee for misconduct, warning her about the potential consequences.

"Olivia, I'm just worried," he said last night. "You know I agree with you, but if you report them… it's risky."

His words echoed in her mind as she grabbed his keys and tossed them into her bag. After a moment's hesitation, she pulled on her coat and gloves, braced herself against the cold, and trudged out to her car.

"Good morning Livvy! Mulder not coming down this morning?" her landlord said from his truck as he continued to plow the driveway.

3

"Nah, getting him out in the snow is impossible. Thanks for plowing early this morning," Olivia said.

"No problem. I thought I'd get a jump on things in case you were heading off to school early. Do you want me to get Mulder to come out later?"

"No, that's ok. I don't think he'd appreciate that, and I'll be back soon anyway, so I'll take care of him. Thanks again!" Olivia said.

Her landlord waved as he kept plowing, and she backed out of the driveway.

Olivia lived about a ten-minute drive from the campus, and the trip was easy. Boston usually prepares for snow, and the city had already begun clearing the roads. While driving to the lab, her mind wandered, and the dream of the stone wall resurfaced. It had been a persistent dream for years, almost daily, sparking a feeling of familiarity that she didn't understand.

When she arrived outside of the lab, Maya, the administrative assistant, was outside loading boxes of paperwork into her car. Maya, impeccably dressed, had worked at the lab for fifteen years. Despite the snow today, she wore a designer sweater in a striking shade of blue, and pressed slacks that clung to her figure. Her heels, though impractical for the weather, added a touch of sophistication to her ensemble. Her blonde hair was meticulous, pulled back with a stylish, jeweled hair clip.

Olivia couldn't help but feel a tinge of self-consciousness as she glanced at her reflection in the side mirror of her car. She passed a comb through her unruly brown curls, finding amusement in the irony that she worried the committee might perceive *her* as unprofessional.

She watched Maya for a few minutes before focusing on the laboratory building. The conference room, positioned at the front of the building, had a large picture window that allowed Olivia to spot her committee's gathering spot. A beta fish used to live in a small bowl on the windowsill, but Maya took him home. Olivia used to tune out of her meetings in the conference room by watching the fish.

The longer she had worked on her graduate degree, the more she learned about her mentor, Dr. Karen Lynch, and the less she felt compelled to engage in the lab meetings. It had become clear that Dr. Lynch fabricated and falsified data, rendering most discussions irrelevant, as her mentor didn't actually conduct any research. So, more often than not, Olivia stared at the beta fish. As expected, nobody in the building would make weekend trips to feed the fish, so Maya had brought him home a few weeks ago. So, unfortunately, Olivia couldn't just stare at the fish today.

What Olivia saw today through the picture window was Bradley Parker, wearing a fitted sweater—the kind that screamed *look at me* rather than subtlety or taste. His tailored, charcoal-gray pants were used to highlight his tall, lean frame and his choice of horn-rimmed glasses, that he didn't need, only added to the spectacle.

He had no business being there today, as he was not on her committee. His office was miles away at a satellite campus. She felt a sinking pit in her stomach and trembled. What should she do? Should she just leave? Quit her program? How was she supposed to have her committee meeting when she thought Bradley might be there to bring up their "confidential" discussion?

Olivia took several deep breaths and a giant swig of her coffee. When she talked herself into getting out of her car, she delayed her entry into the building further by sauntering over to chat with Maya.

"Hey Maya! What are you up to today?" Olivia asked.

"Oh, well, I'm being *sent* downtown, of course, in the middle of this snowstorm, to deal with these student surveys. You know what Karen is like," Maya said. "I saw her in there talking with Bradley just now, and she looked absolutely pissed. I'm sure you're gonna have fun at your meeting." She gave a sly smile, nodding subtly toward the building.

Olivia tilted her head to the side and gave Maya a strange look.

"You all right?" Maya asked.

"Uh… yeah. It's just… I swear I've heard you say that before. Déjà vu, I guess," Olivia said, though her mind raced. The words tugged at a distant memory, something she couldn't quite place. Had she heard it in a meeting? A lecture? The nagging familiarity gnawed at her, but the harder she tried to grasp it, the more it slipped away, like trying to hold water in her hands.

Shrugging, Maya carried on loading the cardboard boxes of student surveys into her car.

"Anyway… thanks for the heads-up about Bradley. Just what I needed to hear before my meeting. I should say I'm surprised that she's making you travel in this weather, but I'm not," Olivia said.

"Yeah, I know. I had hoped she would become a better person after she married that psychologist, but I guess that was just wishful thinking," Maya said.

"You know, I was already dreading this meeting, and now—" Olivia stopped, feeling a subtle rumbling beneath her feet.

Then a shockwave rippled through the air. The force of the explosion knocked them to the ground, and they tumbled across

6

the parking lot. The deafening roar echoed in her ears as she lay on the ground, disoriented. It was a struggle to push herself up from the ground; she was too dizzy and weak to move. She felt a warm, sticky sensation near her hairline, and her hand came away smeared with blood.

She shifted onto her side, turning toward the laboratory building, where flames and smoke billowed upward from the rubble. Her heart raced as she saw Maya lying unconscious at the far end of the parking lot and what she thought might have been Bradley's legless body nearby. The acrid stench of burning debris permeated the air, making her nostrils burn, while the thick dust and smoke made it difficult to breathe. Darkness closed in at the edge of her vision, the distant echo of sirens fading.

And then there was only black.

CHAPTER 2

"What the fuck?" Special Agent Rachel Quinn said into her cell phone.

Special Agent Ted Mitchell, her partner, rolled his eyes and looked at her, palms up, one eyebrow arched in silent question. He mouthed the word "Problem?", his voice barely audible, almost imperceptible.

"We need to go downtown immediately. Someone blew up a fucking university lab," she said as she disconnected the call.

Mitchell's lips twitched in a half-smile, his demeanor calm. "Luckily, we don't have to go too far this time."

Rachel gave him a dry look, her eyes narrowing slightly. After a decade defusing literal bombs as a Special Agent Bomb Technician with the FBI, her patience for dark humor in moments like these was thin.

"So, what's the situation?" Mitchell asked, his chair creaking as he pushed back from his cluttered desk. His worn leather jacket hung over the back of the chair. He joined Rachel by the door, lines etched deep into his face from years of intense investigations. "Think it's another domestic terrorist?"

Rachel's jaw tightened as she shook her head. "Let's not rush to conclusions without more information."

"Right," Mitchell said. "Because you never jump to conclusions."

They'd been partners since the beginning—ever since the Boston field office had assigned him as her mentor when she first arrived. With a significant twenty-year age gap between them, Mitchell brought a wealth of experience to their partnership. He wasn't a bomb technician, but his deep knowledge of explosives and years in the criminal investigation unit made him an expert in everything that could go wrong.

Rachel rolled her eyes and sighed, running a hand through her tousled hair. "But it sounds like a mess," she said, almost to herself.

She glanced at Mitchell, but his expression didn't mirror hers. Beneath the surface, she caught a shadow of doubt in his eyes—like he could read her thoughts and knew she was holding something back.

"It just happened, so I think we need to move on it fast, maybe look for other bombs at the school," Rachel said.

They were amidst a sea of cubicles in the Chelsea field office; the air filled with the hum of other conversations and the click-clack of keyboards. Papers shuffled, phones rang, and agents moved between desks, all engrossed in their own investigations.

Mitchell's attention shifted to a stack of papers on his cluttered desk. "Good thing we wrapped up that case in Minnesota," he said, sliding a completed report into a manila folder. "Now onto the next crisis, it seems."

"I have to finish a report too, but this is the priority."

"Any word about what kind of explosive we're dealing with?"

"Not yet," Rachel said, frustration creeping into her voice. "But we won't know until we get there. ATF is likely on their way."

"Well, let's not waste any more time than," Mitchell said, as he reached for his jacket slung over the back of his chair.

Rachel followed suit, slipping into her own jacket and preparing herself for what lay ahead. They moved with purpose, each step echoing as they gathered the specialized equipment, their movements efficient and practiced. Rachel grabbed her toolkit, which included her standard items like screw drivers, drill bits, and flashlights. Mitchell secured his tactical vest, adjusting the straps with practiced precision. She didn't entirely believe that her specialized ninety-pound protection suit was necessary, but she always kept it in her trunk. With their gear in place, they headed for the elevator, their movements synchronized like a well-oiled machine.

Once they were outside and settled in Rachel's car, Mitchell glanced over at her, his expression serious. "I can see it on your face. You think it's him, don't you? You always think it's him."

Rachel couldn't shake the unease that settled over her like a heavy blanket. Every callout came with its own uncertainties, but this one felt different. They always did. It stirred memories of a bomber she'd encountered in Georgia during her first case—a man who had haunted her across the country for the past decade. Despite her relentless pursuit, she had never caught him, a failure that weighed heavily on her conscience and gnawed at her daily. Every new case reignited the same nagging suspicion. And yet, she scolded herself for always jumping to thoughts of him.

"Shut the fuck up."

As they trudged through the snow toward the university, Mitchell said, "You know, if you keep swearing like that, the money in your kids' swear jar might just cover their college tuition."

———————— ❖ ————————

Rachel, being a Boston native, didn't drive cautiously in the snow, but by some stroke of luck, they arrived safely. Mitchell, originally from Florida, always entrusted Rachel with the driving duties. Despite spending fourteen years with the FBI in Boston, he never quite grew accustomed to the snow.

Amidst the winter backdrop, the small campus appeared striking, with just five red-brick buildings. Two buildings housed classrooms and the campus library. The third building, usually abuzz with student activity and home to classrooms and a small cafe, was unusually quiet this morning, with students noticeably absent. There were beautiful courtyards between the buildings, adorned with benches and pine trees covered in fallen snow.

Rachel drove past the main academic buildings, heading toward the nearly hidden research facilities tucked at the back of the campus. Her eyes scanned for signage that might hint at their purpose. One read "Research Labs & Offices." The other, its lettering weathered and half-faded, stated "Advanced Physics Research – Linear Accelerator."

She slowed, squinting at the second sign. "Linear accelerator." The term stirred something in her memory—faint, undefined, and oddly unsettling. She couldn't recall exactly why it sounded familiar, especially since she'd never been to this university before. But the feeling lingered, like she was brushing up against something she should remember.

As they approached the research area, a scene of chaos and commotion interrupted the winter tranquility of the campus. Thick plumes of smoke billowed into the frigid air from the building that housed only labs and offices, obscuring the surroundings, while yellow caution tape cordoned off the area. Flashes from police lights and the red glow of ambulance and fire truck beacons lit the scene in pulses. Members of the press had converged, cameras and microphones poised to document the unfolding drama, their breath visible in the crisp air. A curious crowd of onlookers had gathered nearby, their faces a mix of worry and fascination. A sharp sense of urgency hung over everything as the search and rescue team, aided by dogs, dug through the rubble.

Rachel and Mitchell stepped out of the car, taking in the scene before them. Without hesitation, Rachel jumped into action, determined to locate the first responders who could get them up to speed. She found a group of officers attempting to keep the press at bay.

"Hello officers, we're with the FBI. Could someone fill us in on the situation?" Rachel said above the noise.

"Officer Kirkland, over in the grass, can help you out," one officer said as he pointed over toward one ambulance.

Rachel and Mitchell jogged over to the ambulance to find Officer Kirkland as the press leaned over the yellow caution tape, shouting questions and clamoring for information. As they crossed, Rachel's sharp eyes glimpsed someone standing absolutely still among the reporters, a compact figure cloaked in a hooded sweatshirt. It was him. The bomber she had been pursuing. She saw him for just a split-second, but he slipped into the crowd, disappearing before she could move.

Rachel scanned the crowd of reporters, trying to locate him. She approached the yellow caution tape, positioning herself so she could get a better view. But as she pushed forward, the crowd seemed to swallow him whole. The man in the sweatshirt had vanished.

The press was relentless, bombarding her with questions as she turned her attention back to Mitchell. He cast a cautious glance her way, his expression asking, *What's on your mind?*

Rachel shook her head as they continued toward Officer Kirkland. The bomber's taunts lingered in her mind, echoing from Georgia to Virginia to Massachusetts. She still thought about him daily, even seeing him in places where he shouldn't be.

"Officer Kirkland, I'm Special Agent Quinn and this is Special Agent Mitchell with the FBI. Can you tell us what happened?"

"We have limited details on the explosion's cause. We're still working on finding other survivors… or victims," he said.

"Bradley Parker was dead at the scene. A student, Olivia, and one professor, Dr. Karen Lynch, were still alive. Olivia was unconscious but didn't appear seriously injured—at least externally. Dr. Lynch, though, was severely burned," Officer Kirkland read from his notebook.

"Oh, and Maya is here receiving treatment," he gestured toward a tall blonde woman sitting on the ambulance's back bumper.

"Thank you for the information. Have you interviewed anyone yet? Any witnesses?" Rachel asked.

"We've interviewed a few onlookers, but no one has a clear account," Officer Kirkland said, nodding across the street toward two people speaking with another officer. "We've isolated a few individuals for further questioning."

As Officer Kirkland spoke, Rachel's eyes flicked toward the two individuals across the street, standing with another officer. She nodded in understanding, then scanned the sea of faces again, searching for any sign of the man she thought she had seen earlier.

"They suspect this might not have been an accident," Kirkland said as he jotted down details about the two witnesses and handed the information to Rachel.

"Well, I appreciate your help, Officer Kirkland," Rachel said.

"Of course, Agent Quinn. We'll do everything we can to assist. My little sister goes to this school."

———◆———

Rachel and Mitchell quickly crossed the street, weaving around the press to reach the two individuals Officer Kirkland had held for them to interview. According to his notes, they were Dr. Arthur Lloyd and Dr. Tina Williams, both researchers in the physics department whose offices were located in the building with the linear accelerator.

As they approached, Rachel guessed Dr. Lloyd was in his sixties. He wore a neatly pressed suit with a perfectly knotted tie. His professional look completed by distinctive white hair and thin-framed glasses, as if he'd stepped straight out of a scientific journal.

In contrast, Dr. Williams seemed the embodiment of eccentricity, dressed in a mismatched ensemble of a colorful blouse, loose slacks, and a lab coat. Her short, heavy-set frame only emphasized the difference between them. But it was her unkempt salt-and-pepper hair that caught Rachel's attention. It gave her the look of a stereotypical mad scientist.

When Rachel introduced herself, both professors offered polite nods, but neither smiled. Dr. Lloyd adjusted his glasses, avoiding her eyes, while Dr. Williams clutched her coat tighter around her, glancing briefly toward the damaged building. They looked rattled—but beneath that, there was something else. Rachel caught the sharp glint in their eyes, not quite fear. Interest.

"I understand you don't think this was an accident," Rachel said.

"Of course not. That building's just offices and computer labs—with whiteboards. No chemicals, no chance of an accidental explosion," Dr. Lloyd said.

Rachel watched as Dr. Lloyd and Dr. Williams exchanged uneasy glances while trying to piece together what might have happened.

"But you don't work in that building, correct?"

"No, we work in that building," Dr. Williams said, gesturing toward the sign for the linear accelerator.

"What kind of research do you do with that accelerator?" Rachel asked.

"Oh, we don't use it much anymore," Dr. Williams said. "We've all been conducting research with high-energy physics, computer programs, competing for Department of Energy grants."

Rachel's attention sharpened as she listened, intrigued by how little they seemed to use the linear accelerator—and by what those Department of Energy grants might really be worth.

"The linear accelerator speeds up charged particles—electrons, protons—to incredibly high speeds. It can even collide them, which could potentially cause a tremendous explosion," Dr. Lloyd said, glancing at Dr. Williams. "So I suppose we're lucky she didn't choose to blow up that building."

15

Concern was etched on their faces, a quiet recognition of how narrowly they'd avoided disaster. They still looked shaken, no doubt imagining how different things might have been if the explosion had happened in their own building.

"Who is she?" Rachel asked.

"It has to be Olivia, Dr. Lynch's graduate student," Dr. Williams said, shaking her head, her voice unsteady. "She's always so quiet, dressed in black, listening to that headbanger music. It's always the quiet ones."

Rachel noticed Dr. Williams trembling, still visibly shaken. But there was a sharp edge to her voice—an unsettling certainty that hinted at more than just fear.

Dr. Lloyd nodded in agreement. "Bradley Parker confirmed her arrogance and reluctance toward completing her PhD. He said that she's miserable here and has been spreading rumors about Dr. Lynch and her committee chair, Dr. Kingsley."

"What type of rumors?" Rachel asked.

"Well, we don't want to gossip…" Dr. Lloyd said.

Rachel furrowed her brow as she jotted down notes. She wondered if gossiping was exactly what they wanted to do. For such intelligent professionals, their eagerness to implicate a student was surprising. But in her line of work, nothing was off the table. Maybe they were pointing fingers to protect themselves.

"Wait a second," Mitchell said. "Isn't she a physics student? What makes you think she'd even know how to use chemicals to blow up a building?"

"You can find anything on the internet," Dr. Williams said, her tone implying the obvious as she glanced down at the ground.

Mitchell shook his head, looking between them, which prompted Rachel to step in and steer the conversation forward.

"Do you know if anyone else was supposed to be in the lab today?"

Dr. Lloyd leaned back, thoughtful. "I'm uncertain about the attendees, but Olivia had a committee meeting planned with Dr. Lynch, Dr. Kingsley, and Dr. O'Brien. It was Dr. Lynch's team in the building, and they have their own schedules."

Dr. Williams nodded in agreement. "And Maya, of course."

"Thank you for your time," Rachel said, extending her card toward them. "If you think of anything else, please call us."

Mitchell remained silent throughout the conversation, quietly observing the professors and forming his own impressions. Rachel hadn't made up her mind yet, but she hadn't ruled out the possibility that the student, Olivia, was involved. They crossed the street again and returned to the ambulance, where Maya was still receiving treatment.

"Hello, Maya," Rachel said. "We're from the FBI, and we were wondering if you'd be willing to answer a few questions."

Maya regarded them for a moment before answering, her voice uncertain. "I'm not sure how much help I'll be. I didn't see anything. Olivia and I talked outside, and then… I was on the ground across the parking lot."

"So, you and Olivia weren't inside the building?"

"No," Maya said. "We were right by my car when all hell broke loose."

"Any idea who was in the building?"

"When people come in, they have to sign in with me," Maya said. "Dr. Lynch, Dr. Kingsley, and Dr. O'Brien were all there for Olivia's committee meeting. Bradley was there to meet with Dr. Lynch."

She paused, taking a deep breath before continuing. "Dr. Franklin Collins—he's got a lab in the building—was there too. Brittney, one of Dr. Lynch's postdocs, called in sick this morning. The other postdoc, Sofia, and the lab tech, Ethan, hadn't shown up yet. They don't usually come in before ten."

"Could this be an accident?" Rachel asked.

"I'm not sure. You mean like a gas line explosion or something?" Maya asked.

"Well, some of your colleagues seem to think someone may have done this on purpose."

"Dr. Lynch is nuts. I wouldn't put it past her to blow herself up," Maya said.

Rachel seized on the comment. "Do you think Dr. Lynch could be involved?"

"I don't know, but she is a crazy bitch. She married a psychologist just to score free therapy." Maya paused. "I think I'm gonna throw up."

"Alright, Maya. We appreciate your cooperation."

Rachel and Mitchell stopped to update Officer Kirkland and then walked back over to Rachel's car.

"What do you think?" Rachel asked Mitchell.

"Let's not take any chances. We should station an officer outside both Olivia's and Dr. Lynch's hospital rooms," Mitchell said. "We should also assign someone to find the postdocs and the lab tech."

As Rachel sped away from the university toward the hospital, Mitchell dialed the field office. If Olivia or Dr. Lynch were involved in the explosion, there was a real risk they'd vanish before anyone uncovered the truth.

CHAPTER 3

The roses, shrouded in mist, remained beyond Olivia's reach. However, this time, she thought she saw a subtle hint of snowfall before she awoke. The harsh buzz of fluorescent lights overhead filled the room with a relentless, high-pitched hum and her eyes stung with discomfort. A throbbing ache pulsed through her head, intensifying with any attempt to move.

The walls, painted a clinical shade of pale blue, offered no comfort, only amplifying the room's cold, sterile atmosphere. The steady hum of the lights and the rhythmic beeping of machines told Olivia she was in a hospital. As she scanned the room, she thought she glimpsed a mourning dove perched outside the window, its soft cooing faint in her ears. She shut her eyes and shook her head. When she opened them again, the bird was gone and the window revealed nothing but falling snow. Confusion clouded her thoughts as she tried to piece together the fragments of her memory. She couldn't remember how she had ended up here.

She reached out to touch the bandage on her forehead, where the dull pain throbbed, but she couldn't remember how she had sustained the injury. What had happened this morning?

All she could remember was seeing Bradley through the picture window.

Faint voices of hospital staff and patients drifted from the nearby hallway. Now and then, a sudden commotion would escalate into raised voices and hurried shouts as doctors and nurses rushed to attend to an emergency.

The persistent ache throbbed in her head. Closing her eyes, she longed for silence, trying to remember how she had gotten here. As she struggled to concentrate through the pain, a nurse swept into the room, her words an indistinct murmur. Disoriented, Olivia strained to hear through the room's underwater-like sounds, but the nurse was gone before she could make sense of what was happening.

A very tall young man in a white coat entered the room only a few seconds later, marked by an unexpected booming greeting that startled Olivia.

"HELLO OLIVIA," the doctor said, causing Olivia to squint and grimace, pulling her head back to escape the sudden onslaught of noise.

"Oh, I'm sorry, Olivia. I thought you might have trouble hearing. I'm Dr. Richardson," he said as he shined a bright pen-light into her eyes. "Can you tell me what year it is?"

"2020," Olivia said, her voice raspy, faltering.

"2020? Are you sure?"

Olivia hesitated, "Well, yes, I saw a mourning dove and I… my notes and… I thought maybe the river… um… I'm sorry, I think I'm just confused."

"Do you know what city you're in?" Dr. Richardson asked.

"Boston," Olivia said.

"Okay," Dr. Richardson said. "Do you know who the president is?"

"Yes, it's Biden," Olivia said.

"Okay, Olivia. What year is it?" Dr. Richardson asked again.

"2023," she said, her voice trembling.

"Good. Your head injury is a mere bump, as confirmed by the CT scan upon your arrival. We believe you have no concussion, but we're keeping you overnight for observation to make sure."

Olivia shook her head and closed her eyes, a fog of confusion pressing in. The image of a snowy stone wall with roses flashed through her mind again. The doctor scribbled a few notes on her chart, then reassured her he'd return later to check on her.

When Olivia opened her eyes, they landed on a familiar-looking vase with a red ribbon sitting on her bedside table—the kind found in any hospital gift shop. It held a single rose. She didn't expect it was from her family. Her mother had died when Olivia was in high school, and her father had long since moved on, marrying someone only two years older than Olivia. The idea of him traveling to New England, let alone ordering from 1-800-Flowers, seemed far-fetched. She figured it must have been Ethan who'd come by while she was still unconscious.

The nurse returned, and Olivia weakly asked for water. Then, her voice barely audible, she whispered, "What happened?"

The nurse leaned in. "Don't worry, dear. No one will bother you. There's a police officer stationed outside your door to protect you from anyone who may want to harm you."

"What do you mean?" Olivia asked, her anxiety rising as her eyes darted around the room. The nurse's words caught her off guard. *What had happened? Had someone hurt her?*

21

Then, in a sudden, overwhelming rush, the memory slammed into her. The deafening explosion echoed in her ears again, her body jolting with the force of it. She saw herself lying in the parking lot outside the lab, pain stabbing through her skull. The grim image of Maya. The possibility that Bradley was lying there—lifeless. The dream of the stone wall. The mourning dove in the hospital window.

Olivia's heart raced, each beat thundering in her chest. A tremor surged through her—sudden and uncontrollable—like an electric current tingling through her veins, leaving her shaken to the core.

The nurse offered a reassuring smile and a gentle touch. "Oh, honey, don't you worry about a thing right now. I'm just going to give you a mild sedative so you can rest a bit before we wake you to check your vitals."

"Wait... where's Ethan? Is he okay?" Olivia asked, her speech beginning to slur as the nurse slowly pushed the sedative into her IV. A wave of uncertainty washed over her as her consciousness slipped away.

Rachel and Mitchell reached the hospital in record time, thanks to Rachel's aggressive driving. The recent snowfall had led to a surge in car accidents, adding to the hospital's already chaotic atmosphere. The hospital staff shortage made it difficult to find someone to help them locate Olivia and Dr. Lynch. Everyone appeared overwhelmed and preoccupied by the influx of accident victims from the snowstorm and the university explosion.

As they attempted to capture the staff's attention, Rachel froze. Motionless in the hallway stood a small man wearing a hooded sweatshirt, his gaze fixed on her.

"Professor Neil!" Rachel called out. She couldn't believe her eyes. He was here at the hospital right in front of her.

Rachel tried to push her way through the crowd in the ER to reach him. Adrenaline coursed through her veins as she elbowed past people, her focus solely on catching up with the man. But just as before, he vanished, leaving Rachel grasping at space. She scanned the hallway, her heart pounding in her chest, wondering if anyone else had seen him.

"Did you see the short guy in the sweatshirt?" Rachel asked.

Blank stares and confused shrugs were all she received in response.

"Rachel, are you okay?" Mitchell asked.

"He was here!" Rachel said, as her eyes darted around.

"Rachel, I think you're hallucinating again. You suspect him in every bombing, and you conjure him up in your mind."

"Fuck off," Rachel said, brushing past Mitchell on her way back to the nurses' station.

The nurses and hospital staff remained swamped with work, but a receptionist directed them to the fifth floor to speak to Dr. Richardson, who first delivered the grim news about Dr. Lynch's condition.

Dr. Richardson explained that Dr. Lynch suffered severe injuries. She had multiple broken bones, a head injury, internal bleeding, and extensive burns. Emergency surgery halted the bleeding, but she was still in danger. The doctors had placed her into a medically induced coma, and her prognosis was uncertain.

Despite multiple attempts, the hospital couldn't reach her husband today. Rachel suspected that Dr. Richardson thought Dr. Lynch was unlikely to recover, and he was worried she may die before they could get in touch with her husband.

"What about Olivia?" Rachel asked.

"Olivia is in much better shape," Dr. Richardson said. "She may have a concussion, but overall, it seems like she was very lucky."

Rachel emphasized the urgency of speaking with Olivia, signifying her testimony in helping with their investigation into the explosion. However, Dr. Richardson's response remained resolute, as he refused them immediate access.

"Dr. Richardson, the FBI has jurisdiction over this type of crime, and we will speak to Olivia even if I have to contact your boss," Rachel said, while Mitchell's cell phone began ringing and he stepped away to take the call. Rachel reached for her own phone to frighten Dr. Richardson into changing his mind.

"I'm sorry, Agent, but I don't care about your jurisdiction. I prioritize my patient's well-being, and you will not be speaking to her tonight unless you want to have me arrested," Dr. Richardson said before he walked away.

Rachel stood there staring after the doctor, astonished that he just walked away. Despite her frustration at not being able to speak to Olivia right away, she couldn't help but be impressed by Dr. Richardson's dedication.

"What did the doctor say?" Mitchell asked as he walked back over, ending his call.

Rachel let out a sharp breath. "He's refusing to let us talk to her tonight. I even threatened to call his boss."

"Well, you did what you could. It's okay," Mitchell said. "I just got off the phone with Officer Kirkland. Search and rescue pulled three bodies from the rubble."

He paused. "Doctors Kingsley, O'Brien, and Collins couldn't be identified at the scene because of their injuries, but based on what Maya told us, I'm assuming it's them. Also, ATF has been working through the debris. Kirkland overheard someone mention a pipe bomb."

"So, this was not an accident?"

"Nope," Mitchell said. "After I spoke with Kirkland, I called a couple of uniforms we'd tasked with finding the postdocs and the lab tech. Sofia, one of the postdocs, was still in bed. Because of the snow, she said she had no plans to go in. She found out about the explosion from the officer. According to him, she'd just woken up... and just wanted to go back to sleep."

"Are all academics like this?"

"Oh, you're just biased. You know you can't stand these pretentious university types," Mitchell said with a sly grin, trying to lift Rachel's spirits.

Mitchell was right. Rachel had always struggled to relate to people who seemed too wrapped up in academia. In her experience, their conversations often veered into esoteric territory— more about sounding intelligent than actually communicating.

Being an FBI agent in Boston, a city overflowing with universities, hadn't helped. She'd encountered plenty of so-called academics whose polished credentials masked far darker motives. Chief among them was Professor Eric J. Neil, the bomber she'd been chasing for years. He always outmaneuvered her, his presence haunting every corner of her investigation. He was the reason her bias had hardened against academics.

"Where were you just now?" Mitchell asked, noticing Rachel's distraction.

"Sorry. What were you saying?"

"The uniforms still haven't found the other postdoc or the lab tech," he said, his expression tightening. "And we should probably start looking for Dr. Lynch's husband too—the hospital says they can't find him either."

As they walked out into the hospital parking lot, Rachel said, "I'm going to meet with some uniformed officers to help locate Dr. Lynch's husband, the postdoc, and the lab tech. You're going back to the university?"

"Yeah," Mitchell said, adjusting his jacket. "I need to gather a bit more info from the ATF at the scene."

"You think we'll pull an all-nighter?"

"There isn't much we can do in the middle of the night. Go home and wait for officers to reach out if they find anything," Mitchell said.

Rachel hesitated, torn between the demands of the investigation and her need to go home. The loss of life from today's bombing weighed heavily on her—but so did the thought of her two-year-old twin girls. She missed them deeply whenever work kept her away, along with her husband, Alex, a fellow Boston native.

"Alright. I'll drop you off at the university. Then I'll plan on coming back here tomorrow to speak to Olivia," Rachel said.

"Sounds good," Mitchell said as he climbed into Rachel's car.

Like a shot, Rachel rushed toward the university, her mind consumed by the case. During the drive, she contemplated the growing list of missing individuals, and wondered whether this investigation was spiraling into something far more complex than suspected—perhaps more than just the act of a bitter, disgruntled graduate student.

CHAPTER 4

March 2013

Rachel joined the FBI straight out of college, entering Quantico shortly after graduating from Boston University at twenty-three. Prior to this, she had only worked at her boyfriend's family plumbing company. After completing her training at Quantico, Rachel opted for the six-week Special Agent Bomb Technician training at the hazardous devices school in Huntsville, Alabama. One of her instructors at Quantico recommended it to her, highlighting the widespread shortage of bomb technicians. Rachel also found the notion of bomb training rather appealing.

Upon becoming a full-fledged Special Agent Bomb Tech, Rachel was luckily assigned to the FBI field office in Boston. However, her first case with Mitchell took them straight to Clarkston, Georgia, marking the end of training exercises and the beginning of Rachel's real-world FBI career.

"We're heading to Georgia," Mitchell said. "There's been an explosion at an Alcoholics Anonymous meeting in a church."

Rachel glanced across the cluttered desks, strewn with stacks of files and paperwork. Her stomach fluttered with a blend of nerves and anticipation. She knew she had to rise to the occasion and prove herself in her brand new role.

They reached Georgia within a few tense hours of flying. As the plane descended into Atlanta, Rachel felt a knot of apprehension tighten in her stomach. Her feeling nervous was unusual, but this case had a foreboding presence even before reaching the scene.

St. Michael's Church on Smith Street in Clarkston, Georgia, was nestled within a modest neighborhood characterized by tidy rows of houses and tree-lined streets. The church itself had once stood as a symbol of faith, its brick facade weathered by time. Alongside the walls, lush rose bushes flourished, their vibrant blooms bursting with bright red color. The petals climbed upwards, creating a stark contrast against the old bricks of the building.

The air carried a faint scent of smoke, a lingering reminder of the recent explosion that had rocked the building. Amidst the lingering smell, the delicate aroma of burned roses added a bittersweet note, a poignant contrast to the acrid smoke. Despite the damage inflicted, the church remained standing. Its once pristine facade was now marred by a jagged hole where one classroom had endured the explosion. The walls, scorched and blackened, held steadfast, a testament to the strength of the structure.

The road leading to the church was cordoned off with bright yellow caution tape, marking the area as restricted. A handful of onlookers, drawn by the unusual activity in their typically quiet surroundings, observed from a distance. The quiet neighborhood was unaccustomed to such commotion.

ATF agents were sifting through the wreckage, their trained eyes scanning for any clues that might point to foul play. Wearing protective gear, they meticulously combed through the debris, collecting fragments of evidence. Prior to the ATF beginning their investigation, emergency medical technicians had already been on site, transporting the wounded survivors to the nearby Emory University Hospital.

"We're clear here, bomb tech," one of the ATF members said to Rachel, noting her obvious flame-resistant clothing and gloves. "We've swept the church; no other bombs."

"Do you have any other details?" Rachel asked, a flush of embarrassment rising as she stood there in full protective gear.

"Just that room," the ATF agent said, pointing. "We found fragments of pipe bombs hidden under the carpet—held together with self-adhesive bandage and suture." He shook his head. "Three people were found dead at the scene. It was apparently an AA meeting. Twelve members were present. The survivors were taken to Emory."

"Did someone from the meeting do this?" Rachel asked.

"That's your department to figure out, doll," the agent said with a wink, his demeanor casual as he continued scouring the remnants of the church classroom.

Rachel blinked, slightly thrown by the agent's choice of words. She wasn't exactly offended, just caught off guard. She exchanged a glance with Mitchell, who smirked at the term *doll*.

Mitchell was thinking aloud, his voice heavy with analytical curiosity. "You know, it's entirely possible that one alcoholic in the meeting had a hand in planting those pipe bombs."

His gaze drifted as he mentally sifted through various scenarios.

"But then again, it's just as plausible that someone else set them off. Alcoholics can definitely have enemies. Some hold grudges against churches. Hell, we can't rule out the possibility of terrorists or even just a random act."

His words hung in the air, prompting Rachel to consider the myriad of possibilities. Mitchell's knack for thinking beyond the obvious was clear as he urged her to explore every angle.

"Should we set up the investigation at the office or visit the hospital to speak with witnesses?" Rachel asked.

"It's a good idea to go to the hospital," Mitchell nodded. "We need to gather witness impressions while the events are still fresh in their minds, before memories fade or emotions cloud their recollections. And while we're there, our tech-savvy agents can dig into the backgrounds of all the victims."

"Hospital it is, then," Rachel said as they got into the car and set off toward the hospital.

———————— ❖ ————————

Emory University Hospital, situated north of the center of Atlanta, was about a fifteen-minute drive for them. The expansive campus boasts state-of-the-art facilities ready to tackle a variety of medical emergencies, including bomb-related injuries.

Ambulances arrived in a steady procession, their urgent wails blending with the constant activity surrounding the hospital. In Atlanta, where emergencies are common, the bombing made no difference at the hospital.

As Rachel and Mitchell stepped inside, they were met with the familiar whirlwind of an emergency room. Doctors and nurses in scrubs darted about, their movements purposeful and efficient as they tended to patients. A symphony of beeping monitors and shouted orders filled the air, punctuated by sharp intakes of breath and the cries of the wounded. In the waiting area, families huddled in quiet clusters, eyes fixed on doors that might open at any moment.

Rachel steadied herself, drawing in a deep breath as they navigated through the emergency room toward the check-in desk. The sharp scent of antiseptic stung her nostrils, causing her to wrinkle her nose in discomfort.

"We're with the FBI," Mitchell said, presenting his badge to the nurse stationed at the desk. "We need to speak to the survivors of the Clarkston Church bomb."

The nurse dialed a number, informing someone that the FBI was there to speak with the bombing victims. After hanging up, she gestured toward the automatic door to her right. As Rachel and Mitchell moved toward it, a doctor entered, her eyes sweeping the room.

"You're with the FBI?"

Before they could respond, a teenage girl burst into the ER, drawing their attention. Her voice was urgent as she called out to the nurse at the check-in desk.

"Where's my mom? My mom?" she asked, her long, unruly brown curls bouncing with each step.

The nurse tried to calm the girl, asking for more information, but panic was written all over the teenager's face. She scanned the ER, repeating, "I need to see my mom!"

Rachel felt a pang of empathy, memories of her own teenage years surfacing—losing both parents had left a mark she still carried. Was this girl's mother one of the bombing victims?

"Take a breath. Was your mom at the Clarkston Church?" Rachel asked gently.

The girl stared at her, stunned, a hint of confusion in her eyes.

"What? No, my mom was in a car accident!"

As a nurse approached and led the teenager away, Rachel felt a wave of embarrassment. She'd inserted herself into the wrong situation, and the heat rising in her cheeks only made it worse.

Mitchell seemed to pick up on it.

"It's okay, Rachel," he said quietly. "Come on. The doctor's taking us to the bomb victims."

They proceeded down the ER hallway, where only curtains enclosed the bomb victims. The ER doctor informed them that a few patients were in surgery, but most only suffered minor injuries. Among them were individuals with superficial burns, cuts, and debris in their skin.

Rachel and Mitchell moved through the survivors, speaking with each one. They listened as the survivors shared their experiences, tears welling in their eyes as they recounted the moments of the church explosion.

"It happened so fast," one survivor said, their voice trembling. "We were just talking—and then there was this deafening explosion."

"I couldn't see anything. Smoke was everywhere," another added. "It was crazy."

The interviews were emotional, each story clearly distressing to the survivors. Rachel listened carefully, taking notes as they struggled to recall what had happened during the explosion. Most were hesitant to say anything about who might be responsible—until they reached a young man having his wounds cleaned.

"My name's Ben, and I'm an alcoholic," the young man said, his voice heavy despite a weak attempt at a smile. The explosion during the AA meeting had clearly shaken him.

"Do you remember what happened?" Rachel asked.

"Yeah, I actually do. I used to forget stuff all the time, but I've been sober for about six months since I started going to these AA meetings," Ben said.

Rachel and Mitchell remained silent, urging Ben to continue with the details.

"I saw Professor Neil being removed from the room," Ben said. "They blocked him at the classroom door, refusing to let him in. He was yelling something about someone's brother, so they pushed him back out to leave the church. You can't bother anyone at the AA meeting. It's protected, confidential. At least it used to be…"

"Professor Neil?" Rachel asked.

"Yeah, he's one of my professors at Emory. He's new, so I recognized him. I was trying to hide from him so he wouldn't see me at an AA meeting," Ben said.

"Anything else happen?" Rachel asked.

"The bomb exploded only a few minutes later. We hadn't even really started the meeting. I think three of us died…" Ben's voice trailed off, his eyes dropping to the floor.

"Okay, Ben. Thanks for your help," Mitchell said, his tone steady, offering quiet reassurance.

When they finished interviewing everyone, Rachel and Mitchell walked out into the ER lobby. Rachel paused, taking a deep breath as she tried to steady herself again.

"A professor?" she asked.

"Nothing surprises me anymore," Mitchell said. "Let's head back to the field office and start digging into the victim's background."

Rachel nodded in agreement, mentally preparing for the research ahead. But she couldn't shake the image of the professor—his face vivid in her mind, even though she'd never seen him before.

———————❖———————

At the field office, Rachel and Mitchell dug deep into the details surrounding the victims of the church bombing. As they sifted through the backgrounds of the AA members, they found no glaring red flags pointing to any suspects. None of them had any criminal history, and there were no signs of hostility among the group members. Several people faced hardship, including divorce and job loss because of alcoholism. However, there was no obvious motive to target them with a bomb.

Throughout the investigation, no outside individuals, anti-church groups, or terrorist organizations came forward to claim responsibility. In fact, no one seemed eager to take credit for the bomb at all, leaving the investigators grasping at straws. Mitchell worried it might be a random act, the case that was notoriously difficult to crack.

"I don't think any of these people were involved, but I've got a feeling about the professor," Rachel said, frustration creeping into her voice. "I can't find anything on his background."

Identifying him was easy: Professor Eric J. Neil, a physics professor at Emory University. But despite the discovery, Rachel couldn't find any connection between him and the bombing victims, the church, the AA group, or Clarkston.

Mitchell nodded, giving her space to follow her instincts. Still, ever the pragmatist, he kept pressing her for a motive.

"Why did a physics professor, unconnected, bomb a church?" he asked.

Rachel was certain they'd find the answer to this question from Professor Neil. With her conviction driving them, Rachel and Mitchell dropped by the professor's office at Emory University unannounced.

As they stepped into the room, they found him seated behind his desk, grading assignments. He had a rather modest appearance, with dark hair, light eyes, and dressed in a simple combination of a sweater vest and slacks.

Upon introductions, Dr. Eric J. Neil insisted on including the "J," emphasizing it in both conversation and correspondence. There was an undeniable smugness about him, as if he considered himself above the two FBI agents standing before him. Yet beneath the polished exterior, Rachel noticed a faint sheen of sweat—a trace of nervousness breaking through.

She got straight to the point, explaining the investigation into the Clarkston church bombing and mentioning that a witness had seen him at the scene. His response lacked sympathy; instead, his self-importance seemed to dominate. Rachel wondered if he was overplaying his arrogance—perhaps to deflect suspicion or throw them off.

"Yes, I'm aware," he said. "I read about it. Unfortunate, of course—but I had no reason to be in Clarkston. I wasn't there."

Rachel caught a slight hesitation, a catch in his voice that didn't match his composed demeanor. His words felt uncertain, like he was making them up as he went.

"Are you sure? A member there said that you were escorted out because you were upset about a brother."

"No, I was never there. And frankly, I'd assume you can't fully trust an alcoholic," the professor said, arrogance creeping back into his voice.

"How did you know they were alcoholics?" Rachel asked.

"I remember reading about it in the news," the professor said.

Undeterred, they pressed further, noting that his department head had confirmed he hadn't shown up for work that day. Rachel watched as the professor's confidence faltered—a flash of fear crossed his face.

"I... uh... well, I had a migraine. I stayed home. You can ask my doctor at University Hospital," he said, avoiding eye contact as he stood and moved to a nearby filing cabinet.

"Are migraines common for you?" Rachel asked.

"Hmm... uh... yes, since I was younger. Now if you'll excuse me, I have a prior engagement," he said, retrieving a briefcase from the filing cabinet and attempting to walk past them.

"Wait, Professor Neil," Mitchell interjected, stepping in front of him. He towered over the professor and blocked his exit from the office. "Could you visit our office to discuss this? Share your insights?"

"No, no. I was not there. I was not involved, and now I have plans," the professor said, pushing past Mitchell to make his escape down the hallway.

Rachel moved to follow him, but Mitchell halted her in her tracks.

"Rachel, we lack evidence, connections, and he may have a valid point regarding the alcoholic kid."

"Are you joking?" Rachel said. She felt deep in her gut the professor had a part in the explosion. "He was nervous, and I think he was involved somehow."

"You've still got nothing concrete," Mitchell said.

Returning to the field office, Rachel couldn't stop thinking about the professor. Her conviction that he was involved in the bombing was unwavering, but Mitchell remained skeptical. He persistently pressed her to explain the professor's actions, specifically planting a bomb in the church. He pointed out again that they came up empty-handed, lacking any connections or evidence. And an alcoholic could make a mistake.

Rachel considered that maybe the bomb tested the professor's nerve, his ability to act without detection. Yet, she admitted the theory lacked solid evidence.

Mitchell continued to sway her and instill doubt, but Rachel's fixation on the professor consumed her thoughts. Her attempts to gather evidence, however, were thwarted. She frequented the professor's office and tried to trail him to his apartment, but he always eluded her. Despite her efforts to remain hidden, he was always aware of her presence, acknowledging her with a melancholic smile and an upward glance.

Mitchell cautioned her to focus on the actual investigation rather than her fixation on Professor Neil. He saw her obsession as tunnel vision, a concern for a new agent like her. He pointed out that her enthusiasm sometimes bordered on new agent impatience.

While keeping her continued investigation into the professor from Mitchell, Rachel stumbled onto a breakthrough: Professor Eric J. Neil's identity didn't exist until a few months ago. The university where he claimed to have earned his physics PhD had no record of him. She suspected he'd either faked or stolen credentials to land his position at Emory.

Rachel hesitated. Mitchell had been skeptical of her focus on the professor, and the idea of bringing this to him only heightened her anxiety. Taking matters into her own hands, she decided to visit Emory University alone—and confront the professor herself.

As she entered the familiar office space, she found him standing by his filing cabinet once more. He held his briefcase in one hand and a flask containing a mysterious red powder in the other.

"Professor Neil," Rachel said, "I have a few more questions for you. Are you on your way out again?"

Without warning or a word, the professor hurled the entire flask of red powder into Rachel's eyes. With searing pain engulfing her, tears welled up and her vision became useless. Panic surged through her as she groped blindly for her gun, her fingers fumbling in the darkness. Desperation seized her as she attempted to force her eyes open, but they remained shut against the burning sensation.

With trembling fingers and frantic cries, Rachel reached for her cell phone in the silent office, trying to dial 911. Every instinct urged her to flee, to find refuge from the unknown threat now looming over her. Yet, immobilized by her incapacitated sight, she found herself trapped.

She stood frozen, straining to catch any sound of the professor amidst the unsettling silence. Footsteps approached from down the hallway, responding to her frantic cries as individuals rushed into the room.

"Oh my God, what happened?" one voice asked.

"Professor Neil threw powder in my eyes," Rachel said, her voice tense with pain, her eyes still shut.

"He's not here," another woman observed as she reached out and took hold of Rachel's elbow, offering support. "Let's get you to the lab. They have an eye wash there."

Grateful for the offer, Rachel allowed herself to be guided to the nearby lab, where she flushed her eyes with the soothing wash. Despite the initial agony subsiding, her eyes remained red and inflamed. Because the woman recognized Rachel needed more treatment, she took her to the nearby University Hospital.

With Mitchell's arrival, the situation became clearer: Professor Neil had hurled capsaicin powder into Rachel's eyes, akin to pepper spray. Fortunately, it was determined that her eyes hadn't suffered permanent damage, requiring only a regimen of triple antibiotic drops three times a day for recovery.

Rachel was certain now—she'd been right about the professor all along. They should have trusted her gut.

Mitchell didn't say a word, but his silent fury was unmistakable.

They remained in Georgia for about a week, scouring the area for any sign of Professor Neil. But their efforts proved futile—he had disappeared. Despite extensive searches, they found no trace of his car, his apartment, or anyone who might have known him. With their reports on Professor Neil filed, they boarded a plane to Boston.

Back home, Rachel faced the harsh consequences of her actions. The FBI reprimanded her and suspended her without pay for two weeks because of her rule-breaking escapade in Georgia. As part of her punishment, she attended mandatory sessions with the FBI psychologist.

Rachel tried to accept her mistakes and move forward, but she was determined that she'd catch Professor Eric J. Neil. Although she had told the FBI shrink she would let it go, she knew she wouldn't.

CHAPTER 5

CLARKSTON GEORGIA GAZETTE
Mysterious Sinkhole Baffles Experts.
By: Emily Granger
March 19, 2013

CLARKSTON — Early this morning, residents of downtown Clarkston awoke to the startling sight of a massive sinkhole that appeared overnight. In the heart of Smith Street, the sinkhole measures twenty-five feet in diameter and an estimated depth of forty feet. City officials and emergency services have cordoned off the area, issuing a public warning to avoid the vicinity because of the risks of further collapse.

Emory University geologist Dr. Ronald Vickers called the sinkhole an anomaly, unlike typical collapses. Its characteristics didn't match those of erosion or water displacement. "This is something we haven't seen before," Dr. Vickers said. "The walls of the cavity are unusually smooth, almost as if they were... cut. These conditions wouldn't result from natural processes."

City engineers have inspected the surrounding infrastructure for damage, and while there are no immediate reports of injuries, the abrupt collapse swallowed a number of vehicles and sections of sidewalk.

Several witnesses claim to have heard a low, mechanical hum before the collapse, followed by a deep, resonating "pop" akin to a firework. Around 2:15 a.m., others reported a strange, metallic taste in the air. "It felt like everything was shaking for a second, like a minor earthquake," recalled Jasmine Walker, a resident whose apartment faces Smith Street. "I heard a pop, then saw a massive hole when I looked outside."

Authorities are calling for calm and assure residents that an investigation is underway, though details remain scarce. Early theories include the failure of old sewer lines or the collapse of forgotten tunnels beneath the city, but city historian Margaret Green was quick to refute those claims. "There have been no records of any tunnels or mines beneath Smith Street. If there were, we'd have known about it," Green stated in an interview with Clarkston Courier. "It's all very peculiar."

Unconfirmed reports of objects reappearing from the sinkhole deepen the mystery. Several onlookers saw flashes of light in the hole, followed by the surfacing of corroded artifacts. These included a pocket watch, rusted goggles, and a tarnished key, all with unfamiliar designs and inscriptions. Officials, however, have denied these claims, citing the debris in the sinkhole as rubble from collapsed infrastructure.

Despite the city's reassurance, rumors of the sinkhole's origin are spreading like wildfire on social media. Speculation ranges from the plausible to the absurd, with theories involving hidden wartime bunkers, alien activity, and even time travel.

One of the more bizarre accounts comes from a local blogger, Zachary Denton, who claims that the sinkhole might result from a "temporal anomaly." In a blog post, Denton argues the sinkhole aligns with a series of unexplained occurrences from the 1930s, documented in old town records. "In 1937, near Smith Street, witnesses reported a disturbance. Accounts describe strange mechanical noises, an inexplicable power outage, and a loud popping sound at 2:15 a.m.. It's the exact same description," Denton wrote. "I'm not saying it's time travel, but something weird is happening."

Denton's theories, while dismissed by experts as "fringe fiction," have nevertheless gained traction among residents, fueling a growing fascination with the sinkhole's true origins.

"There's definitely a pattern," said Susan Fischer, a local history enthusiast who runs the online forum Clarkston Mysteries. "Minor details line up. They found a pocket watch near the hole, but the watch looks like it's been sitting in seawater for decades. It is not documented as being there in the past."

For now, the official explanation remains mundane: a collapse because of old, neglected infrastructure and ground instability. City officials and geologists will hold a press conference later this evening to address public concerns and outline plans for stabilizing the area. Experts remain baffled by the sinkhole, gaining more questions than answers.

Authorities rerouted traffic, and they closed businesses around Smith Street. For residents, the incident serves as a stark reminder of the hidden, unexplored depths beneath their feet—and perhaps even beneath time itself.

"You can look at it as a geological anomaly," Dr. Vickers said, his voice tinged with curiosity. "Or a reminder that some things are best left buried."

CHAPTER 6

Olivia's night had been unusually dreamless, a stark departure from her norm. The nurse had roused her twice, but each time, she'd drifted back into a deep sleep. But still no dreams. Morning brought a food service worker bearing scrambled eggs, whole wheat toast, and orange juice. It was only then that she realized she hadn't eaten since sharing toaster waffles with her dog the previous day. The aroma of eggs alone spurred her to devour the meal.

Her head still throbbed, but the pain no longer pinned her to the bed. Dr. Richardson had visited in the morning, wielding his bright penlight that stung her eyes. She answered all of his questions correctly this morning, securing his approval for her to be discharged.

Olivia hadn't ventured beyond her room since being admitted, and she hesitated to inquire further about the police officer the nurse had mentioned. In her mind, avoiding the topic might enable her to simply leave the hospital. She knew discussion of the incident was inevitable, but she was tired, and had to get home to her dog. Poor old Mulder had spent an entire night at home alone, left to his own devices.

Regrettably, yesterday's dust and shredded fabric marred her clothes, prompting her to buy a gray sweat suit from the gift shop. She dressed and was ready to make her way to the nurses' station to sign her discharge papers. Her possessions were minimal, as everything else remained in her car back at school, except for her phone. Thankfully, her phone had weathered the ordeal with only a cracked screen and about a 20% charge left.

While seated on the hospital bed, Olivia opened the Uber app to arrange her ride home when a woman's voice in the hallway abruptly seized her focus. The woman was informing the police officer she intended to interrogate Olivia at the field office, releasing him from duty. Olivia froze, briefly toying with the irrational idea of climbing out of the window before dismissing it.

The woman who entered the room appeared to be in a hurry. She entered with an authoritative presence, her quick and purposeful steps commanded attention. She was about the same height as Olivia, but dressed in a well-tailored gray suit, paired with a deep purple blouse. Sensible, flat shoes hinted at practicality. Her straight, shoulder-length black hair framed her face, and her striking blue eyes provided a noticeable contrast to her dark hair, giving her a distinct and intriguing presence.

"Hello, Olivia," the woman began, flashing her badge. "I'm Special Agent Rachel Quinn with the FBI. I need to ask you a few questions about what happened yesterday."

"I don't know how much I can tell you," Olivia said, "It's all a blur. I was outside, the building blew up, and next thing I knew, I was here."

"You don't remember anything? Nothing different? No sounds, no people?" Rachel asked.

"Not really… I spoke with Maya outside, and then I was here," Olivia said.

"So, you don't have any theories? Any explanations for what happened?" Rachel asked.

"I don't know… maybe some kind of accident? Like some hazardous chemical or some kind of high pressure? I don't know…" Olivia said, her voice faltering as she closed her eyes. She inhaled, then pinched the bridge of her nose, as if warding off a headache.

Rachel's expression hardened, her tone serious. "Olivia, this wasn't accidental; witnesses implicate you."

"What?! That's insane!" Olivia's eyes widened. "I would never do anything like that."

"Regardless," Rachel said, "we need to bring you in for questioning."

"I wouldn't even know how to do that!" Olivia said. "Who blamed me?"

"Who do you think would blame you?" Rachel asked.

Olivia's nerves prickled, a knot forming in her stomach. She hesitated, apprehensive about answering any of these questions.

"I… I can't believe you suspect me," Olivia protested, her voice trembling. "Several lab members might be responsible. They're just a terrible group of people."

"Oh yeah? Like who?" Rachel asked, her eyebrows appearing to be arched in skepticism.

"Basically everyone in that lab," Olivia admitted. "They all hate each other."

"Well, I think it's in your best interest to come down to the field office. We need to sort this mess out, and you can shed some light on the so-called *terrible people*," Rachel said.

Olivia felt a surge of fear as the weight of the accusation settled on her. The thought that both her lab colleagues and the FBI might see her as guilty made her stomach churn. But it wasn't just her own predicament that haunted her—she couldn't stop thinking about her dog, waiting alone at home. Unsure whether speaking up might further incriminate her, she hesitated.

"Um… I really need to get home to take care of my dog," Olivia said, her eyes darting between Rachel and the exit. "He's been alone since yesterday morning, no one to take him outside or feed him. I was just ordering an Uber."

Rachel contemplated the situation before proposing a compromise. "Okay, Olivia," she began, her tone softening. "How about I give you a ride? We can stop at your house to take care of your dog. After that, you'll come with me to the field office. How does that sound?"

Reluctance warred in Olivia's mind as she grappled with the decision. She wasn't surprised that someone had tried to blame her—especially after Bradley had disclosed her "confidential" misconduct allegations. Fear pulsed through her veins, but the desire to clear her name burned just as fiercely. With a shaky breath, she nodded, though everything in her resisted.

As they headed to the nurses' station for Olivia's discharge, she felt Rachel's gaze linger on her, scrutinizing. At first, Olivia thought Rachel was searching for someone else amidst the sterile hospital corridors. But as the scrutiny continued, a pang of unease twisted in Olivia's gut. Was Rachel keeping a watchful eye on her, suspecting her involvement in the lab's bombing?

"Alright, let's get moving," Rachel's voice jolted Olivia from her thoughts, pulling her back to the reality of the moment. Together, they trudged through the falling snow towards Rachel's car, each step muffled by the soft crunch of fresh flakes.

———————◆———————

Olivia was taken aback by the mess inside Rachel's car. She had expected a spotless vehicle, mirroring Rachel's own demeanor. Instead, she found food wrappers and empty coffee cups strewn about, cluttering the space. Olivia cleared trash from the passenger seat before she could get in. Oddly enough, the clutter in the car made Olivia feel somewhat more at ease, as it hinted they may have something in common.

Rachel wasted no time and started driving like a bat out of hell, not bothering to even ask Olivia's address before hitting the road. The snow had eased, but foot-high drifts still lined the roads.

"I live over on Huntsman Drive," Olivia said.

"I know," Rachel said.

Of course she knew. I'm a suspect—she probably knows everything about me, Olivia thought, jaw clenched. Her unease was growing as she considered the investigation against her.

They pulled up to Olivia's house, and as Olivia tried to rush out of the car, she said, "I'll just be a minute."

"Oh no, you're not going in there alone. I can help you," Rachel said.

"That's not a good idea," Olivia warned. "Mulder is not a very nice dog, he might bite."

"I think I'll be fine," Rachel said. "And really? Mulder?"

Olivia winced as Rachel slammed the car door shut, her head throbbing from the sudden noise. They headed toward the back stairs of the two-family house.

Then, in an instant, they were stepping into Olivia's apartment at the top of the stairs. Rachel froze in the doorway, confusion flashing across her face, as if realizing she had no memory of climbing the stairs.

"How did we get here?" Rachel asked, her voice low as she stood motionless, looking completely lost.

"Um... we drove?" Olivia had already unlocked the apartment and pocketed her keys when she turned and caught Rachel's bewildered expression.

Rachel shook her head, like she was trying to clear the fog of uncertainty that clouded her thoughts.

"No, I mean, how did we climb the stairs? We left the car, and suddenly we're here. What happened?" Rachel asked.

"What? We just walked up the stairs," Olivia said, casting a puzzled glance at Rachel.

"I don't understand. It's like... we just skipped a beat or something."

Olivia's eyes darted from Rachel to the stairs, uncertainty etched on her face.

"Maybe you were just distracted? Did you not sleep last night?"

Olivia watched as Rachel kept looking between the doorway of Olivia's apartment and the stairs. Maintaining a confused expression, Rachel approached the top of the stairs, peering downward and leaning over the rail silently.

"Huh, I don't know..." Rachel said.

Olivia shrugged as she stepped into the apartment. She made her way to her bedroom, where Mulder lay on her bed, seemingly indifferent to her presence, showing no intention of moving. She had placed pee pads down for him, since he often refused to go outside with her. Olivia cleaned up the used pads and replaced them with fresh ones. She attempted to offer him some kibble, but he turned his nose up at it. Although she offered a walk, enticing him with the leash, he remained motionless, staring at her as if unimpressed by the offer.

With Rachel entering the room, Mulder's demeanor took a sharp turn. He emitted a low growl and arched his back, not welcoming her. Olivia intervened, pushing Rachel out of the bedroom and into the kitchen, where she could prepare Mulder a more appealing meal of his beloved toaster waffles.

"How do you handle such an ornery fucking dog?" Rachel asked, a hint of laughter in her voice.

"He's alright, it's just the way he is. I rescued him about a year ago; now I let him be comfortable in his old age because his early life was hard."

Papers and notebooks cluttered Olivia's apartment, strewn across every available surface—the kitchen table, the living room coffee table, even the kitchen counter. It was reminiscent of Rachel's car, which was similarly cluttered. Rachel appeared at ease, making Olivia wonder if Rachel's home resembled her car.

While Olivia prepared her toaster waffles, Rachel examined her work, rifling through the scattered papers and notebooks. She thought Rachel was disinterested or even irritated that the clutter was all educational.

"What do you study, anyway?" Rachel asked.

"My research focuses on temporal anomalies and Einstein's River of Time theory. I'm looking for geographic areas that already have unusual electromagnetic fields or gravity," Olivia said matter-of-factly.

"Could you repeat that in English, please?" Rachel said, glancing up at Olivia from the papers.

"Sorry. Most people think time moves in a straight line—that you can't change it. But Einstein flipped that idea on its head."

"Okay…" Rachel said.

"Einstein believed time could flow like water in a river—the speed and direction changing depending on what's around it, like obstacles in its path," Olivia said.

"I don't think I get it."

Olivia paused, thinking about how to simplify it.

"Think of it this way," she said, her hands moving gently like river waves. "Imagine time as a river. It flows from past to present to future, just like we experience it every day."

"Got it…" Rachel nodded.

"But his theory states that there are whirlpools in a river. And in time. In the right geographic circumstances, with the right equipment and a bit of luck, a whirlpool in time might be possible. You could travel through time," Olivia said, glancing away, a faint flush creeping into her cheeks.

"You're trying to travel through time?"

"Well, it's just a theory," Olivia said.

"Did you actually do it? Travel back in time?" Rachel asked with a smirk, her voice light with amusement.

"Of course not. The environment isn't so abnormal that you'd just "time jump." Someone has to manipulate something—like electromagnetic fields or something—to change the sur-roundings," Olivia said, avoiding Rachel's eyes, already regretting how it sounded.

Rachel let out a sigh and tossed Olivia's papers back onto the table. Olivia, increasingly embarrassed, decided against further discussion of the topic. She grabbed the plate of waffles and re-treated to the bedroom.

After ensuring Mulder was enjoying his breakfast, she contemplated changing her clothes, but decided the sweat suit was pretty comfortable. She bundled up in a different coat, opting for a heavier one to combat the cold outside, and grabbed her phone charger. She left the scattered papers and notebooks where they lay as they left for the FBI field office in Chelsea.

When Olivia stepped into the FBI office, the aroma of freshly brewed coffee overwhelmed her, competing with the constant hum of activity that filled the room. The office was a vast space, with a grid of cubicles at its center. Agents and other personnel engaged in animated conversations, punctuated by raised voices. The walls were a lackluster off-white color, adorned with a sparse collection of framed awards and photographs featuring smiling officers.

At one end of the room, individual offices with frosted glass windows lined the perimeter, each bearing the nameplate of its occupant. Behind those doors, she knew, were the private offices of high-ranking officials she hoped she didn't have to meet.

Rachel turned to the right, leading her down a dimly lit corridor. Olivia felt a sense of unease creeping over her, the walls closing in as if she were suddenly claustrophobic. The hallway stretched ahead, its brick walls bare, with no doors or exits, creating an eerie atmosphere. Sudden fear gripped her as she imagined something lurking in the dark, ancient corridor—a hidden cell, perhaps—just beyond her sight.

"What's going on? Why are we going down this dead-end hallway?" Olivia asked, panic surging through her as she turned around, narrowly avoiding colliding with Rachel while trying to leave the hallway.

"What?" Rachel asked, a puzzled expression crossing her face, as she caught Olivia by her elbows to steady her.

Olivia spun around again. The brick wall was gone. In its place was a brightly lit hallway, lined with what looked like interrogation rooms. Framed photos of smiling officers hung neatly along the walls. She blinked and took a step back, the sudden shift making her stomach turn.

Rachel looked at her, eyebrows drawn. "Are you alright?"

Olivia shook her head slowly. The hallway swayed slightly. She closed her eyes and took a breath, steadying herself. "Maybe I have a concussion," she said, her gaze dropping to the floor.

As Olivia hesitated, Rachel placed a hand on her shoulder, and resumed leading her down the hallway towards an interrogation room.

"Why this hallway, this locked room?" Olivia asked, glancing toward the crowded and noisy central office. "Can we just sit out there?"

"It's too loud out here, and we need to record your responses," Rachel said.

"Are you going to arrest me? Do I need a lawyer?" Olivia's voice still trembled. Her eyes darted down the hallway, and her hands clenched into fists at her sides. She didn't know what came next—only that she didn't trust any of it.

"Do you think you need a lawyer?" Rachel asked.

"I don't know, I guess not. I mean, I haven't done anything wrong, so maybe I don't need one?" Olivia said, her voice wavering.

A large, imposing two-way mirror dominated the small and unwelcoming room. Olivia took a deep breath, trying to steady her nerves as she took a seat, positioning herself to face the mirror. She wondered who was watching her from the other side.

"Would you like a cup of coffee or water before we start?" Rachel asked.

Olivia, feeling nervous about asking for anything, felt a pang of guilt, fearing they might blame her for something no matter what she said. Despite this, she knew she needed something warm; she was shivering from the chill in the air. So she nodded, her eyes fixed on the table.

"Coffee, please."

Rachel obliged, calling for someone to bring them coffee. As the officer set the steaming cups before them, Rachel settled into the chair across from Olivia, notebook open and pen poised to take notes.

"Alright, Olivia. I'm going to start the recording now," Rachel began. "You said this morning you knew nothing of the explosion. Although, you claimed there were "terrible" people there who deserved to be blown up."

Olivia shook her head. "Th-That's not what I said. You told me witnesses claimed I did it, but I was not involved. I said the lab staff were terrible, and that others—not me—may want to blow up the building."

"So, do you have someone in mind?" Rachel asked.

"I honestly don't know. Who was there?" Olivia asked.

"Doctors Lynch, Kingsley, O'Brien, and Collins, as well as Bradley Parker. Unfortunately, we think they all died in the explosion, except for Dr. Lynch, who was severely injured and may not survive," Rachel said, reading the names from her notebook.

"What about Maya? Is she alright?" Olivia asked, her heart clenched with worry, and she shifted in her seat.

"Maya is fine. A few scrapes were her only injuries. They didn't even take her to the hospital," Rachel said.

"What about Brittney, Sofia, and Ethan?" Olivia asked, her voice betraying her obvious nervousness as she glanced around the room, her fingers fidgeting with the edge of her sleeve.

"Sofia was at home, so she was unharmed, but we haven't been able to locate Brittney or Ethan. We also can't seem to contact Dr. Lynch's husband," Rachel said.

With an earnest expression, Olivia leaned forward, through worsening nerves.

"This isn't something Ethan would do. Brittney, Sofia, and Aiden, Dr. Lynch's husband, are a different story. Th-They've all been... affected by the people who died in that explosion," she said, unable to control a slight stutter in her voice. "If you're considering me as a suspect, you need to consider them as well. Th-They all have a motive."

"Why are you so sure about Ethan? Could your relationship with Ethan be influencing your opinion of him, leading you to protect him?" Rachel asked, raising an eyebrow.

It surprised Olivia that Rachel was privy to her relationship with Ethan. She had attempted to keep it discreet, but everyone had somehow caught wind of it.

"No, I'm not protecting him," Olivia said. "Ethan is genuinely a good person, and he has no reason to harm anyone in the lab."

"But you have a motive, because something affected you like the others?" Rachel asked.

"No, th-that's not what I mean." Olivia shook her head hard, voice cracking as she tried to find the words. Her hands curled into fists at her sides.

"That's not what I meant," she repeated, more quietly this time.

"What I mean is, there's a whole lot of inappropriate stuff going on in that lab—things you haven't uncovered yet. Because you've been focused on me and my relationship with Ethan, you haven't been able to look into the others," Olivia said, her words rushed but careful.

Rachel, calm as ever, leaned in, one brow arched in skepticism. Olivia glimpsed something—doubt, maybe—in her eyes.

"Well, in that case, why don't you enlighten me about the lab's secrets?" Rachel's voice dripped with sarcasm, and Olivia couldn't tell whether she was being challenged or dismissed entirely. Did Rachel believe anything she said?

Olivia leaned back in her chair, nerves still taut.

"We're probably going to need a lot more coffee," she said with a nervous smile, hoping to lighten the atmosphere.

CHAPTER 7

August 2018

Olivia became self-reliant in her final year of high school. Her mother passed away when she was seventeen, leaving her father preoccupied with his own grief. He often seemed distant, focusing his attention on women barely older than Olivia. She found herself at a crossroads. She entertained the idea of just staying home and finding a job, but also contemplated pursuing a medical career. When she got accepted to an undergraduate program on a scholarship, she enrolled as a pre-med student.

However, an introductory physics course caught her attention. In her professor's lab, Olivia explored quantum entanglement, Einstein's theories, and approximate solutions of Einstein's equations for gravitational waves. Motivated by these experiences, she made the pivotal decision to switch her major to physics. Olivia had reservations about becoming a doctor, anyway. She had always been so shy and she wasn't sure she even had the aptitude for the profession.

As Olivia further explored quantum physics, her fascination with the universe grew. Each new revelation seemed to affirm her belief in determinism; that the universe planned or predetermined everything. Encouraged by her academic success and newfound passion, she considered looking into pursuing a PhD after finishing her undergraduate studies.

Just before her undergraduate graduation, she was taking part in job fairs and graduate school expos. She focused on New England, renowned for its prestigious STEM research institutions and many physics opportunities. She engaged with many recruiters from various institutions, but one university stood out in their relentless pursuit of her. They went to great lengths, treating her to dinners and sending her merchandise from the school, like jackets and coffee mugs.

Olivia's first encounter with Dr. Karen Lynch had occurred during one of the recruitment dinners, before she had committed to pursuing her PhD at the institution. The dinner took place within the refined ambiance of an elegant, high-end restaurant. Faculty members engaged Olivia in discussions about their institution, their voices blending with the gentle clinks of silverware and the hum of conversation that filled the room. Against this backdrop, Dr. Lynch stood out, not for her flamboyance, but as a reserved individual, seldom uttering much during the evening. She had come across as rather unassuming.

Olivia sat at a table with pristine white linens, illuminated by the soft flicker of candlelight. Eager to learn more about her potential mentor, she leaned forward as she tried to direct a series of questions to Dr. Lynch.

"So, Dr. Lynch," Olivia began, her voice carrying a hint of eagerness, "what inspired you to pursue physics?"

Dr. Lynch's eyes shifted toward Olivia, then back to the group with a neutral expression. It was as though she was weighing her words carefully before responding.

"Well," a professor to Dr. Lynch's left chimed in, "I believe the interdisciplinary nature of physics attracted Dr. Lynch. Isn't that right, Karen?"

Dr. Lynch nodded, her lips forming a polite smile. Olivia felt a bit of disappointment at the lack of direct engagement.

"But was there something that sparked your interest? Anything personal or educational?" Olivia pressed to glean more information from Dr. Lynch.

Dr. Lynch's eyes drifted from Olivia to the other professors gathered around the table, as if urging one of them to jump in. Then, with a subtle shift of focus back to Olivia, she remarked, "It's difficult to pinpoint just one."

As the conversation threatened to stall, Olivia tried to change the subject to the university by asking a few general questions. "I know you've been in New England for quite some time. Could you share what draws you to this university, especially in terms of its physics research?"

Dr. Lynch remained silent, turning her attention to the other professors around the table. Another professor spoke up, a warm smile accompanying his words. "Well, Olivia, this university boasts a vibrant research community in physics. The collaborative atmosphere and state-of-the-art facilities make it an ideal place for aspiring physicists to thrive."

No matter what Olivia asked, Dr. Lynch remained silent, allowing other faculty members to interject and provide responses. She figured that Dr. Lynch was just shy.

Olivia had looked into Dr. Lynch before the dinner. She knew about Dr. Lynch's accomplishments in high-energy physics, and how she consistently got research funding and grants. Aware that some distinguished scientists were not outgoing, she thought she understood why Dr. Lynch spoke little. After all, Olivia herself was shy and often reluctant to discuss herself or her research.

As the dinner drew to a close, Olivia felt the universe was nudging her toward attending this university. Boston's status as a leading physics research hub heightened its appeal. And the faculty had expressed an interest in her undergraduate research.

"Olivia, your work during your bachelor's degree has been quite impressive to us," noted one professor. "The computer programming is what caught our attention. And your proficiency in theoretical physics surpasses that of an average undergraduate student. We see you as a valuable asset to our department."

"Yes, and your understanding of Einstein's theories of time travel is the innovative thinking we encourage here," another professor said.

Their eagerness to recruit her left a powerful impression. After reflecting on the evening's conversations, Olivia made her decision: she would begin her journey toward earning a physics PhD at the university that had so clearly wanted her.

Upon completing her BS in physics, Olivia excitedly moved to Boston to begin her graduate studies. On her first day, she had a meeting with Dr. Lynch, who was to be her mentor. As Olivia stepped into Dr. Lynch's opulent, spacious office, the overwhelming grandeur pressed in from all sides. Luxurious furnishings, including a grand, intricately carved desk dominating the space. A plush, inviting couch occupied a corner, complemented by elegant end tables with arranged ornaments. A state-of-the-art computer modernized the otherwise classic decor of the office. The extravagance of the amenities surprised Olivia, considering the professor's position at a small university.

"Good morning," Olivia said as she entered Dr. Lynch's office.

Dr. Lynch looked up, unfocused, as if she had forgotten about their meeting.

"Oh, right. Good morning," she said absentmindedly, her tone lacking any genuine warmth. "You're the new student, aren't you?"

Dr. Lynch's demeanor took Olivia by surprise. She underwent a notable transformation, adopting an air of arrogance that contrasted with the unassuming persona she had presented during their earlier dinner meeting. Yet she maintained her mousy appearance, with her light brown hair neatly pulled back into a simple ponytail, devoid of any elaborate styling. She wore no jewelry, and her outfit—plain slacks and a modest blouse—reflected a deliberate lack of style that seemed at odds with the self-assuredness she projected. Olivia wondered if her recollection of Dr. Lynch from their prior interactions might have been inaccurate.

During their brief encounter, Dr. Lynch explained that, in her initial year, Olivia wouldn't have much chance to pursue her own research ideas. She mentioned that Olivia would be busy with coursework and getting to know the lab's operations. The meeting left Olivia feeling somewhat underwhelmed, as it was rather short and not enlightening.

However, Dr. Lynch's last remark about Isaac Newton's Second Law of Motion stopped Olivia short—she claimed that Einstein, not Newton, had formulated the law. At that moment, Olivia assumed that Dr. Lynch had misspoke. But as time passed in the lab, she would come to understand otherwise.

———————◆———————

November 2019

Olivia's first two years in the program included graduate-level classes that encompassed not only physics but also statistics and ethics—an amusing addition given the lab's somewhat questionable ethical track record Olivia learned about later. Attending and presenting at journal clubs and teaching undergraduate classes were regular features, but primarily she interacted with fellow graduate students during these initial years. She had spent her first few years in the student's office in the other research building that housed the linear accelerator.

That small office had its own distinct vibe, with a few unique personalities. There were only three desks for the graduate students, each with its own computer. A communal whiteboard adorned the far wall, serving as a canvas for various equations. Harsh fluorescent lighting bathed the room, highlighting scratches and blemishes on the beige walls. A mini-fridge with a potted plant on top decorated the corner.

Olivia shared the space with two fellow graduate students, Tom and Abbie. Tom was Dr. Lloyd's graduate student, pursuing a physics PhD like Olivia. He remained reserved and rarely spoke to anyone else in the office, focusing on his own research. His ever-present, noise canceling headphones clung to his ears, sealing him off from the others in the office.

Abbie was a vibrant presence in the office. Her auburn hair cascaded down her shoulders, exuding an air of approachability that invited conversation. Unlike her counterparts, she was pursuing a master's degree in physics education, which explained why she was always so bubbly and open. Often eager to engage in discussions and share her knowledge, Abbie's enthusiasm for teaching physics was helpful during Olivia's first year of courses. Her support and guidance also aided Olivia in preparing for her first journal club presentation.

A journal club serves as an important educational forum where participants discuss published articles, aiming to stay updated with the latest research findings. The meetings help students to develop critical thinking skills and promote evidence-based practice. During these sessions, students take turns presenting papers, followed by discussions and questions to ensure they comprehend what they just presented.

Olivia, a regular attendee of such journal clubs, found them to be a mix of formality and informality. While the atmosphere was relaxed, your mentor added a layer of accountability. The mentor's role varied from providing supervision and encouragement to occasionally challenging students to defend their understanding of the presented material. This dynamic kept students on their toes, but sometimes lead to public humiliation.

Olivia was nervous as she prepared for her presentation. Although a minor event, the physics department expected everyone in the department to attend the journal club. But when Olivia was standing at the podium about to begin, she noticed that Dr. Lynch was absent. Even Olivia's committee members failed to show up, except for Dr. O'Brien, who sat in the back of the room, slumped in one of the plastic chairs. His rhythmic breathing showed he had likely fallen asleep. It was just Dr. Willams and Dr. Lloyd, and just the two other graduate students, who had made the effort to attend.

Olivia confidently presented her chosen journal article to her peers. With each slide she clicked through, her enthusiasm for the subject shone through. She had poured hours into understanding every nuance of the paper, and it showed. As she spoke about the intricacies of the research, everyone engaged in an animated discussion, sharing their insights and critiques. The atmosphere was casual, and Olivia thought the knowledge exchange was valuable. Each presentation was also a chance to refine her public speaking skills and help to develop her teaching abilities.

However, Olivia's mentor's conspicuous absence disappointed her. Did the absence reflect her mentor's lack of interest in her progress? Or was she swamped with her own research and grant writing? Olivia wondered if she should ask Dr. Lynch about not attending or just let it go? As the discussion wound down, Olivia let it go and returned to the student's office.

When Olivia entered the office, Abbie offered a warm congratulation on her presentation as she settled into her seat in front of her computer. As she focused on her statistics project, Dr. Williams' entrance interrupted the quiet hum of the room. The professor made her characteristically loud entrance, clad in her usual mismatched, brightly colored clothing covered with a lab coat. Dr. Williams' salt-and-pepper hair defied gravity, each strand seeming to have a mind of its own, untouched by even the suggestion of a comb.

"Olivia, that presentation was truly exceptional!" Dr. Williams said, her eyes brightening as she spoke.

"Thank you," Olivia said. She gestured towards Abbie, seated at her desk nearby. "Abbie was a tremendous help."

Dr. Williams shook her head with a smile. "Nonsense, Olivia. I've had the chance to look into some of your undergraduate research, and I must say, you possess remarkable potential."

Olivia's cheeks flushed with embarrassment as she looked down at her shoes.

"I've been considering a project for my lab," Dr. Williams said, "And I believe your expertise could be invaluable. Would you be interested in collaborating?"

"Of course, Dr. Williams. What exactly do you have in mind?" Olivia asked.

"I'm looking to develop a computer program similar to the one you used during your previous research," Dr. Williams said. "I believe it could revolutionize our research methods."

"I can help with that," Olivia said. "I could probably get something set up for you over the weekend."

"That would be fantastic! I'll email you the details. Once again, great job on your presentation," Dr. Williams said as she turned to leave the student's office.

Olivia was excited to be an actual part of the physics department here at the university, relishing the opportunity to contribute beyond just attending classes. Having honed her skills in computational particle physics as an undergraduate, she went on to work in program synthesis—a method that constructs programs using computer algebra systems, or CAS. This experience wasn't just a feather in her cap; it was a testament to her dedication and expertise in physics.

"Olivia, you really need to tread carefully," Abbie said.

"What do you mean?"

"It's this whole thing with the Department of Energy's five-million-dollar grant for high-energy physics research. Everyone's scrambling for it." Abbie had leaned in, her voice dropping to a whisper.

"You mean that DOE grant?"

Abbie nodded. "Exactly. Dr. Lynch's practically got her claws out for it. If she catches wind that you've been helping Dr. Williams, and she ends up snagging the grant ahead of her, there could be… repercussions."

"Repercussions? Like what?" Olivia asked, worry creeping into her voice.

"It might not mean getting the boot, but trust me, you don't want to get on Dr. Lynch's bad side. She'll make your time here a living nightmare if she loses that grant to Dr. Williams," Abbie said.

Olivia found the allure of participating in such innovative research and the chance to help secure such a lucrative grant irresistible. She saw it as a priceless opportunity to advance her career. Fueled by confidence and ambition, Olivia was certain her performance would impress Dr. Lynch. However, her understanding of academia and Dr. Lynch at that moment was mistaken.

January 2020

Olivia received the email from Dr. Williams outlining the specifics needed to set up the computer program. It was a straightforward task, one she had already mastered during her undergrad years. She was eager to contribute to actual research efforts and to get her name on a grant application. After all, collaboration was the cornerstone of scientific progress, or so she thought.

Olivia could not stop thinking about what Abbie had said. She was worried, but she wanted to work on this computer program and seize the grant opportunity. Fearing potential conflicts with Dr. Lynch, Olivia cautiously expressed concern to Dr. Williams about assisting her. Dr. Williams reassured Olivia, stating that the program encouraged collaboration among graduate students and faculty. She even promised to inform Dr. Lynch of Olivia's help, ensuring there would be no misunderstandings.

Olivia felt better, convincing herself that moving forward was the right choice. After all, she had worked on this during undergrad and her instructors had already published it. She believed she could share it with Dr. Lynch or anyone else in the department. She was adding a few specifics as requested by Dr. Williams and could adapt the program for anyone in the department if necessary.

Over the weekend, Olivia completed the task and sent the revised program to Dr. Williams on Monday. In a gracious thank you note, Dr. Williams assured Olivia that she would add her name to the grant application. Olivia was thrilled, knowing that this addition would enhance her CV and potentially lead to future postdoctoral fellowships.

However, despite her promise to Olivia, Dr. Williams only informed Dr. Lynch of Olivia's help after submitting the grant applications. It was only then, in a moment of self-congratulation, that Dr. Williams revealed to Dr. Lynch how Olivia had played a pivotal role in her application process. This revelation served as more than just an innocent boast; it was a calculated dig aimed at Dr. Lynch's ego.

The betrayal ran deep in the scholarly world, where collaborations were not just about sharing resources but also about trust and mutual respect. Dr. Williams' decision to sidestep Dr. Lynch and enlist her student's help was a clear breach of that trust. It underscored the cutthroat nature of academia, where individuals would stop at nothing to gain an edge over their rivals. The audacity of Dr. Williams to flaunt her underhanded tactics in Dr. Lynch's face was a testament to the lengths people would go to in pursuit of success.

Neither Dr. Williams nor Dr. Lynch broached the subject with Olivia, leaving her in the dark about the unfolding drama. She didn't get the details until Abbie—an unlikely source, being a master's student who rarely entered Dr. Lynch's building—spoke up.

"Olivia, you shouldn't have helped Dr. Williams," Abbie said as soon as Olivia entered the student's office.

"Why? What's going on?"

"Well, it's not just a simple disagreement they're having about you helping Dr. Williams with no one asking Dr. Lynch," Abbie said.

"But I had checked with Dr. Williams about that. She said collaboration with grad students was fine and that she was going to tell Dr. Lynch," Olivia said, but her palms were growing clammy.

"Well, she didn't. Probably on purpose," Abbie said.

"What do you mean?"

"They have a not-so-happy history. It's a deep-rooted feud that has stretched back for years," Abbie said.

"Really?" Olivia's eyebrows shot up in surprise.

She had never imagined there was any real tension between Dr. Williams and Dr. Lynch. Abbie's revelation made her stomach churn. Had she, without knowing it, stumbled into a much larger conflict?

"Yeah. Dr. Lynch once tried to shut down Dr. Williams' lab just to claim it for herself," Abbie said. "There are also rumors that

Dr. Lynch sabotaged Dr. Williams' grant application. People said that Dr. Lynch went so far as to pay someone to tamper with the requirements that were already completed."

"Wow. That's... underhanded, to say the least," Olivia said.

"And Dr. Williams didn't just let it go. She constantly criticizes Dr. Lynch's methods," Abbie said. "She'd denounce Dr. Lynch's work, suggesting that Dr. Lynch fabricated all of her data. She's trying to tarnish Dr. Lynch's reputation among other researchers, hoping people wouldn't want to work with her."

Olivia was at a loss for words. It was becoming apparent that the conflict between the professors went beyond professional differences; it was personal—they hated each other. She wondered if helping Dr. Williams had damaged her relationship with her mentor.

"Like I said before, you should have treaded carefully..." Abbie's words hung in the air.

The story left Olivia reeling. She worried she had gotten tangled in a conflict she couldn't handle. Plus, Olivia was a little surprised that Abbie knew all these things, since she was just a master's student.

The bitter rivalry that had once simmered beneath the surface was now laid bare before her, casting a shadow over her own aspirations in the competitive arena of academia. Olivia felt hurt when she reflected on Dr. Williams' true motives for involving her. It became apparent that it wasn't about genuine collaboration or needing her help; it was a strategic move to undermine Dr. Lynch. She felt like Dr. Williams had manipulated her as a pawn in a larger scheme. Now, she worried about hidden agendas and ulterior motives in every interaction and exchange.

"Dr. Lynch is definitely pissed with both you and Dr. Williams," Abbie said. "But she deals with things in a passive-aggressive manner, so don't count on her addressing you."

Olivia attempted to email both Dr. Lynch and Dr. Williams to understand if either of them was upset with her. Despite her attempts, both parties remained silent. It seemed Abbie was right about the passive-aggressive behavior.

Olivia, receiving no replies or feedback, felt uncertain about what to do next. She continued attending classes, immersing herself in the preparation for her upcoming qualifying exam. Yet, as she glanced at her name on the grant application, a swell of pride enveloped her. But worry lingered. What if Dr. Williams secured the grant? Would Dr. Lynch see Olivia as a rival rather than a mentee? And if Dr. Lynch won the grant, would she overlook Olivia's contributions? Wasn't it Dr. Lynch's duty to guide Olivia toward independence in navigating the competitive world of grants and research? With these questions swirling in her mind, Olivia sensed potential trouble ahead, hinting that fate might have other plans for her.

CHAPTER 8

September 2016

Assigned to investigate a bomb at Virginia Tech's computer lab, Rachel and Mitchell arrived in Roanoke, Virginia. An FBI agent for three years, Rachel had gained a reputation for her proficiency in solving explosive cases. She and Mitchell had formed a formidable team in the streets of Boston. But their expertise extended beyond New England; they were often called to help in many states across the country.

Consistent with their multi-state practice, the ATF searched the campus corporate research center after arriving. They had yet to uncover any additional bombs or imminent risks.

The explosion had originated at the Thunderbird cluster, a section within the research center equipped with many computer clusters and servers. The blast, thankfully, only damaged the infrastructure. The aftermath revealed a scene of technological wreckage rather than human casualties.

"Why do they need us here?" Rachel asked Mitchell as they pulled up to the campus.

Her eyes scanned the scene, noting the multitude of personnel present—officers, FBI agents, ATF members. Amidst the crowd, she also spotted two Special Agent Bomb Techs from the Virginia field office, distinguishable by their protective gear. The situation appeared well under control, so why had they been called in?

"'Cause we're just that good," Mitchell said with a smirk, his sarcasm not lost on Rachel as he glanced at her from the passenger seat.

They parked the car and stepped out, making their way towards the bomb scene. Rachel surveyed the area, again noting the many officials already present, leaving her uncertain about whom to approach. Her gaze drifted to an old stone church a few blocks away, its walls covered with climbing rose bushes.

"Are those churches in every bumfuck town in the South?" Rachel asked, knowing Mitchell hailed from Florida.

"Hey!" Mitchell said, his eyes widening in mock offense. "Blacksburg, Virginia, is not some bumfuck town. And yes, every southern town has those churches."

They pressed forward, heading straight for the computer lab where the damaged wall offered a partial view of the debris strewn inside. A technician greeted them before they had the chance to start a conversation.

"Special Agent Quinn, right?" a young female technician called out, catching Rachel off guard.

"Yes..." Rachel said, surprised that someone from Virginia was familiar with her.

"I reached out to you guys. My name is Nikki, I'm a new bomb tech. During our investigation here, we found pipe bomb fragments. But there's more..." she said, holding up a piece of light blue fabric.

Rachel, transfixed by the technician's colorful fabric, barely noticed the smoke curling from the bombed lab. She glanced around and spotted fragments of fabric scattered throughout the wreckage with some snagged on twisted pieces of metal.

"Is that what I think it is?" Rachel asked.

"It's a blue self-adhesive bandage," Nikki said. "I also found remnants of some kind of suture used to hold the bomb pieces together."

Rachel's stomach dropped as recognition set in, her breath catching in her throat. She'd heard this before. In response to the bomb tech, she was silent, her attention glued to the fabric, mouth ajar.

"I just finished bomb tech training, and we discussed your Georgia case with the pipe bombs that had blue bandages and sutures," Nikki said. "It's pretty rare, so I think this might be the same guy."

"Professor Eric J. Neil. Thank you for reaching out to us," Rachel said.

"No problem!" Nikki said. "We've got a lot of things under control, but when I spotted this bandage, I figured it was worth giving you a heads-up. I'm happy to help with anything you need once I'm finished here."

With that, she resumed searching through the wrecked computer lab. Rachel and Mitchell stepped back a few paces from the bomb scene, giving themselves some space to discuss the situation.

"So, you think it's the professor again?" Mitchell asked.

"Yes. We've been over this. Light blue bandages and sutures on pipe bombs were unheard of until the incident at the church in Georgia," Rachel said.

"Do you think he's a doctor?"

"Well, he insisted on being called 'doctor,' but he wasn't medical; he was a physics professor," Rachel said. "But he also falsified his credentials to land his job at Emory."

"But I think finding sutures within bomb debris suggests he has access to medical supplies you can't really buy at a drugstore," Mitchell said.

Rachel hesitated, not sure how to respond to Mitchell. Suppose the bomber was a doctor. The thought churned in her mind. Why would a doctor target a church and then a computer lab? She had spent the past three years searching for him, unbeknownst to Mitchell. She thought she had looked everywhere, but found no trace of him. No evidence of him involved in other bombings, no bandages on bombs—nothing. But what if he had struck elsewhere in the meantime, flying under her radar?

Rachel felt uneasy considering further investigation. Last time she chased this guy in Georgia, he attacked her with pepper spray. Since the Virginia FBI field office had sufficient staff, her and Mitchell's trip to Virginia seemed unnecessary. The bomb tech had reached out because she said she recognized the Georgia case. Rachel suspected that the new tech's memory was likely more for Rachel's rule-breaking in Georgia than for the case itself.

"Looks like officers, a sketch artist, and student witnesses are over there," Mitchell said, gesturing to a nearby group. "Lets see if they have suspect information."

Rachel glanced over and nodded in agreement.

———————◆———————

Together, they approached the investigators, who were amid questioning two young student witnesses. Not wanting to disrupt the flow, Rachel and Mitchell displayed their badges when the investigators looked over at them. With a nod of acknowledgment, the investigators returned their focus to the witnesses, prompting them to continue speaking.

"…he was running toward us. Dressed in sweats and a hooded sweatshirt, he seemed like a runner to us, but appeared exhausted, almost on the verge of passing out," the student witness recalled.

"Yeah, I even made a comment that it looked like he was trying too hard or maybe he was a new runner. I believed he ran with someone, maybe a trainer," a second witness said—the first's girlfriend.

"I didn't see another guy. Right after the sweaty guy went past us, there was a loud explosion in front of us, and we saw smoke and fire," the boyfriend said.

"I immediately called 911. We thought maybe there was an electrical problem within the computer labs. We were on our way there," the girlfriend said.

"But I knew it was that guy who set it up and was running. He looked so scared and sweaty, and I realized he was running so he wouldn't blow himself up," the boyfriend said.

"You've seen his face?" the investigator said.

"Oh, yeah," the boyfriend witness confirmed, shaking his head.

"Alright, if you could describe him to the sketch artist, that would be helpful."

The sketch artist, dressed like a starving artist with wild hair, a large notebook, and several different sized pencils, stepped forward. He positioned himself in front of the witnesses, a slight distance away from the investigators, and began sketching.

Rachel and Mitchell introduced themselves to the Virginia FBI investigators, explaining why they had traveled from Boston. They clarified that a bomb technician had reached out to them because of finding a bandage and suture on the bomb fragments, similar to a case they had investigated in Georgia three years ago.

"You think this is the same guy?" the investigator asked.

"I do," Rachel said. "He escaped in Georgia, and until today, we haven't seen suture on pipe bombs, so I believe it's him again."

The investigator seemed skeptical of Rachel's assertion and adopted a rather questioning tone. "Do you know why he does it? His motive?"

She hesitated. With Mitchell, she'd built a solid track record—but Georgia was proving different. And she hated not having an answer.

"No. We found nothing in Georgia, and our investigation here has just begun," she said, sarcasm curling her words. The way he spoke—like she was a rookie—grated more than she let on.

The sketch artist finished his composite sketch much faster than Rachel expected, cutting off any potential for the conversation to turn confrontational. He handed the investigator the drawing based on the witness descriptions. The investigator examined it, but it didn't seem to provide him with much help. He then turned it toward Rachel and Mitchell.

Rachel's heart skipped a beat as she recognized the face in the sketch—it was unmistakably Professor Eric J. Neil. She glanced at Mitchell, who wore a knowing expression, shaking his head, confirming her suspicion.

"Professor Eric J. Neil," Rachel said, her voice more steady this time.

"This is your guy?" the investigator said.

"Yup. That's the guy from Georgia," Rachel said.

"So, what next?" The investigator's tone had shifted, abandoning any trace of condescension. He appeared eager to collaborate with Rachel to catch the bomber.

"I'm certain he works at this university. In Georgia, he faked his ID and landed a job at Emory, so I'd wager he's doing the same here at Virginia Tech," Rachel said.

She entertained the idea of recounting her failed attempt to apprehend him alone, but she didn't want to admit her mistake.

"Let me gather a handful of officers, and we can canvas the university with this image to see if we can locate or at least identify him," the investigator proposed, sparing Rachel from having to recommend that no one search for him alone.

The investigator used his cell phone to organize a large group of officers. Using provided composite images, the investigator created two- to three-person teams to search the school. They were all instructed to cover various campus areas, including a nearby hospital, in case the suspect was a doctor.

Rachel and Mitchell interviewed several classrooms, the cafe, and a few labs, but no one recognized the sketch artist's image. The search stretched into hours, yet they relished the coffee and snacks when at the cafe.

"You wanna take a break or keep going?" Mitchell asked.

Rachel felt exhausted, but couldn't bear to give up. She needed to find this guy. She rolled her eyes and sighed.

"Let's finish these last two buildings; then, we'll eat. Or maybe we should check out the hospital."

Rachel and Mitchell entered a lab where a few students were engaged in various tasks. The space had a few cluttered lab benches with equipment, computers scattered around the room, whiteboards with scribbled notes, and a few stools and desk chairs.

"We're Special Agents from the FBI, investigating the explosion at the computer lab," Mitchell announced, as they both displayed their badges.

"We use the Thunderbird all the time; we're lucky we weren't over there," one student remarked.

"Everyone was lucky," Mitchell acknowledged. "No one got hurt; only the building, computers, and some servers were destroyed."

Rachel pulled out the sketch artist's drawing and handed it to the students. They passed it around, shaking their heads in confusion until it reached the last young woman, who studied it longer than the others.

"Yeah, this is that professor... uh... professor... oh, I can't remember his name," she struggled. "You know, the one who doesn't really work here, the locum professor."

"Locum professor?" Rachel asked.

"Yeah, like a substitute teacher," she clarified as she passed the image back to the first student.

"Oh yeah, it does look like him... um... Professor Lucas," one student said.

"Right! Professor Lucas."

"Professor Lucas," Rachel echoed.

"Yes. He's brand new. He doesn't really work here; he just fills in. But he's always in this lab, constantly using our EMF meters."

"Your what?" Rachel asked.

As they stood, the students excitedly pointed to the equipment on the far side of the lab. "Electromagnetic field radia..." the young woman started, but a sudden commotion cut off her words. Someone near the equipment jumped from the floor, surprising everyone. In the process, he knocked over a large shelf with a loud crash, sending equipment tumbling and breaking on the floor before darting out the door.

Escaping the computer lab, he sprinted through campus, weaving between students and faculty. Rachel and Mitchell burst outside and spotted him running ahead. They chased after him, with Rachel pulling out her gun as they pursued. The suspect, wearing a hooded sweatshirt, gripped a rectangular metal object topped with a black ball the size of a baseball. Though he resembled Professor Eric J. Neil in stature and hooded sweatshirt, Rachel didn't see his face.

Just as they were gaining ground, just in front of them, Rachel saw a group of uniformed students on the campus lawn. Clad in camouflage, they appeared to be Army but were likely ROTC cadets conducting a drill. Mitchell, having been in the military, told her during the flight down that Virginia Tech has one of the largest Corps of Cadets in the nation, with several hundred students taking part in formations.

The man in the hooded sweatshirt bolted directly into the formation of cadets. Rachel swore under her breath as she realized what he was trying to do. The students always remain steadfast in their formations, refusing to budge as the fleeing suspect dives through their ranks. Amidst the sea of cadets, it was impossible to see the professor.

Determined, Rachel pushed through the formation while Mitchell maneuvered around them, both searching for the man in the hooded sweatshirt. She scanned the ranks, her eyes flashing from one face to another.

"Rachel!" Mitchell's voice cut through the formation from the other side of the cadets.

Rachel emerged from the formation, only to see the suspect sprinting back toward the scene of the computer lab bomb, as if completing a large circle.

They resumed their pursuit, their footsteps pounding against the ground as they continued to sprint after him. Rachel's eyes remain locked on him, driven by adrenaline as they continued the chase. The suspect made a beeline for the stone church ahead, vanishing inside as the heavy door slammed shut behind him.

With his speed, Mitchell took the lead, circling around the building to intercept the professor if he tried to escape out the back. Meanwhile, Rachel charged forward into the church.

Inside, emptiness and darkness enveloped Rachel. The air hung heavy, cold and still. She scanned the dimly lit room, pews extending toward the pulpit. Finding no one, she moved quickly through the church, checking behind each pew and peering beneath the fabric-covered pulpit. Her search yielded nothing. Mitchell arrived just as Rachel slipped out the back door.

"He didn't come out?" Rachel asked, breathless from her search.

"No," Mitchell said, scanning the area outside. "There's no one out here. He has to be hiding inside."

They entered the church again through the back door and found more investigators coming in through the front, having joined the pursuit upon hearing about their chase. They all worked together, combing through every corner of the church. However, they found nothing, only rows of empty pews.

After the FBI called off the search of the church, Rachel and Mitchell found themselves in a familiar predicament reminiscent of their case in Georgia. They remained in Virginia for about a week, scouring the area for any sign of Professor Neil, or Professor Lucas, or whatever his real name may be. Despite their efforts, they came up empty-handed once again. The professor left behind no evidence or traces of his identity. He remained unknown, even to locals. He again vanished without a trace.

"How the fuck did he just disappear?" Rachel asked.

Mitchell remained silent as he handed her the report to sign. Accepting the end of the investigation was becoming difficult for Rachel. Reluctantly, she signed off on the documents detailing their failures before they headed back to Massachusetts.

During the flight back to Boston, Rachel's determination hardened into obsession. She couldn't stop thinking about capturing the professor, despite her repeated failures. She avoided speaking to Mitchell, anticipating his criticism—and knowing he wouldn't help her anyway. Part of her wanted to redouble her efforts; another part doubted she could succeed alone. *How does someone just disappear? How do we catch him?* She had no idea what to do next.

CHAPTER 9

September 2016
WNRC 94.7 FM RADIO REPORT
LIVE AT FIVE

Richard Malone: "Good evening, Blacksburg. It's five o'clock, and you're tuned in to *Live at Five* on WNRC 94.7 FM. I'm Richard Malone, and as you know, it's been a pretty tumultuous day here. We've got updates on that mysterious flash flood that struck the South Fork Creek area yesterday afternoon, causing extensive damage and multiple injuries. Six residents are hospitalized, three are in critical condition, and one person is still missing."

Deborah Wilcox: "Richard, I'm out here in South Fork, and it's like nothing I've ever seen before. The residents are shaken, confused, and honestly, just seeking answers. There was no rain yesterday, no storms on the horizon, and yet, this sudden flood hits out of nowhere. Families barely had time to react before the water was already inside their homes."

Richard Malone: "Let's get right into what we know so far. Authorities have confirmed there was no warning—no heavy rainfall, no issues reported with the creek upstream, and no broken infrastructure like a dam failure. And yet, South Fork was underwater in minutes."

Deborah Wilcox: "And, Richard, it's not just the absence of weather events that's strange. According to a few residents I spoke to, the water didn't rise like it would with a typical flood. They described it as if the creek had been released all at once. One neighbor, who's lived by the creek his whole life, said he's seen nothing like it."

Richard Malone: "So it's not just a flash flood—it's behaving in a way that defies what you'd expect from a natural event. That's unusual. And Deb, you've mentioned earlier about federal authorities being involved. What can you tell us about that?"

Deborah Wilcox: "Yes, Richard. The FBI was already in town yesterday, before the flood. I've spoken to a few locals who saw them coming into Virginia Tech in response to a bombing in a computer lab. Luckily, the damage was limited to computers and servers; no one was injured. When questioned, the Bureau says they are conducting a 'routine investigation' and are not involved with a 'not routine' flash flood."

Richard Malone: "This isn't speculation; the timing suggests something more significant than coincidence. Federal authorities arriving, and then hours later, we have this unexplained event. Have they released any information on their involvement yet?"

Deborah Wilcox: "No, nothing concrete. They've been pretty tight-lipped, Richard. It's adding to the tension in the community, with people wanting straightforward answers. I sense more is happening behind the scenes, and we are uninformed. Local law enforcement are the only organization saying they're working closely with federal agencies to determine the cause of the flood."

Richard Malone: "You know, Deb, I've been going through some calls we've gotten today, and the theories are already rolling in. Everything from the computer lab bomb, underground reservoir breaches to—believe it or not—some kind of experimental technology mishap."

Deborah Wilcox: "Technology mishap? That's… new. I haven't heard that one yet."

Richard Malone: "Yeah, someone called in earlier suggesting that the surge of water could have resulted from an electromagnetic anomaly. I'm not sure where these theories come from, but people are scrambling to find explanations for what happened yesterday. There's a small online group whispering about something incredible—a time traveler."

Deborah Wilcox: "Time traveler? You're kidding."

Richard Malone: "I know, it sounds ridiculous, but it's out there in the rumor mill. Probably a joke or one of those conspiracy theory forums."

Deborah Wilcox: "Well, considering what we've seen, it's almost understandable why people are reaching for the most outlandish explanations. And it's not just the flood itself that's worrying people, Richard. There's also been talk of some strange sounds just before the water surged. Several residents mentioned hearing what they described as a low, mechanical rumbling, but with no source in sight."

Richard Malone: "Did any experts comment on that?"

Deborah Wilcox: "Not officially, but I spoke with Dr. Alan Graves, a hydrologist at Virginia Tech. He said the flood patterns matched nothing he's ever seen in his thirty years of studying regional waterways. He called the sudden rise 'anomalous,' which, if you read between the lines, means they're at a loss for an explanation."

Richard Malone: "Anomalous is right. Community tension seems to stem from this. Deb, any news on the missing resident?"

Deborah Wilcox: "The search is still ongoing. Teams have been working throughout the day to comb through houses and surrounding areas. The missing resident is an elderly woman in her seventies who lived near the creek. Family members have been assisting in the search, but there's been no sign of her yet."

Richard Malone: "That's heartbreaking. We'll continue to hope for the best there. For those just tuning in, we're talking about the sudden and unexplained flash flood that hit South Fork yesterday, causing injuries and leaving at least one person missing. No storms, no rain. The creek surged without warning, and authorities are still searching for a cause. This all happened just hours after federal agents arrived at Virginia Tech for what they're calling an unrelated investigation."

Deborah Wilcox: "It's a lot for this community to process, Richard. Difficult times prompt a search for understanding; however, closer examination frequently generates further questions."

Richard Malone: "You're absolutely right, Deb. And for now, all we can do is keep pressing for answers. We've got Dr. Gregory Morrow lined up next to give us his perspective on the unusual water patterns and shed some light on the events of yesterday. And folks, if you've got theories, questions, or information, we're here, and the phone lines are open."

Deborah Wilcox: "And Richard, before I go, one last thing. There's been a lot of speculation out here—some are connecting this flood with those odd power surges we had. Nothing concrete, but people haven't forgotten that. Whatever's happening, it feels like there's more beneath the surface."

Richard Malone: "Agreed, Deb. And I have a feeling this story is far from over. Thanks for all your hard work today, and stay safe out there."

Deborah Wilcox: "Thanks, Richard."

Richard Malone: "For everyone listening, stay tuned to *Live at Five* on WNRC 94.7 FM. We'll be back after this break with more updates and insights from experts. You will not want to miss this."

CHAPTER 10

December 2020

In the beginning, Olivia had thought that Dr. Lynch might feel proud that her student took part in a grant competition. However, Abbie had warned her that academia is sometimes cutthroat, especially when concerning grant money. Abbie referred to it as "publish or perish"—if Dr. Lynch didn't secure grants through groundbreaking publications, she'd perish. Abbie thought that Dr. Lynch might retaliate since Olivia assisted Dr. Williams, her competitor. However, Dr. Lynch remained silent, continuing to ignore Olivia and skip her presentations, though she did attend her qualifying exam.

The PhD qualifying exam was to assess Olivia's understanding of physics and her ability to conduct her own high-level research. Passing this exam is required before one can advance to the next stage of their graduate program where they start their own dissertation research.

Olivia had only briefly encountered the members of her PhD committee before the qualifier. She had met both Dr. Edward Kingsley and Dr. Sean O'Brien in person on campus, and the outside member, Dr. Walker, she knew only through interactions with Zoom.

Dr. Kingsley, a man of British origin, possessed an air of smug pretentiousness that was hard to ignore. His aristocratic demeanor was further highlighted by his distinctive British accent, which he never seemed to lose despite years in the United States. He stood at six-foot-two, with a lean build that added to his imposing presence. His salt-and-pepper hair, slicked back, added an extra layer of refinement to his appearance. His wardrobe, always filled with expensive suits, was a testament to his obsession with perfection. He preferred designer ties and cufflinks that often bordered on ostentatious, which only further emphasized his sense of superiority.

Dr. O'Brien looked disheveled. He was of average height, but carried a few extra pounds that gave him a rumpled appearance. With unkempt hair that looked like it hadn't seen a comb in days, and a perpetual five o'clock shadow, he often appeared as if he were on the brink of nodding off. His wardrobe stood in sharp contrast to Dr. Kingsley's—rumpled shirts, stained jeans, and scuffed sneakers made it clear he had little interest in fashion. There were rumors circulating that he might have had a penchant for alcohol, given his occasional slurred speech and the faint scent of liquor that lingered around him.

Olivia's success in her qualifying exam came with surprising ease. Dr. O'Brien seemed disengaged, almost as if he had been asleep throughout the process, and Dr. Kingsley appeared indifferent to the proceedings. Likewise, Dr. Lynch remained silent, asking Olivia no questions.

With her qualification secured, Olivia was eager to start her own independent research. However, her excitement was short-lived as she began attending lab meetings with Dr. Lynch's team, and she came to realize the lab's corruption.

❖

February 2021

Olivia's transition into Dr. Lynch's lab meetings marked a significant shift in her academic career. She had spent her first few years in the student's office in the research building that housed the linear accelerator. Aside from the computer program she crafted for Dr. Williams, she didn't take part in much research; her focus was on attending classes.

Olivia's first lab meeting as a part of Dr. Lynch's team took place in a conference room with a large picture window and a pretty, blue beta fish. It was then that she first encountered Dr. Lynch's two postdoctoral fellows, Brittney Turner and Sofia Mendoza. Brittney had begun her postdoc a year earlier, while Sofia had joined the team about six months ago. After introductions, Dr. Lynch dominated the conversation, allowing little room for others to take part. Her demeanor remained arrogant, and her remarks regarding the statistics she used in her most recent grant application were consistently inaccurate.

Brittney, with a distinctive blonde pixie cut and buck teeth, appeared to be a complete sycophant during the meeting. She seldom uttered a word in response to Dr. Lynch, except to praise any statement made by her, regardless of its accuracy. Sofia, a tiny young woman, sat silently, taking notes. She was from the Philippines, but she said that her family had moved to the US when she was just a baby.

Dr. Franklin Collins, another member of the group who had his own lab in the building, also attended the meeting. He was a somewhat portly man with an unkempt shock of graying hair. His glasses perched precariously on the tip of his bulbous nose, his expression bore a perpetual vacant stare. When Dr. Lynch had finished, he ventured into discussions about various experiments he purported to have completed that left Olivia perplexed because of their complete lack of coherence.

Despite Olivia's genuine curiosity and attempts to ask questions, both Dr. Lynch and Dr. Collins dismissed her, attributing her inquiries to her status as a new graduate student who didn't grasp the intricacies of research. Their words stung.

"This is how things are done. Exclude negative data or it looks like you don't know what you're doing," Dr. Lynch said, "Repeating computer programs from your undergraduate studies doesn't equate to competence. You are simply naïve and inexperienced."

"Welcome to academia," Dr. Collins said with a smirk.

As the meeting concluded, Dr. Lynch and Dr. Collins nonchalantly exited, leaving Brittney with instructions to send her work to Dr. O'Brien for revisions. Dr. Lynch tasked Olivia with submitting her research plan, implying her "stupid questions" showed incompetence and that she needed to refocus.

Olivia sat in stunned disbelief as the meeting drew to a close, her jaw scraping the floor. Dr. Lynch's glaring statistical errors were an affront to Olivia, who had just completed a rigorous statistics class. Olivia also recalled Dr. Lynch's previous blunder regarding Newton's law, casting a shadow of doubt over the professor's competence. Was Dr. Lynch, the supposed expert, an impostor?

These disconcerting thoughts swirled in Olivia's mind, leaving her bewildered. It didn't go unnoticed by Brittney, who, with a smug smirk, broke the silence.

"Something on your mind, Olivia?" Brittney's tone dripped with sarcasm, and she seemed to relish Olivia's evident confusion.

"I... I don't really know what just happened," Olivia said, her words uncertain. "Did I misunderstand everything that I've learned so far?"

"Are you serious?" Brittney said, raising an eyebrow. "You realize they don't know what they're doing, right?"

Sofia, still looking down at her notebook, let out a soft giggle.

Olivia's faith in Dr. Lynch's reputation as a renowned physicist wavered, doubt creeping into her mind. She felt a knot form in her stomach as her brow furrowed and her lips pressed into a thin line.

"But Dr. Lynch is a well-known physicist. Her papers have revealed many breakthroughs, and she's secured more grants than most physicists on the East Coast."

"Yeah, she got those lying on her back," Brittney said, and Sofia giggled once more.

"Are you kidding?" Olivia asked, her eyebrows shooting up in disbelief. She was dumbfounded, her mouth falling agape again as she struggled to process this unexpected news.

"What do you think? Who do you suppose she's fucking here to keep this job?" Brittney said with her biting sarcasm, her disdain clear as she headed for the door.

Olivia remained speechless, torn between disbelief and doubt, especially given Brittney's abrupt about-face from fawning over Dr. Lynch during the meeting to criticizing her afterward.

Before leaving the conference room, Sofia leaned in close to Olivia, her voice barely above a whisper. "Don't worry about it, Olivia. Just keep your mouth shut and do what she says, or Dr. Lynch will ruin your life."

CHAPTER 11

Wanting to question Olivia, Rachel hesitated, but then decided against it. Olivia's bitterness and anger were clear, and her disparaging remarks about her colleagues created a vivid picture. She didn't just criticize them; she portrayed them as caricatures straight out of a cartoon—ugly, arrogant, portly, and with buck teeth.

In her years with the FBI, Rachel had learned that when individuals like Olivia started talking, it was best to just let them continue. They would often incriminate themselves in their own words, and Olivia seemed on the verge of revealing something significant. Rachel believed Olivia could have been capable of planting a bomb in the research building.

Just as Olivia took a deep breath, poised to share more, Rachel's phone buzzed with a text from Mitchell, asking her to take a break to speak with him outside the interrogation room. She felt a pang of annoyance, torn between the desire to uncover the truth from Olivia and her interest in the updates from Mitchell.

"Why don't we take a quick break, Olivia? I could use some more coffee," Rachel said.

"Yeah, I could use a break and some more coffee," Olivia said with relief in her voice.

Rachel turned to the officer accompanying them. "This officer will take you for a bathroom break, and I'll refill our coffees."

In the bullpen, Rachel found Mitchell waiting.

"How's it going?" he asked.

"So far, so good," Rachel said. "She's furious and really talking."

"Was she involved with the explosion?" Mitchell asked.

"I don't know yet. Maybe," Rachel said. "Her attitude about the people in that lab is truly hostile; she hates them. But I haven't decided whether I believe she actually planted a bomb."

"I've got some info for you before you continue with her." Mitchell leaned in to share some crucial updates.

"The ATF found fragments from likely three different pipe bombs and—" Mitchell began, but Rachel interrupted before he could finish.

"Pipe bombs? Did they find bandages or sutures?" Rachel asked, eyes bright with urgency.

"Not that I know of," Mitchell said. "But they found some remote detonators that were probably connected to cell phones, so anyone near the building could have set them off."

"So, Olivia could have done it from just outside to make it look like she wasn't involved?" Rachel asked.

"Yup," Mitchell said. "Unfortunately, we're still waiting on the identification of the bodies recovered from the rubble. The DNA and dental records are still pending. We also had a conversation with Dr. Richardson this morning, and he told us Dr. Lynch is stable, still in a coma, but at least not getting worse. However, we still can't find her husband. He's not answering his cell phone, he's not at home, and apparently he called his office yesterday and took personal time for the rest of the week."

"That's interesting," Rachel said, thoughts sparking one after another.

"We also haven't been able to find Brittney or Ethan. Brittney's apartment has been empty for days, but she apparently stays most days with her boyfriend at his apartment downtown," Mitchell said. "We spoke to him, but he's a lawyer in the middle of a murder trial, so he didn't know if she didn't come home last night. We also went to Ethan's address, which wasn't actually a residential address—it was a UPS store."

"Well, shit. Where the fuck are these people? Is Sofia still at home? I'd like to ask her some questions about Olivia."

"Sofia was supposed to come down to answer questions, but she hasn't shown up," Mitchell said. "She's also not answering her phone."

"Perfect," Rachel said, rolling her eyes. "We need to send an officer over to pick her up."

Mitchell nodded in agreement before continuing.

"We've also got a plan in motion," Mitchell said, a determined look in his eyes. "We're going to flag license plates, issue BOLOs for their cars, and maybe try to track cell phones while you continue with Olivia. Meanwhile, I'll head over to the morgue to see if I can persuade the medical examiner to expedite the DNA on those recovered bodies."

Rachel nodded. "Sounds good. Keep me updated."

"So, do you still think it's the professor?" Mitchell asked. Rachel sighed, rolling her eyes skyward again, like patience might be hiding there.

"Yes, it could still be the professor. But it could also be any of these people we're investigating. This is a fuckin' mess."

Mitchell laughed, pointed at the swear jar, then briskly headed for the exit, pulling out his phone as he went.

After watching Mitchell's quick exit, Rachel turned her attention to the coffeepot, filling both cups to the brim. The rich aroma of fresh coffee filled the air, briefly jolting her awake. She also picked up a couple of granola bars and a banana, intending to boost both her and Olivia's energy levels.

With the coffee cups and snacks in hand, Rachel reentered the interrogation room where Olivia sat, waiting for her. Rachel leaned forward, her eyes locked on Olivia's.

"Alright, Olivia, are you ready to continue?"

CHAPTER 12

January 2022

After completing her classes nearly four years into her PhD program, Olivia was assigned only to her mentor's lab. But far from feeling free to pursue her research, she now sensed herself trapped within its walls. She submitted her meticulously crafted research plan as requested by Dr. Lynch, hoping for guidance and mentorship. Instead, Dr. Lynch sent her an e-mail containing a "revised" research plan that was a laundry list of mundane lab duties—maintaining computers, cleaning whiteboards, and conducting simple experiments with predetermined outcomes that would construct Olivia basic dissertation.

Dr. Lynch's advice carried a firm tone, constantly reminding Olivia that her stipend came from the lab budget and that she had no choice but to do as she directed. She insisted Olivia should abandon her fanciful experiments, as Olivia was, in her view, incapable anyway. According to Dr. Lynch, Olivia would find greater happiness if she surrendered her silly ambitions and just did what she was told.

That's precisely what Olivia elected to do. She was assuming more of a role as a silent spectator rather than an active contributor. Olivia had always been quiet and reserved, reluctant to stand up for herself. She shied away from confrontation, always opting for the easier, quieter path.

Though she was angry with herself for not taking action, she leaned on determinism to justify her inaction. No matter how hard Olivia worked, it always seemed like the universe had other plans.

Oddly enough, as Olivia said less and less, both Dr. Lynch and Dr. Collins were more and more pleased, reinforcing Olivia's behavior. They appeared to appreciate Olivia more when she became a passive presence in meetings who found peace in gazing at the bright blue beta fish, who she named Walter. Walter swam around in his fishbowl, which featured a live plant serving as both a lid and an underwater canopy.

As the days turned into weeks and then into months, Olivia became invisible, almost like a ghost haunting the lab. She found that when everyone remained silent and didn't argue with Dr. Lynch, choosing instead to agree and do what they were told, an unusual calm settled over the lab.

Olivia battled a deep sense of depression, considering that she might have to abandon her graduate program. But she couldn't just turn back now. She had come too far to waste everything she'd worked for. She knew that if she could endure a bit more time in silence, she could escape.

However, while she remained subdued in the lab, Olivia's mind raced with ideas. The resources offered by the school's library and computer facilities were too valuable to abandon, even in the face of her stifling environment. Tucked away in the quiet seclusion of the student's office, safe from prying eyes, she focused on her own research.

Olivia harbored a deep-seated fascination with advancing Einstein's theories concerning the river of time. Her focus lay on the intriguing concept of whirlpools, where changes in the environment might induce changes in time itself.

She aimed to explore whether specific locations on Earth possessed unique peculiarities that, with her addition of electro-magnetism, might trigger forming these temporal whirlpools. However, she questioned whether creating whirlpools even mattered. With Olivia's firm conviction in the universe's pre-determined nature, she struggled to see how whirlpools could genuinely facilitate any meaningful change.

These thoughts spurred her to do more research in secret, adding another layer of complexity to her already full plate of experiments. With so many investigations to juggle solo, self-doubt crept in. She wondered whether her hypotheses were far-fetched, especially since Dr. Lynch and Dr. Collins repeatedly emphasized her supposed ignorance.

Olivia figured it mattered little at this point because no one was overseeing her research, anyway. She didn't have any actual work to do in the lab—just updating computers.

Olivia seldom ventured into Dr. Lynch's office, avoiding her, save for the obligatory lab meetings. Yet, there was one computer that had resisted her updates, requiring Dr. Lynch's password. After procrastinating for far too long, Olivia mustered the resolve to tackle the issue. She ascended the stairs leading to Dr. Lynch's office, determined to just get it over with.

Approaching Dr. Lynch's half-open door, Olivia had intended to knock once and make a quick request for the much-needed password. However, her plans took an unexpected turn when she looked into the office.

Dr. Lynch was bent over her ornate desk, Dr. Kingsley behind her with his expensive pants around his ankles. They attempted to keep their passionate encounter quiet, but with the door left open, discretion was out of the question. Olivia stood in stunned silence, her eyes widened in disbelief. Their disregard for secrecy was unmistakable. Was Brittney telling the truth about Dr. Lynch's proclivities? Dr. Lynch had tied the knot with a psychologist a few years back, and Dr. Kingsley, a father of two boys, was also married. Their involvement with each other was bad enough, but displaying it in the lab was utterly revolting.

In her haste to escape the surreal scene, Olivia turned and almost sprinted back down the stairs. In her mad dash, she collided with Dr. Collins, whose office was next to Dr. Lynch's.

"Oh, Olivia, I'm sorry. I had to use the bathroom, so I wasn't at my usual post. You didn't see anything you weren't supposed to, did you?" Dr. Collins inquired with a lecherous grin as he glided past Olivia and back into his office.

Still in shock, Olivia, her face pale and her hands trembling, dashed to the neighboring building, her heart pounding with a mix of fear and adrenaline. She sought refuge in the familiar surroundings of the student office. Her breaths were coming in short, rapid gasps as she struggled to regain her composure. Unfortunately, Abbie was there gathering her things to leave, and she could sense that something had rattled Olivia.

"Hey Olivia, are you okay? You're as white as a ghost," Abbie remarked.

"Yes, yes, I'm fine," Olivia said. "I just don't feel well today. I might be coming down with something."

"Oh, well, I hope you feel better. Maybe you should go home to rest," Abbie said.

"Yeah, I think I'll do that," Olivia said.

"I'm leaving early today too, since it's my anniversary. Hey, did you see my husband on your way over here?" Abbie said.

"Oh, I didn't know you were married. Are you talking about Tom?" Olivia said, her eyes flicking toward the other graduate student's desk, her expression curious as she nodded in its direction.

Abbie chuckled. "Oh, no! I thought you knew! I'm married to your committee chair, Edward Kingsley!"

Olivia's stomach plummeted, and she felt as though she might be sick. She had just walked in on Dr. Kingsley and Dr. Lynch in flagrante on Dr. Lynch's pristine desk—on Dr. Kingsley's anniversary, no less. Should she tell Abbie what she just saw?

"Oh, Olivia, you need to go lie down right now; you look terrible," Abbie said.

Unable to face Abbie any longer, Olivia said nothing further and rushed from the student's office to lock herself in the bathroom.

August 2022

After Olivia witnessed Dr. Lynch and Dr. Kingsley's affair, the lab's status quo remained unchanged for what felt like an eternity. Day after day, Olivia had to maintain her silence. She cringed every time she watched Dr. Kingsley entering the building and ascending the stairs to Dr. Lynch's office.

As time went on, her struggle to conduct her own research in secrecy grew challenging. She steered clear of the student's office to avoid encounters with Abbie, leaving her with no choice but to spend time in the building with Dr. Lynch and Dr. Collins, who kept a watchful eye on her.

On the bright side, Dr. Lynch only appeared for lab meetings and her occasional rendezvous with Dr. Kingsley, usually once or twice a week. Dr. Collins, however, remained an unpredictable variable. He'd sometimes make unannounced visits to ensure everyone was toeing the line, keeping Olivia cautious and paranoid during her own clandestine experiments.

Part of Olivia's routine was entering the conference room for their dreaded weekly lab meeting. But this time, there was an unexpected addition: Dr. Sean O'Brien. The sight of him stopped her cold. Her fingers tightened around the notebook in her hand.

She assumed they had discovered her use of the lab computers, and that Dr. O'Brien—being on her committee—was there to join in the reprimand. But then she noticed the unmistakable signs: he was clearly intoxicated. Surprisingly, no one in the room seemed to even acknowledge how drunk he was at ten in the morning. Olivia just played along, pretending as if everything were normal.

Dr. O'Brien rambled loudly about the certificates on the wall, slurring his words, and even dozed off briefly with his head on the table, snoring, before resuming his commentary on the lab's projector. Still, no one reacted.

"Good morning, everyone," Dr. Lynch began, her voice brimming with enthusiasm. "Today, I want to congratulate Dr. O'Brien on his recent publication in Nature Physics."

She distributed copies of the paper around the table, her eyes gleaming with pride. Olivia glanced over at Dr. O'Brien, whose head was resting on the table, finding him an odd choice for such commendation.

"Dr. O'Brien will join us today to discuss his latest research developments and share insights into the art of publishing. His work truly embodies perfection," Dr. Lynch said.

Olivia blinked, unsure if she'd heard correctly. Was Dr. Lynch serious? Was this actually happening? Dr. O'Brien reeked of whiskey, his eyes glassy and unfocused—exactly like the rumors always claimed. There was no way his work was flawless. Yet around the table, heads bobbed in calm agreement, as if this were all completely normal.

Brittney, however, struggled to conceal her reaction. She stared at the paper, her mouth agape, and let out a small grunt before quickly regaining her composure. Olivia cast a questioning look at Brittney, but by then, Brittney had already reverted to her sycophantic facade, masking her true feelings.

Olivia then examined Dr. O'Brien's paper and understood Brittney's response. The paper was identical to the one Brittney had written and sent to Dr. O'Brien for revisions, as per Dr. Lynch's request. Dr. O'Brien had appropriated Brittney's work and published it under his own name, without even so much as an acknowledgement at the end.

Olivia kept her expression neutral, though revulsion twisted in her gut. Dr. Lynch was stealing her postdoc's work to prop up Dr. O'Brien. No one in the room flinched. The space pressed in on her, its walls lined with framed degrees and research awards that now felt like a cruel joke

Given what she'd seen in the lab, Olivia wasn't entirely surprised—but the pressure to stay composed was real. What did catch her off guard was Brittney's reaction, or rather, the lack of one. They were all expected to stay silent, but Olivia couldn't understand how Brittney managed such calm when she herself was barely holding it together.

At the conclusion of the meeting, Brittney stood up and left the room, not speaking to anyone and leaving her notebooks on the table. Dr. Lynch and Dr. Collins continued to shower Dr. O'Brien with accolades.

"I must say again, your work is truly remarkable, Dr. O'Brien," Dr. Lynch said.

Dr. Collins chimed in, "Indeed, it's a shining example of dedication and excellence."

As they walked out of the room, their voices carried just loud enough to sting.

"Let's hope this meeting was as productive for the rest of you," Dr. Lynch said, pausing mid-turn to glance over her shoulder. "Perhaps you'll catch up to Dr. O'Brien one day."

Dr. O'Brien himself, that Olivia now thought of as an alcoholic plagiarist, remained slouched in his chair, snoring softly, his disheveled appearance a clear sign of his personality.

Sofia shook her head while looking down at the table, grinning knowingly as she gathered her notebooks.

"I told Brittney not to send her work to Dr. O'Brien," Sofia said, flipping her pen between her fingers. "But she didn't listen. You know that paper he published last year in the *Journal of Applied Physics*? That was mine."

Olivia's eyes widened. "What?!"

"I sent my work to Dr. O'Brien for revisions, and that's when he told me…" Sofia's voice turned slurred and sarcastic as she mimicked him, "'Your work cannot allow for rigorous conclusions as the underpinnings are very weak and it's a waste of my time to revise.'"

Olivia didn't move. After what she'd seen at the lab meeting, the words barely registered as surprising.

"And then he published it as his own," Sofia said.

Olivia was at a loss for words. In a strange way, she felt relieved she wasn't the one writing papers or grant proposals—especially now, knowing Dr. Lynch had a habit of handing them off to Dr. O'Brien to pad his publication record. But why? Did he have some leverage over her? Was she sleeping with him too?

Olivia considered contacting the university ombudsman to discuss the things she'd witnessed in the lab. However, she dismissed that idea and called it an early day. The prospect of continuing to hide in the lab for the rest of the day was too much for her. Besides, she had an early start the next morning—8 a.m. sharp—as she was responsible for training the new lab tech, Ethan Delano.

CHAPTER 13

Rachel leaned back in her chair, her eyes never leaving Olivia, who sat across the table. The room was silent save for the hum of the overhead light, casting a harsh glow on the table between them. Rachel had been listening intently, jotting down notes, her pen scratching on the pad as she was trying to piece together the narrative being spun before her. However, her patience was wearing thin. Abruptly, she leaned forward, her eyes narrowing as she placed her hands flat on the table with a deliberate thud.

"You know, I've been sitting here, listening to you paint quite the picture about everyone in your lab," Rachel said, her tone measured but skeptical. "But here's the thing—I think you're using them as a smokescreen."

"What?" Olivia said as she fidgeted nervously. Sweat beaded on her forehead, her hands trembling slightly. Rachel watched her compulsively chew on her lower lip and tug at the sleeve of her sweatsuit.

"Well, you've spent the last hour taking us on a trip down memory lane, mentioning everyone in the lab except yourself or Ethan," Rachel said. "It sounds to me like you're more interested in protecting someone—maybe yourself—than in telling the truth."

"We did nothing wrong," Olivia said, her voice quivering, her eyes dropping to the table. Her shoulders slumped, and her face tightened as if she was fighting back tears.

"Right..." Rachel said, glancing down at her notes. "So, Dr. Lynch was having an affair with your chair, who happens to be married to... Abbie, your fellow student. Did you ever tell her that her husband was cheating on her?"

"No," Olivia said.

Rachel flipped through her notebook, her tone businesslike. She didn't bother with pleasantries.

"And Dr. O'Brien is a drunk who steals papers, Dr. Williams hates Dr. Lynch, and no professor in the lab knows what they're doing," Rachel said, raising an eyebrow and folding her arms across her chest.

When she looked up from her notebook, she saw Olivia crying; tears dampened her sweatshirt sleeve as she tried to wipe her eyes.

"So, tell me, if it wasn't you, who was it? Which one of them do you want to point the finger at today?" Rachel's voice cut through the tension in the room, her tone firm and devoid of any warmth.

"I don't know. I just wanted to tell you about them, all the bad things that they did. I didn't do it, and I think one of them did," Olivia said, her voice quivering as tears streamed down her face. She wiped her cheeks with the back of her hand, trying to steady her breath.

"And another thing," Rachel pressed on, leaning forward, "you've also been very vague about your 'secret' research. Are you lying about doing that, too?"

Olivia recoiled, her body language betraying her distress. She clamped her mouth shut, her fingers trembling as they pressed against her forehead. With her eyes squeezed shut, tears escaped, tracing silent lines down her cheeks.

Seeing this, Rachel realized she might have pushed too hard. She knew she should have just allowed Olivia to keep talking. Given time, she might have confessed or even implicated her boyfriend Ethan, whom she was just about to talk about. Now, seeing Olivia so overwhelmed, Rachel worried that her approach might have backfired, shutting down any chance of uncovering the truth.

"I'm sorry, Olivia, I'm sorry," Rachel said, her voice softening as she tilted her head slightly, offering a small, hesitant smile. Olivia didn't respond. She stared at the floor, hands clenched in her lap.

"I apologize for being rude. Sometimes my FBI training kicks in too strongly," Rachel said, attempting another small smile. "I can be an impatient bitch sometimes. My partner always tells me I jump to conclusions."

As Rachel spoke, the officer in the room handed Olivia a box of tissues. Olivia took several, dabbing at her eyes and blowing her nose, her breathing steadying as she calmed down.

"Okay. Let's try a different approach," Rachel said, her tone much gentler. "I get it. It's important that we get a complete picture of all the suspects so we can figure out who's responsible. You're key to that."

"Anything. I'll do or tell you anything," Olivia said as she looked up, her eyes swollen and red. "I didn't do it and I'll do anything to prove that."

"That's great, Olivia. Thank you," Rachel said, her tone still gentle. "Maybe just start with your secret research. You mentioned earlier something about time-traveling whirlpools. Is there anything else you're researching?"

"Well, I've been searching for locations across the United States that have unique characteristics, like variations in gravity, to determine if a whirlpool could be formed there," Olivia said.

"Yeah, I think you told me that, too," Rachel said, nodding.

She wanted Olivia to share more, but was careful not to press too hard for fear of shutting her down again. After a brief pause, she dug deeper, despite the risk.

"But you also keep saying that nothing matters, like you don't have any control?" Rachel asked.

"I believe in determinism, like everything is planned and you can't change it," Olivia said, her voice cracking as she inhaled, the last of her tears subsiding.

"Why do you believe that?" Rachel asked, carefully keeping her voice calm, her expression open.

"It feels like my whole life has been a pre-arranged plan. My dad always said that fate was something beyond our control. I learned more in high school and college, so I started trying some computer projects here," Olivia said.

"Oh yeah?" Rachel asked, feigning interest. She had convinced herself that Olivia was responsible for the lab bombing. She suspected that Olivia's belief in determinism justified her actions in her own mind—as if having no control of fate absolved her of guilt, making her feel disconnected.

"Yes," Olivia said, brightening as the conversation shifted to her research. "There's a good 2020 paper from Los Alamos National Laboratory that basically disproves the so-called butterfly effect."

Rachel gave a small nod, her expression urging Olivia to continue.

"You know, where stepping on a butterfly could transform the future?"

Again, Rachel nodded, her pen poised over her notebook, trying to capture every detail.

"Well, in their experiment, they used a quantum computer to simulate time travel. They made changes in the past and then returned to the present, but nothing changed."

At that moment, unexpectedly, Rachel had a strong feeling that this had all happened before. She was sure she and Olivia had had this very conversation before. She could vividly recall Olivia's words, 'but nothing changed,' spoken in this very room, at this very table. But they had only just met.

"So, I've been working on computer programs to repeat what they did, and I think it worked well," Olivia said.

The words 'You actually believe we can't change anything?' echoed in Rachel's mind as if she had already spoken them. Déjà vu plagued her; this conversation felt familiar, yet impossible. Maybe her anticipation of her own words came from her firm belief in free will rather than fate. Feeling dizzy, she closed her eyes for a moment, trying to anchor herself back to reality. She took a deep breath, trying to steady herself as she struggled to hold back the words she was thinking, but she couldn't control herself.

"You actually believe we can't change anything? That we don't have choices?" Rachel finally voiced aloud.

"Not really. The universe is deterministic," Olivia said. Rachel could see a faint blush tinting Olivia's cheeks, as if she felt embarrassed by her own assertion.

"I'm sorry, Olivia, but I kinda think that's bullshit. We all have choices," Rachel said.

"I know. A lot of people don't agree with me; I've had this debate many times at school," Olivia said as she attempted a smile, amusement tugging at her features for an instant, but it didn't quite take hold.

Rachel's dizziness faded, and her mind snapped into sharp clarity, as though she had overcome some unknown ailment. Like she had just shaken off an inexplicable fog.

"Okay, Olivia. I'm sorry for being impatient earlier—I just feel better now that you've been honest about your research," Rachel said, hoping to ease the tension enough for Olivia to keep talking. "Are you ready to tell me more about your time at the lab?"

Despite her conciliatory tone, Rachel strongly suspected Olivia was involved—likely with Ethan, who was still missing. But her deeper suspicion lingered on Professor Neil, especially since the latest attack happened in Boston.

CHAPTER 14

April 2019

For the next three years, Rachel exhaustively searched for the elusive professor. Despite her relentless pursuit, she hit dead ends time and time again. Her determination bordered on obsession, driving her to continue the hunt even when others questioned her motives.

Although she tried to keep her investigations under wraps, her quest didn't go unnoticed. In fact, it landed her in hot water with the FBI, who accused her of neglecting her current duties in favor of chasing after a case they deemed all but closed. Rachel was walking a tightrope between her professional obligations and her personal mission, risking her reputation, and even her job.

"I know you are hell-bent on catching the professor, but you can't just ignore everything else," Mitchell said. "It's getting harder and harder to cover for you."

"I'm not ignoring anything," Rachel shot back.

"Yes, Rachel, you are. You've got other cases gathering dust while you chase after a ghost," Mitchell said, his voice firm.

Rachel knew the professor was still out there, just beyond her reach. His presence seemed to linger around her. She became hyperaware of her surroundings and she often thought she caught glimpses of him in the crowd, only for him to disappear like a ghost, as Mitchell said. Every so often, mysterious cards or trinkets would appear for her, unlabeled and with no sign of who sent them, leaving her to wonder if someone was taunting her or if she was losing her mind.

Rachel attempted to heed Mitchell's advice and concentrate on her current cases, but she just couldn't manage it. Despite her best intentions, something forced her to keep searching for the professor. But the routine chaos of the FBI persisted, with new challenges cropping up daily.

Such a challenge emerged when they were called to investigate an explosion at the Kendall/MIT subway station on Boston's red line. The devastation was clear as they arrived at the scene, with twisted metal and shattered glass strewn across the platform, and the acrid smell of smoke hanging heavy in the air. Emergency responders attended to the injured, their quick, efficient movements contrasting with the commotion surrounding them. The investigation revealed that two individuals died in the explosion, while several others sustained minor injuries.

Dressed in her specialized bomb technician gear, Rachel combed through the entire subway station. Hidden under the victims' bench, she discovered only a few pipe bomb fragments, lacking further explosive evidence. She couldn't help but scour the area for specific medical supplies like light blue bandages and sutures, but she came up empty-handed.

After completing her thorough assessment of the scene, Rachel peeled off her protective gear and rendezvoused with

Mitchell to investigate the lives of the victims. They dug into the backgrounds of the two deaths that resulted from the bombing. Their investigation revealed that the victims—college professors—had no clear connection to each other, similar to the survivors. The duo interviewed both the victims' family members and coworkers. No one could provide a plausible motive for anyone to target them. They were both well-respected college professors, a fairly typical occupation in this region of Massachusetts, considering the number of universities.

As they returned to the FBI field office, Rachel felt a knot of disappointment tighten in her stomach. Despite their efforts, they had found nothing substantial, leaving her frustrated and a little angry. Before she could even sit down at her desk, a tech greeted her and handed them the subway's CCTV footage.

As they huddled around the screen, Rachel felt a strange sensation creep over her, a mix of déjà vu and nervous anticipation. It was as if she knew what the video would show, though she couldn't say why. She shook her head to refocus, but had to sit down to ease her dizziness as they started watching.

The footage showed the explosion victims seated on the bench. But just beside the bench, a slight figure crouched against the wall, their face concealed beneath the hood of a sweatshirt. The mysterious figure suddenly sprang to their feet, moving at a quick pace that bordered on a frantic dash, just moments before the bomb went off. It appeared as if they were attempting to shield their identity from the CCTV cameras on the platform as they kept their face obscured beneath the hood.

As he was racing up the stairs to escape the station, he glanced upward, inadvertently exposing his face to the camera. His expression was one of panic, his outstretched hand reaching for someone ahead, revealing his face. His mouth was moving as if he was shouting at the person.

"Holy shit!" Rachel said as she caught sight of his face.

Mitchell shook his head in agreement, sharing Rachel's shock about who they saw.

"That's him!" Rachel said. "He looks even more panicked this time, thin, scared, like he's aged twenty years. Why does he keep doing this? Why does he keep blowing things up? He's killed at least five people we know of."

"Yeah, Professor Neil, or whatever his name is, looks rough," Mitchell said.

Rachel and Mitchell rewound the CCTV footage repeatedly, having to go back to scrutinize every frame. While reviewing the earlier footage, Rachel noticed that the person the professor was reaching for had walked past him by the bench, wearing a hat and keeping their eyes low, maybe also evading the cameras. However, unlike Professor Neil, that person's face never appeared in the footage.

"See how he started running right before the bomb went off? Maybe he panicked because he fucked up this time," Rachel said.

"Yeah, because he didn't want to blow himself up," Mitchell said.

"Or maybe he jumped up to chase that other guy."

"Got any ideas who that other guy is?" Mitchell asked.

"I have no idea. Maybe nobody, considering how crazy Professor Neil looks on this footage," Rachel said.

"Well, let's start where?"

"MIT," Rachel said.

"What? Why?"

"He's done this before. He fakes his credentials and lands a job at a university. MIT is the closest to that subway station," Rachel said

"Hmm... Alright, let's go," Mitchell said in a high-pitched voice with a shrug. His lips curved into a small, wry smile, hinting at his willingness to try.

As they arrived at MIT, Rachel had a strong gut feeling that the professor was there. It was déjà vu again—she was sure it was MIT, though she couldn't explain why.

Rachel and Mitchell canvassed the physics section with CCTV images. Within moments, a professor recognized the man in the footage.

"That's Professor Aron. I just saw him heading to his office," he said, pointing down the hall.

Mitchell wasted no time calling for backup, and they headed straight to Professor Aron's office.

Unwilling to wait for backup, Rachel strode into the office, hoping to find Professor Aron. However, he wasn't there. Seated at the professor's desk was his teaching assistant, who was expecting Rachel's arrival.

"Professor Aron has left for the day," the assistant said. "But he thoughtfully left this card addressed to you."

The card addressed to Rachel listed an address in the terminal storage warehouse district where they could find him. Rachel wasted no time. She knew they needed to act fast and redirected the backup team to meet them there.

When Rachel and Mitchell arrived, they found the backup already on scene, with the SWAT team and the ATF also dispatched, just in case the professor was planning another bomb.

114

The location yielded only a lifeless, abandoned warehouse—no people, no bombs, no electricity, nothing.

However, a harsh spotlight illuminated an elegant pedestal positioned at the center of the otherwise empty warehouse. A petite hourglass stood atop it, no taller than Rachel's hand. It was cradled in a crafted mahogany frame, etched with the image of a serpent devouring its own tail. Delicately engraved on the wooden base, in sophisticated cursive script, was a single name: *Rachel*.

Forensics combed the warehouse and the professor's office at MIT. Despite their thorough search, they again found no leads—no car, no apartment, no digital trace. As always, no one knew who he really was. No fingerprints. No explosives. No documents. Absolutely nothing.

Rachel stared at the hourglass etched with her name. He had left nothing behind but her name and a symbol of time slipping away. Her breath caught. This wasn't just a disappearance. It was a message.

He doesn't just run. He controls when he disappears.

CHAPTER 15

April 2019

CBS BOSTON CHANNEL 5 EVENING NEWS

SPECIAL REPORT

Daniel Harris: "Good evening, Boston. I'm Daniel Harris. Tonight, we begin with breaking news from Cambridge, Massachusetts, where a powerful and mysterious seismic event has rocked the Kendall Square area, resulting in tragedy and widespread confusion. Let's go live to our field correspondent, Jane Parsons, who is at the scene. Jane?"

Jane Parsons: "Daniel, it's an incredibly chaotic scene here. At around 5:47 p.m., an unexpected seismic event shook the streets near the entrance of Kendall Square Station. Officials are describing it as a 'localized earthquake,' but the specifics are still unclear. Tragically, we can confirm that seven cyclists lost their lives in this incident, with more than a dozen injured, many critically. Witnesses describe hearing a deep rumble, followed by a sudden, violent shaking. Many also reported 'strange electrical noises' and flashes of light emanating from the subway entrance. Moments before the ground shook, witnesses reported an explosion of light and a deep, echoing hum from beneath the street. One witness, an MIT student, described the sound as an electric current surging through the air before the tremors began. First responders arrived within minutes, but the damage had already been done. The collapse of parts of the street brought down bike racks, trapping several cyclists under the wreckage. There is still no official word about the cause of this mysterious event."

Daniel Harris: "Thank you, Jane. MIT has released a statement showing that no construction or experimental activity was taking place in or around the station at the time of the incident. However, several witnesses have mentioned experiencing a buzzing sensation and hearing what they described as an 'electromagnetic hum' moments before the quake hit. Officials are not yet addressing these accounts. Joining us now is Dr. Claire Robertson, a geophysics expert from Harvard University. Dr. Robertson, what can you tell us about these reports of an electromagnetic disturbance and the possibility that it might have triggered this seismic event?"

Dr. Claire Robertson: "Thank you, Daniel. Initial findings suggest that the 'localized earthquake' description is unusual. While small, isolated quakes aren't impossible, the reports of electromagnetic interference are curious. In some rare cases, seismic activity can induce electrical disturbances, but is not typical of this nature. It's possible there was an interaction between underground infrastructure and electrical systems, or even an energy release from below the station. However, this is all speculative until we have more data."

Daniel Harris: "Thank you, Dr. Robertson. We're also hearing unconfirmed reports of an explosion that may have occurred within the subway station itself. Police and emergency personnel haven't commented on a connection between the explosion and the seismic event, but sources say they are investigating it. Governor Foley addressed the incident earlier this evening, urging the public to remain calm and to avoid spreading unverified information. We now turn to Governor Foley, who joins us live. Governor, what can you tell us about the situation and the state's response?"

Governor Foley: "Our hearts go out to the families of the victims in today's tragic incident. We are working closely with the MBTA, MIT, and local emergency services to determine the cause of what happened. At this time, we are asking everyone to stay clear of the area and to follow updates from official sources."

Daniel Harris: "As more details emerge, questions remain about the exact cause of this incident. Some social media users speculate about a possible electromagnetic anomaly or interference with underground electrical lines, but these claims remain unsubstantiated. What we know is that residents reported feeling a powerful surge of energy just before the quake, with one witness describing it as a 'static charge in the air' that made the hairs on their arms stand up. Again, MIT has issued a statement denying any connection between the incident and recent experimental research on campus, particularly projects involving electromagnetic fields and high-energy physics. Still, the unusual characteristics of this event have led to increased speculation among the public. Police have confirmed that there was no known warning before the quake and have not provided additional information on the reported explosion within the subway station. Investigators from the National Transportation Safety Board and local authorities are now working to determine whether the explosion was a contributing factor or a coincidental event. This incident has left the Cambridge community shaken and in mourning for the lives lost today. As investigations continue, we will keep you updated with the latest information. For now, the cause of this mysterious event remains unknown. I'm Daniel Harris, and this is CBS Channel 5 Evening News."

CHAPTER 16

January 2023

Olivia arrived at the lab at 8 am, and Ethan was already waiting for her outside. He stood just a few inches taller than Olivia, his dark brown hair tousled, framing an angular jawline that sported a hint of a scruffy beard. As Olivia stepped out of her car and approached him, he greeted her with a warm smile, revealing charming dimples.

"Olivia?" he asked, extending his hand as she approached the front door.

"That's me," Olivia said, clasping his hand. "You must be Ethan."

"That's right. It's very nice to meet you. I'm excited to work here," Ethan said, his smile broadening as they shook hands. He held her hand for a moment longer than usual, his warm smile persisting. She had a hard time looking away from his expressive hazel eyes, which lit up genuinely as his smile reached them.

Ethan was casually dressed in jeans and a navy blue cable-knit hooded sweater. Olivia couldn't deny that she found him handsome, but she pushed those thoughts aside.

She had a short-lived relationship with a boy during her final years of high school. At eighteen, she wholeheartedly believed that she was in love with her soulmate, only to have her heart broken when he left for college in California. When she went to college, she dated a little, but she prioritized her grades above all else to keep her scholarship.

Olivia seemed to be disenchanted with most college guys, as their primary interests revolved around partying and sex. While not a prude by any means, she had one-night stands, but had grown tired of them as well. There was, however, a teaching assistant from her thermodynamics class whom she dated for nearly the entire semester. She thought they had a connection, but as time went on, she became restless and, true to her pattern, grew bored with the relationship.

Unfortunately, that romance ended in a messy breakup. He accused her of only dating him to manipulate her grades. Determined to avoid repeating any such situation, she had no intention of getting involved with anyone she worked with.

Olivia led Ethan into the quiet laboratory building, finding it empty as usual this early in the morning. Olivia had been the de facto lab tech, and she wasn't sure how this was going to work now that the lab had the budget to hire a dedicated technician. She assumed they would share the work, considering Dr. Lynch would never offer her research opportunities. But she was worried that there wasn't enough work to go around.

She gave Ethan a tour of the offices, explaining the required computer updates and whiteboard cleaning. They also toured the linear accelerator building, also tasked with cleaning Dr. O'Brien's lab. As they walked out of the building, Ethan seemed very comfortable, occasionally scanning his surroundings but mostly keeping his attention fixed on Olivia.

"Do you have questions?" Olivia asked, her voice wavering. Ethan's intense gaze made her nervous, yet she felt comfortable around him, especially appreciating how politely he held doors open for her.

"I'm actually familiar with most of this lab equipment."

"Oh, really?" Olivia asked.

"Yeah, I've worked as a physics lab tech. I've handled a lot of equipment maintenance, calibration, and even some repairs."

"So, you're quite experienced, then?" Olivia said. She panicked, fearing that Ethan's expertise might overshadow her role as the laboratory maid.

Ethan noticed her concern and smiled, his expression kind. He paused their walk, gently turning her to face him.

"Yes, I'm comfortable handling the technical side of things here," he said, placing his hands on her shoulders. "It sounds like we'll complement each other's roles well."

Olivia almost felt a bit of a spark when Ethan touched her, and a sense of relief followed. She recognized she would be the one cleaning the whiteboards, while Ethan would handle the lab equipment.

She couldn't help but laugh at herself for ever worrying that her status as a PhD student might hinge on her ability to clean whiteboards. Olivia realized in that moment that she had accepted her fate, just blending into the background of the lab like a quiet church mouse.

Over the course of the next two weeks of working closely together, Ethan frequently complimented Olivia on her band T-shirts—from Rage Against the Machine to Korn—and shared his love for aggressive rock. And interestingly, he was also a huge Pink Floyd fan. Seizing on these conversations as the perfect opportunity, he asked her out.

"Since we both have such great taste in music, how about we catch a live show together this weekend?" Ethan asked with a smile.

Olivia politely declined his date invitation. She explained her reservations about dating someone she worked with. To her relief, he respected her decision and continued their relationship as if he had never asked her out.

Curious about her work, Ethan asked about her research daily. Olivia, feeling somewhat embarrassed about her limited lab responsibilities, brought up her aspirations to work on Einstein's river of time theories.

"Really?" Ethan asked with excitement. "Are you studying whirlpools? Like, trying to change the environment to travel back in time?"

"Exactly!" Olivia said. "I'm amazed you're familiar with it."

Olivia had developed a genuine interest in him. His intelligence and support made her feel at ease. In the weeks that followed, Ethan had noticed the affair between Dr. Lynch and Dr. Kingsley, as well as Dr. O'Brien's consistent inebriation, yet he remained silent about it all. Olivia placed her trust in Ethan, especially because of his discretion.

She immersed herself in her private research, knowing she could rely on Ethan's help without fearing he'd expose her secret activities. He often helped to keep her work under wraps, further solidifying the trust between them.

He also encouraged her to write up her experiments and submit them in a grant application. Hesitant, Olivia debated with him, explaining Dr. Lynch's attitude toward her and the fact that she would never get her approval.

"What's the worst that could happen?" Ethan said, his unwavering faith in her research clear.

"Dr. O'Brien could publish it under his name and then I'm screwed."

"Then don't include everything—just some superficial details," Ethan said.

It was a compelling idea, one that persuaded her to take the chance. Olivia submitted a small grant application during a lab meeting, downplaying it as a brief attempt to secure some funding for the lab.

"Why are you even writing anything, Olivia?" Dr. Lynch said. "You should work with the lab tech, and you'll just graduate. Stop trying to do things you're not qualified to do."

Olivia overheard Sofia's giggle just before Dr. Lynch's surprising change of heart.

"Actually…" Dr. Lynch said, "it might benefit the lab if we can secure you a training grant. I'll review it and send it back before I submit it."

Olivia left the lab meeting grinning so hard her cheeks hurt. The moment she spotted Ethan, she rushed toward him and practically launched herself into his arms.

"I assume it went well; I've never seen you this happy," Ethan said, his smile revealing those endearing dimples and his hazel eyes glowed.

"Yes! She said she was going to look it over because it would look good for her if we got a training grant!" Olivia said, surprised by her own words.

"So, now that we've convinced Dr. Lynch that you have valuable ideas, would you consider having dinner with me?" Ethan asked.

"Of course I will!" Olivia said, unable to resist any longer.

Their pent-up attraction led to an unexpected kiss right there in the hallway. Olivia's breath caught as their lips met, sending a thrilling jolt down her spine, momentarily silencing her. Ethan turned to leave, but then pivoted back toward Olivia, presenting her with a single rose. He continued to beam with that warm, dimpled smile and whispered his heartfelt congratulations before he walked away. Alone in the hallway, Olivia felt only her heart fluttering.

Their first date was a night to remember. Ethan had chosen a quaint little Italian restaurant in the city, with soft ambient lighting and cozy booths. Olivia had always loved Italian food, so finding out that Ethan shared her enthusiasm felt like a fortunate coincidence. There were just a handful of other diners, ensuring a quiet atmosphere for their meal.

As they settled into their secluded booth, a candle on the table danced and cast a soft, inviting glow. Their conversation flowed effortlessly, as if they had been close friends for years. Olivia discovered Ethan's love for travel as he shared fascinating stories about his trips abroad. She slipped into the role of an eager listener, although she shared a few anecdotes from her upbringing in a small southern town.

The meal they ordered was exceptional, and Ethan's choice of this Boston favorite was spot on. Before their entrees, they shared a platter of bruschetta, featuring toasted bread topped with diced tomatoes, basil, and a drizzle of balsamic glaze.

As they savored the bruschetta, Olivia's excitement was obvious, as was her nervous energy. She picked at her food, taking small bites and occasionally glancing around the restaurant. Ethan noticed her fidgeting and offered a reassuring smile, hoping to ease her nerves.

"Isn't combining flavors just incredible?" Ethan said. "The tanginess of the tomatoes with the sweetness of the balsamic glaze."

"Absolutely. It's really delicious."

Their conversations continued as they moved on to their main courses, but Olivia's stomach fluttered with butterflies, her anticipation of being with Ethan overshadowing her usual enjoyment of Italian food. She nudged her food around the plate, flustered by how intensely she felt drawn to him. As they dined, Olivia couldn't help smiling at Ethan's quick wit and the warmth behind his dimpled grin. The way he looked at her left no doubt—and made her blush at nearly everything he said.

She admired Ethan's choice of the mushroom risotto, but with her own fettuccine Alfredo, she only managed a few bites before pushing the plate aside.

"I'm sorry, I guess I'm just not that hungry," Olivia said, her cheeks flushed. "Maybe I overdid it with the bruschetta."

"No worries at all," Ethan said with a nod, reaching across the table to give her hand a squeeze. "Italian food can be filling."

As dessert arrived, Olivia laughed at his jokes and stories, feeling her nerves gradually ease as she relaxed in his company. She shared a warm cappuccino and a slice of caramel cheesecake with Ethan. They lingered, losing track of time long after the last crumb disappeared. Caffeine jittered through Olivia as they bundled up to face the chilly night.

"Where to next?" Ethan asked as they walked toward the exit.

Olivia pondered for a moment, then suggested, "How about a stroll through Boston Common?"

"That sounds perfect," Ethan said, his face lighting up.

The night air was crisp, and the stars shimmered overhead. They held hands, their fingers interlocking naturally, as they meandered along the sidewalk. Streetlights glowed, city life hummed distantly. Olivia felt comfortable in Ethan's presence, and they walked together in contented silence. Their hands stayed connected, warm and steady, as they entered the park, a serene world of moonlit paths covered with an untouched blanket of snow.

They walked the winding paths, the world fading behind them. Olivia sensed a burgeoning connection, despite how little time they'd known each other. She especially enjoyed this comfortable silence. When they reached the center of the park, Ethan turned to face Olivia, his eyes locking onto hers. With a soft, meaningful touch, he cupped her face, drawing her closer into a kiss. Time stood still as they held each other.

When he broke the kiss, the smiles they exchanged conveyed a deep understanding of one another. Their hands still linked, Olivia walked with him toward the cars, unsure what this connection meant. Her short time with Ethan had lifted her from the depths of her depression. Maybe, with his support, she could handle her current situation in the lab. Maybe destiny had other plans for her than enduring this predicament forever. Instead, this could be the start of something remarkable—a journey they'd take side by side.

CHAPTER 17

January 2023

Their second date came the very next day. Their attraction had been undeniable since before their first date, and they both couldn't wait to see each other again outside the lab. Ethan suggested they meet at a little cafe in the city, right down the street from the university. The atmosphere was warm and inviting, with a crowd of college students and the gentle melodies of soft jazz music playing in the background.

As Olivia stepped into the cafe, a flutter of butterflies still danced in her stomach, though her nerves had settled. She spotted Ethan already seated at a corner table, a dimpled smile lighting up his face as he stood to greet her. He pulled out her chair, and they exchanged a warm hug before settling into their seats.

Over cups of steaming coffee and delicate pastries, they engaged in lively conversation. They discussed a wide range of topics, from their favorite books and movies to their thoughts about their fellow lab mates. Ethan's passion for science fascinated Olivia, and she could sense his genuine interest in her research.

As the day progressed, they found themselves lost in each other's company, sharing stories and laughing as they completely lost track of time. Olivia felt a deep sense of connection with Ethan, again as if they had known each other for a lifetime. After leaving the cafe, they again took a leisurely stroll through a nearby park. Ethan slipped his hand into Olivia's, their fingers intertwining, as they continued to walk and talk.

By the end of the second date, it was clear to Olivia that something special was growing between them. They shared a sweet kiss beside Olivia's car. Olivia needed this relationship after her challenging times in the lab, and Ethan seemed perfect for her.

Their third date took a bit of a turn. They opted for a visit to a local museum, trying to embrace something different for the both of them. While meandering through the exhibits, they talked more about their complete lack of comprehension of art.

"I have no idea what that's supposed to be," Olivia admitted, casting a playful glance at Ethan as she gestured towards an abstract painting.

"Me neither," Ethan confessed, shaking his head in agreement, his laughter joining hers.

Their laughter filled the air throughout their visit, bonding them over their mutual bafflement at the abstract art on display. Turns out, they enjoyed the experience more than they expected.

Afterward, they skipped their traditional stroll through a park, and instead headed back to Olivia's apartment, craving a more intimate setting. Inside her apartment, they continued their intellectual exchange, poring over research papers and discussing Olivia's research.

As the evening wore on, they found themselves drawn closer together. In the quiet of her apartment, bathed in the soft glow of lamplight, Olivia couldn't shake the pull she felt toward Ethan. Though they'd only known each other a few months, she was certain—she was completely in love with him.

Their first night together had been a blend of tenderness and fiery passion, unfolding naturally from the bond that had grown between them. The air in her living room had practically crackled as they sat close on the couch—every glance, every brush of skin, charged with anticipation. Their chemistry was undeniable.

Their eyes locked, and the tension in the room grew. Time seemed to slow down as they leaned in closer, drawn together by an inescapable magnetism. A dimpled smile curled at the corners of Ethan's lips, and the air seemed to thicken with desire. He reached out, his fingers grazing her forearm, sending a shiver down her spine. Olivia bit her lower lip, a subtle invitation.

They gingerly removed their clothes piece by piece, their skin inching closer with each piece of fabric they shed. An unexpected surge of nervous excitement jolted through their veins. Their breath mingled, creating a warm and intoxicating blend of eager anticipation. It was a languid, desire-filled dance, as they intertwined, moving with hesitation and nervousness, slowly exploring each other.

Ethan's hands embarked on a slow journey, their gentle touch caressing Olivia's collarbones, tracing the contour of her belly, and following the curves of her hips. Simultaneously, Olivia's hands threaded through the soft strands of Ethan's hair, and her arms encircled his shoulders in a tight embrace. Their bodies moved in perfect harmony, as if following an unspoken rhythm. Their connection blazed like fireworks, igniting sparks that set Olivia's heart racing with a surge of adrenaline. With every motion and touch, Olivia felt like her skin was on fire. As they moved in unison, their passion intensified, reaching a feverish crescendo. They found themselves breathless, their chests heaving as they clung to the edge of the couch.

Afterward, as they cuddled close, struggling to fit on the couch, Olivia experienced a complex mix of emotions. She felt completely satisfied, the aftermath of their intimate encounter leaving her feeling fulfilled and loved. Yet, beneath that comfort, a curious apprehension lingered in the back of her mind. Ethan, with his charm and attentiveness, appeared to be almost too perfect. Olivia wondered if it was her own insecurities playing tricks on her. She recognized those old doubts that haunted her—fear, self-sabotage, the thought that she had no control over her fate.

In her moments of introspection, she tried to convince herself that she could brave whatever challenges the universe had planned for her. The upcoming months at the lab were likely to be terrible, but with Ethan by her side, she felt a newfound sense of strength. Olivia pushed aside her doubts and fears, embracing her love for Ethan, even in the face of her uncertainties. She brushed aside the irrational thoughts lurking in the recesses of her mind. She no longer wondered if the stars had aligned—she felt it, steady and certain: she wanted this, wanted *him*, in her life.

Olivia and Ethan spent almost all of their time together, and their relationship continued to deepen over the next few months. Ethan was always trying to make Olivia laugh, and he made the lab atmosphere so much more relaxed when they worked on her research. Outside of the lab, they continued going out to various restaurants, to the movie theater, and they visited the Museum of Science frequently.

However, they spent most of their time at Olivia's apartment. Ethan lived in Springfield, so he often spent the night with her to avoid the train commute. Even though Mulder, Olivia's cantankerous terrier, was more irritable lately because of a pair of mourning doves nesting on her window air conditioner, he surprisingly didn't growl at Ethan. Mulder didn't exactly like Ethan, but he tolerated him better than most humans.

Ethan's cooking skills played a huge role in winning over the canine critic. Whether Ethan was preparing a meal or they opted for Chinese takeout, Mulder seemed to appreciate the change in cuisine. Mulder was also calmer with the quieter music that Ethan preferred. Ethan often played Pink Floyd both at her apartment and in the lab, with *The Final Cut* being his favorite CD. Olivia wasn't initially into it as she listened to harder rock, but over time, she appreciated it.

Olivia had fallen head over heels for Ethan. She had believed that her high school sweetheart was her soulmate, and since then, she hadn't dated seriously. But Ethan was entirely different, leagues ahead of her immature high school boyfriend.

What set Ethan apart was that he could almost read her mind. He had such a considerate nature, even during arguments. He accepted Olivia for who she was without trying to change her. But it might have been his remarkable patience and kindness toward Mulder that won her over. Even when the old terrier attempted to bite him, Ethan just laughed.

Olivia had crawled out of her depression with Ethan's support. With his encouragement, she had submitted that small grant application that Dr. Lynch had accepted. During lab meetings, while Olivia stared at the beta fish, she often thought of Ethan, which seemed to help speed up time. He promised her a spring release from the lab, providing she remained inconspicuous. However, Dr. Lynch shattered Olivia's dreams once again.

At the next lab meeting, Dr. Lynch cleared her throat and said, "By the way, I went ahead and submitted Olivia's training grant. Fingers crossed—it might actually get funded."

Olivia blinked. *What?*

Dr. Lynch offered a tight smile, already moving on to the next agenda item. She didn't distribute copies for anyone to review—not even Olivia. She hadn't bothered to share the final version before submitting it.

Although Olivia knew she should probably stay quiet, she made her way up to Dr. Lynch's office to ask about the application's status.

Olivia gently broached the topic, asking if Dr. Lynch had made any revisions to the application. She hoped to understand where she might have gone wrong.

"No, Olivia. The grant application is in great shape. I believe we have a significant chance," Dr. Lynch said.

"Do you think I could get a copy of the submission, maybe just for my CV?" Olivia asked.

"Sure, I'll email it over to you," Dr. Lynch said, already turning back to her phone and resuming her usual habit of ignoring Olivia.

Olivia returned to the lab where Ethan was waiting, eager to check her email. She spent over an hour repeatedly refreshing her inbox. Finally, Dr. Lynch's email arrived, containing the grant submission. Olivia's initial reaction was one of confusion; it seemed like Dr. Lynch had sent her the wrong document. The content was radically different from what Olivia had originally submitted. It was full of experiments that nobody in their lab had ever undertaken, each yielding extraordinary results.

The application was a persuasive masterpiece, highlighting Olivia as an exceptionally promising student researcher, thanks to the incredible experiments she supposedly conducted under Dr. Lynch's mentorship. Olivia felt baffled, but Ethan remained quiet, seemingly unsurprised.

"I have to go ask her about this, find out what's going on," Olivia said

"I don't think that's a good idea, Olivia."

"What do you mean? This is *NOT* the grant I submitted. I didn't write any of this or perform these experiments. Yet, my name is on it," Olivia said, fury building with each word as she turned to leave.

"Wait…" Ethan attempted to interject, but Olivia was already halfway up the stairs to Dr. Lynch's office.

"Excuse me, Dr. Lynch?"

"Yes, Olivia. What do you want now?" Dr. Lynch said, her impatience clear.

"I was just wondering if maybe you accidentally sent me the wrong grant application. This one you emailed is not the one I wrote," Olivia said.

Dr. Lynch rolled her eyes and let out an exasperated sigh.

"Olivia, the application that Dr. Kingsley and I wrote is far superior to what you attempted to submit. How do you think we secure so many grants? I always win. It's how academia works," she said, tilting her head slightly, as if explaining something to a child.

"I'm too busy to deal with you right now," Dr. Lynch said, and with that, she stood, ushering Olivia out of her office, and shut the door.

Outside Dr. Lynch's office, Olivia was both hurt and surprised, tears welling up in her eyes. She berated herself, thinking, *I'm so stupid,* over and over, like a broken record. It was painfully clear now—Dr. Lynch had never intended to mentor her.

Dr. Lynch and Dr. Kingsley weren't just dismissive. They were deceitful. They fabricated their data to secure grants and publications, rarely setting foot in the lab themselves, other than to have sex on her fancy desk.

Olivia now understood how Dr. Lynch financed the luxurious decor in her office and her frequent stays at five-star hotels during conferences in exotic destinations like Dubai. She certainly wasn't spending the grant money on lab equipment or experiments.

Olivia stormed back into the lab with her face flushed, anger and tears overtaking her. Ethan, waiting for her, looked genuinely concerned as he spoke up.

"I'm sorry, Olivia. I miscalculated," Ethan said.

"What are you talking about? You did nothing wrong. It's everyone else in this lab. I'm going to the ombudsman, and I'm going to report them," Olivia said.

A flash of panic crossed Ethan's face as he tried to dissuade her. "No, Olivia! You can't do that. They'll blacklist you. They've done it before."

"What do you mean?" Olivia asked.

"I just mean that they've probably done it before. I just assume, given how no one in this lab has spoken up. Academic retaliation is a genuine issue—I read about it in the paper last week."

"I'm doing it. The conversation is confidential, and they can help me figure out what to do." Olivia had decided—no more second-guessing.

"Olivia, please think about this. You only have a few more months until you graduate. Just focus on getting out."

Olivia continued to cry while Ethan clutched her to his chest, as if he could shield her from the pain. Over the years, she had tolerated the lab's tumultuous atmosphere, knowing that she had already accepted her fate. However, something inside her refused to let go this time. The situation had gone from bad to worse. Dr. Lynch and Dr. Kingsley's affair, Dr. O'Brien stealing work from the postdocs, and now the revelation that all of their research might be fraudulent.

Olivia had suffered silently within the confines of the lab, but she couldn't accept the thought of another student being tricked into joining their ranks. The next day, Olivia emailed Bradley Parker, the ombudsman, to arrange a meeting.

CHAPTER 18

"Wait a minute," Rachel interrupted. "Are you trying to say they just make up all their experiments?"

"Yeah, that's exactly what I'm saying," Olivia said, her fingers nervously toying with the edges of her sweatsuit. "They literally don't do any actual research."

"But I thought that real scientific research had to be repeatable," Rachel said, leaning forward. "I thought other scientists should be able to replicate the experiments and achieve the same results."

"Ideally, yes; realistically, no," Olivia said, her eyes fixed on the table.

"But that makes no sense," Rachel said. "If nobody else can replicate their experiments, wouldn't any supposed breakthroughs just be… shaky, at best? How could she become some famous researcher with no big discoveries?"

"If you were ever a PhD student, you'd get it," Olivia said. "I looked into this while considering a transfer, but learned how often science can be fake. Around 30% of researchers admit to what they call 'questionable practices,' and about 75% admit they've witnessed fraud by fellow researchers. Of course, they never get into trouble."

"Seriously? That many scientists fake their work?" Rachel asked. "Then why were you planning to report them if you thought nothing would happen? Wouldn't someone eventually catch on? Expose their fraud?"

"I wanted to file a report to protect prospective students. I didn't actually think they'd get in trouble. They've been doing this for years," Olivia said. "Unfortunately, most researchers are more driven by money—funding—than genuine discovery. They're almost never caught."

Rachel sat in silence for a few minutes, mulling over Olivia's words. She wasn't sure if she could trust what Olivia was saying. Though Rachel hadn't worked in research, living in Boston—a city with a lot of universities—she had encountered plenty of shady academics. Was Olivia telling the truth? Or was she exaggerating to justify her own actions? Rachel still suspected Olivia's involvement in the bombing, and this explanation about bad researchers added a layer to the puzzle, potentially giving Olivia a motive.

Rachel abruptly changed the subject, focusing her attention squarely on Olivia, watching closely for her reaction. "So, you're in love with Ethan?"

Olivia blushed, placing her hand on her forehead and looking down at the table. She let out a small laugh and attempted a faint smile. "Yeah, I guess I am."

"And he's in love with you?" Rachel asked.

"I believe he is, though he's never said it."

Rachel hesitated to push too hard, wary of Olivia's tendency to clam up, but she couldn't resist asking, "So, he could have easily hurt the lab people for you?"

"No! He would never do that," Olivia said, her eyes wide. She kept fidgeting with her shirt sleeves, and Rachel worried she might fray them.

"Okay, I'm sorry, Olivia. Let's take another quick break. I'll grab you some more coffee."

"No, thank you," Olivia said, her attention fixed on the floor as if searching for an escape from the uncomfortable conversation.

"Alright, I'll be back in just a minute," Rachel said as she stood up to leave the room.

Exiting the interrogation room, Rachel found Mitchell waiting outside, his arms folded across his chest.

"Now are you convinced she did it?" Mitchell asked.

"Pretty much. I think her and Ethan might have done it together."

"I didn't catch your entire interrogation, but to me, it seems like she didn't really tell you anything," Mitchell said, his eyebrows raised as he leaned against the doorframe.

"We're just taking it slow, hoping she'll open up more. I think she'll eventually admit it."

"Come on, Rachel. You've got to remain more objective. Do you truly think Olivia was more inclined to plant those pipe bombs than the other suspects that we can't actually find?" Mitchell asked, rubbing his temple.

"Yeah, yeah, I know, 'be objective,' but I can't shake this gut feeling that she's involved."

"You also always think the professor is involved," Mitchell said.

"Fuck you. What's the latest update?" Rachel asked.

Mitchell brushed off her rude response, a smile creeping onto his face as he uncrossed his arms and began his update.

"First, we tried to bring in Sofia, but she's not responding at her apartment. Because we have no justification for breaking in, we've requested the landlord conduct a welfare check, given her car is still there."

Rachel stood in silence, her attention fixed on Mitchell as he delivered the update.

"As for Aiden, who is Dr. Lynch's husband, Ethan, or Brittney, there's been no sign of them yet," Mitchell continued, his tone matter-of-fact. "Their cars haven't turned up, and our officers are scouring hospitals, hotels, train stations, airlines, toll cameras, and CCTV footage, leaving no stone unturned."

"Are you kidding me? We haven't located any of them yet?" Rachel asked.

"I know, Rachel, but we're doing everything we can to track them down," Mitchell said. "I spoke to Dr. Williams again. Despite Olivia's claims, she completely denied ever working with her and continued insisting that it must have been Olivia who triggered the explosion."

"Do you believe her?" Rachel asked.

"No. I think we need to bring her in for further questioning."

"Agreed," Rachel said. "Olivia did just claim that all researchers are liars. Let's set that up. What about the victims from the explosion?"

"Oh, yeah, we identified the victims as doctors Kingsley, O'Brien, and Collins, as we suspected, from Maya's info. And then there was also Bradley, which we already knew."

"Alright. Keep searching for the missing, and I'll continue with Olivia. She'll give us good information—we just need to go slow and let her finish," Rachel said.

"Sounds good," Mitchell said as he turned to leave. "We're also searching Olivia's apartment, too, so I'll keep you updated with any findings."

Rachel nodded as she turned and headed to the vending machine to grab a couple of bottles of water. She then turned to re-enter the interrogation room. Olivia glanced up at her but remained silent.

"We have identified the deaths from the lab explosion. It was doctors Kingsley, O'Brien, and Collins, as well as Bradley," Rachel said, hoping that informing Olivia about the deceased might prompt her to confess her involvement.

Tears welled up in Olivia's eyes once more. "I thought I saw Bradley in the parking lot after the explosion. I knew he was dead," she said, her entire body trembling as she wiped her eyes with her sweatsuit sleeves.

Rachel again hesitated to rush Olivia, fearful that it might cause her to freeze up. After waiting for Olivia to calm down, she resumed the recording.

"Alright, Olivia. The recording is back on. Take your time and continue whenever you're ready."

CHAPTER 19

February 2023

After receiving a reply email from Bradley, Olivia felt a bit of uncertainty creeping in. Maybe she was overstepping her bounds. Perhaps trying to change the universe's plan wouldn't work. She then considered whether she was on par with Brittney and Sofia, the two postdocs. Maybe they were all comrades, suffering through the same less-than-ideal academic environment.

In the presence of Dr. Lynch, Brittney donned a mask of flattery. However, once out of earshot of the rulers, she unleashed a torrent of ruthless criticism and gossip. Sofia, known for her silence, warned Olivia to be silent. It occurred to Olivia that perhaps, like herself, they were enduring their time in the lab, counting down the days until they could escape.

Olivia considered telling Bradley she had made a mistake and changed her mind. But before replying, she thought it might be wise to seek the counsel of the postdocs. She could meet privately with Brittney or Sofia to get their thoughts on meeting with him. With that in mind, she held off on replying.

Olivia planned to catch the postdocs after their next agonizingly pointless lab meeting. She sat through another session of mind-numbing discussion, eyes drifting to Walter the beta fish, until Dr. Lynch snapped her attention back. Olivia was assigned to train Sofia on a specific computer program—essential for moving forward with her grant application. She nodded, used to fading into the background as she handled her technician duties. But then, a light flickered in her mind: this could be the perfect chance to speak with Sofia privately.

When Olivia entered the computer lab to train Sofia, she found both Sofia and Brittney huddled over their cluttered desks, surrounded by glowing computer screens. The air hummed with the soft whir of machinery. Sofia beckoned Olivia over with a careless wave of her hand.

"Olivia, I need you to run these simulations for me," she said, her tone leaving no room for argument.

Surprised by the abrupt demand, Olivia hesitated for a moment.

"Um, okay. Dr. Lynch said I should show you how to do it so you can finish your grant work."

Olivia didn't think that Dr. Lynch had suggested that she should bear the full brunt of Sofia's workload, especially considering Dr. Lynch's comments about Olivia being less than competent. The situation reminded her of Dr. O'Brien's habit of appropriating the postdocs' work.

Sofia's lips curled into a condescending smirk. "I don't have time for lessons, Olivia. Just get it done."

With that, Sofia's attention drifted back to Brittney, eager to resume their gossip session without further interruption.

Olivia's newfound confidence, bolstered by the support of Ethan, emboldened her to push back against Sofia's unreasonable demands.

"I'm sorry, but I have my research to focus on," Olivia said, refusing to let the postdoc treat her as a glorified errand girl, a role Dr. Lynch had assigned her.

Sofia's mask of indifference cracked, revealing a trace of annoyance.

"Right, like you actually have important research to concentrate on. But have it your way."

"Are you still interested in learning the computer work for your grant?" Olivia asked.

Sofia huffed, shook her head while she shot Olivia a dirty look, then resumed her gossip session with Brittney. Upon seeing this, Olivia turned to leave.

As she exited the computer lab, Olivia felt a strange mix of disappointment and satisfaction. She was disappointed that she couldn't discuss Bradley with either Brittney or Sofia, yet triumphant in finally standing her ground. The realization that they had morphed into a replica of Dr. Lynch left Olivia disheartened. It was becoming clear to her that the lab wasn't fostering genuine research, but rather nurturing a culture of misconduct and unethical behavior.

Her own newfound assertiveness surprised Olivia. She was proud of herself, knowing that she had taken control of her situation in the lab, a transformation she credited largely to Ethan.

Later that afternoon, Olivia made her way back to the computer lab after assisting Ethan with the updates in the linear accelerator building. She was excited about continuing to work on her project, which aimed to challenge the butterfly effect theory. For years in the lab, she'd worked on a program to simulate time travel to prove that changes to the past wouldn't alter the future. She encountered some challenges along the way, but recently, her experiments aligned with the findings of the Los Alamos National Laboratory, supporting the notion that the butterfly effect might not exist after all.

As she entered the computer lab, a sinking feeling settled in her stomach. She discovered Sofia and Brittney huddled together around her computer, their heads bent close, whispering. With growing horror, Olivia watched as their fingers danced across her keyboard, executing commands with a disturbing sense of purpose. Before she could intervene, their laughter echoed through the lab.

"What are you doing?!" Olivia asked, her voice trembling as she rushed to intervene. She had spent hours of painstaking effort developing a complex computer program designed to simulate time travel with unparalleled precision.

Sofia shrugged, a smug grin plastered across her face.

"Oops, sorry about that," she said. "We thought it was just some old code lying around. Didn't realize it was something you needed."

"Looks like you'll have to start from scratch, Olivia," Brittney joined in with a sneer, rubbing salt in the wound. Their laughter lingered in the air as they left the computer lab.

As Olivia witnessed the callous destruction of her work, a bitter realization settled over her like a suffocating fog.

"You're just like Dr. Lynch," Olivia said, her voice thick with contempt. She locked eyes with Sofia, unleashing her pent-up frustration.

"You've learned well from her, haven't you? The manipulation, the deceit," Olivia said. "You don't have any work to do, either. You can just make it up or have someone else do it for you."

"Whatever you say, Olivia," Sofia said, feigning innocence. With a final smirk, they left Olivia alone in the lab to grapple with the aftermath of their sabotage.

A heavy silence settled over the lab, broken only by the hum of equipment whirring and the rapid thud of Olivia's pounding heart. Despite her efforts to contain her rising panic, Olivia's hands trembled. She was so absorbed in her thoughts that she didn't even notice when Ethan entered the computer lab. He approached her, his gentle touch an attempt to soothe her wounded pride.

"Don't let them get under your skin, Liv," Ethan said. "I can help you rebuild the program."

Olivia remained silent, not even acknowledging Ethan's presence. She just stared at the computer screen where the post-docs had destroyed her program.

"At least they didn't steal it," Ethan said. "Your work's solid, and now they can't take credit. They're not even smart enough to be anything but petty."

Olivia stood there, considering conflicting thoughts. Every time she stood up for herself, it seemed to backfire. Should she just swallow her pride and stay silent? A part of her whispered yes. She replied to Bradley's email anyway and set up a meeting.

The day Olivia scheduled the meeting with Bradley coincided with the weekly lab meeting. Bradley accepted the invitation to visit the smaller campus, noting that he already had another appointment planned for the same day. This gave Olivia a glimmer of hope, as she thought that this second meeting might mark when someone else dared to speak up.

They agreed to meet in the building with the campus cafe, and Bradley suggested they could find an empty classroom to discuss their matters privately. Olivia was relieved that Bradley agreed with her insistence on secrecy. She feared that any witness would suspect that she was reporting them for misconduct or at least having discussions about reporting them.

The lab meeting unfolded in its customary fashion, but today's gathering included Dr. Kingsley. Dr. Lynch and he discussed their most recent grant application, along with plans for an upcoming conference in Switzerland. Olivia, as per her usual habit, tried her best to tune out their conversation, but one particular detail pierced through the monotony.

"I'm considering calling an exterminator to deal with those pigeons," Dr. Kingsley casually mentioned.

"Pigeons? I haven't noticed any pigeons around. Are you contemplating hiring someone to kill wild birds?" Olivia asked.

"They're nothing more than flying rats shitting all over my car."

"So, you're advocating killing wildlife just to avoid washing your car?" Olivia asked.

"Well, well, well, Olivia, what's your problem today? Have you just found out you can speak?" Dr. Kingsley fired back, with a hint of mockery in his British accent.

"Enough," Dr. Lynch intervened, putting an end to their escalating exchange.

Olivia let the argument drop, storing this new piece of information away. She knew it would make for an interesting addition to her growing list of grievances to discuss with Bradley during their meeting. While it might not qualify as scientific misconduct, it served to further highlight the less than admirable aspects of their personalities. Dr. Lynch concluded the meeting with her usual condescending remarks, and she and Dr. Kingsley headed upstairs to her office.

As Olivia left the lab building, en route to the cafe, she attempted to find the supposed pigeon infestation but found nothing. However, she could hear the soft cooing of mourning doves, but couldn't find them. A wry smile crossed her face as she thought, *Dr. Kingsley is such an idiot.* With a soft laugh and a playful shake of her head, Olivia entertained the thought that Dr. Kingsley might just proceed with his exterminator plans, blissfully unaware of the protected status of mourning doves in Massachusetts. She couldn't help but feel a certain satisfaction at the prospect of these birds continuing to grace his car with their unexpected gifts.

As Olivia stepped into the cafe, she easily found Bradley. She had browsed through his photos on the university website beforehand, but the pictures didn't do him justice. He wore an extremely bright, form-fitting sweater and tailored charcoal-gray pants. His distinctive horn-rimmed glasses commanded attention. It appeared as if Bradley relished being the center of attention. Olivia raised an eyebrow at his attention-grabbing fashion sense, considering that his job called for confidentiality and discretion.

"Hello, Mr. Parker?" Olivia said as she approached his table.

"Yes, Olivia?" he said, rising from his seat and offering his hand.

"Yes, it's a pleasure to meet you. Thank you for agreeing to meet here. I wanted to keep this informal," Olivia said.

"No problem at all. I noticed an empty room, 102, when I arrived. We can talk in there," Bradley said.

They left the small cafe and went downstairs to room 102, which was tucked away in a secluded corner. It was the most remote room in the building, providing them with the utmost privacy.

"So, Olivia, what's on your mind?" Bradley asked, taking a seat a little too close to her.

Olivia laid out the troubling events that had unfolded in her lab over the years. She argued that these weren't isolated incidents, but part of a larger pattern. She detailed Dr. Lynch and Dr. Kingsley's brazen affair—technically not misconduct, perhaps, but wildly inappropriate. Then came Dr. O'Brien: his drunkenness, his blatant theft of postdoc work, tantamount to plagiarism. To cap it off, Olivia described Dr. Lynch and Dr. Kingsley's involvement in submitting grants containing fabricated information—an unmistakable instance of scientific misconduct.

"In my ethics class, they emphasized that staying silent is as problematic as actively taking part in misconduct. So, I really just needed to discuss all of this with you and get your advice," Olivia said.

"I don't know, Olivia. Do you have any proof?" Bradley asked.

"Well, not really..." Olivia hesitated before responding. "Wait, there are no laboratory notebooks or computer records documenting the experiments they claim to have conducted on their grant applications. Couldn't that be proof of fraudulent work?"

"Your lab is small, Olivia. If you decide to pursue a formal complaint, they'll know it was you who reported them." Bradley leaned in closer.

"Aren't you supposed to keep any complaints confidential?" Olivia asked. "There are at least three of us that could have made a report."

"It's difficult to keep such things secret, unless…" Bradley said, nibbling his lower lip as he moved closer to Olivia, placing his hand on her arm.

She froze for a second, then stepped back toward the door, her eyes locked on Bradley's sudden movement.

"It's ok, Olivia. If you want to make a complaint, no one will hear us in here. I use this room a lot," Bradley said, continuing to advance towards her, grabbing the bottom of her shirt.

"Uh, I need to get back to the lab. I'm sorry for wasting your time," Olivia said, quickly pulling her shirt out of his grasp.

She opened the door and rushed out, feeling disoriented and breathless as she wandered around, her mind still reeling. Her heart pounded in her chest as she searched for the exit, her hands trembling. She stumbled upon the way out of the building and began making her way back to the lab, her steps unsteady on the snowy path. She nearly lost her footing several times, her nerves shaken by the unsettling encounter.

CHAPTER 20

Present Day

I knew I wouldn't be able to eliminate everyone with those bombs. I can't believe Dr. Lynch actually survived. It's gonna be a bitch to get into the hospital to deal with her. Well, maybe I won't have to. Maybe I'll get lucky and she won't make it.

Tonight is bitterly cold, and the effort to move quietly is becoming difficult as I crunch through the snow. I approach the poorly lit apartment building, nervous that someone might hear me. My gloved hand reaches into the pocket of my coat, making sure I still have the lock-picking tools I'll need.

I make my way up the icy steps leading to the front door of the building, my breath visible in the frigid air. The cold bites through my clothing, but I can't afford to hesitate. I slip inside, and the lobby appears empty. With swift, quiet steps, I ascend the stairs, making my way to the apartment on the second floor. The lock yields to my practiced touch, and the door swings open without a sound.

I enter silently, closing the door behind me with a soft click. Inside, darkness shrouds the apartment, except for the faint glow of streetlights filtering through heavy curtains and a small night-light in the kitchen. My senses are on high alert as I listen for any sign of movement.

The living room to my left emanates an air of neglect with its sparse furnishings. Faded paint peels away from the walls and the curtains hang askew, granting me the luxury of foregoing my flashlight as the streetlight seeps through the gaps. A threadbare sofa rests against the wall, its only company a solitary end table displaying a series of framed photographs.

As I venture through the kitchen, I see on the counter a trail of half-empty glasses leading the way to a sink filled with unwashed dishes. The counter is also littered with scattered stacks of unopened mail. As I continue through, I hear the radiator click, its metallic sound echoing through the apartment. I pause, listening intently for even the faintest hint of movement. The relentless heat inside the apartment is wearing on me. Despite the cold outside, I wonder how she endures the sweltering heat in this cramped space. I'm sure she likes it hot because of where she's from.

My footsteps are silent as I move deeper into the apartment, heading down the hallway toward the bedroom. Her bedroom is clean and organized, not at all like the disarray in her kitchen. She's sleeping in an enormous bed, cocooned beneath a snug comforter featuring tropical flowers. I strain to detect her breath, barely audible above the clicking radiator.

A television sits on a dresser across from her bed, display-ing a late-night infomercial on its muted screen. On her bedside table, there is another series of framed photographs that appear to tell her life story. From baby pictures with her family in the Philippines to adult photos in Boston—the progression of images was clear.

I creep up to the bed, holding my breath, each step a deliberate endeavor to avoid detection. In the room's stillness, I slowly remove the pocket knife from my coat and unfold it. My breath catches as the blade clicks securely into position.

Beneath the floral comforter, Sofia lay sound asleep on her back, the top of her head peeking out, oblivious to my presence. I inhale deeply, holding my breath to muffle any sound. Slowly, I lower the comforter, revealing her delicate neck. I press my hand against her forehead, ensuring she remains still as I swiftly draw the knife across her tender skin. Her eyes shoot open, but a strangled gasp was all she managed as the blade severed her windpipe. Panic filled her gaze as she struggled to sit up and clutch desperately at her throat.

I lean in, my weight bearing down on her legs, preventing any escape. It was all over before she could comprehend what had just happened to her. I cover her head once more with the comforter, before leaving behind my message for the FBI.

I stepped into the bathroom, cleaned myself up, changed into fresh clothes I'd brought, and then sealed the incriminating coveralls in a plastic bag. I retrace my steps throughout the apartment, leaving it precisely as I had found it, erasing almost every trace of my presence.

With this part of my mission accomplished, I am extraordinarily calm. I pause for a moment, my senses alert to any lingering traces of sound in the air. I feel a pang of satisfaction as I take one last look around before I exit. The lock clicks back into place, and I slip out of the apartment building back into the freezing night.

CHAPTER 21

February 2023

Olivia's mind was still reeling from the recent turn of events. The reality of what had just happened engulfed her, leaving her feeling disoriented and overwhelmed. Now she understood why no one dared to complain. Ethan's cautionary words echoed in her mind. She chastised herself for being so foolish—she should have known better.

As Olivia replayed the encounter with Bradley in her head, she realized she hadn't gone through with making the complaint, and she had even offered an apology to him. Perhaps she could salvage the situation by lying low and focusing on her exit strategy. She had no other viable option, anyway.

Returning to the lab, Olivia immediately emailed Bradley. She expressed her gratitude for his time and emphasized her appreciation for his clarification that there were no issues in the lab, quashing any notion of a formal complaint. She hoped Bradley would interpret this message as a definitive sign she had no intention of pursuing the matter any further.

Olivia hadn't told Ethan about her meeting with Bradley, aware that he wouldn't approve. Instead, she had told him she was going to the cafe for coffee.

"You were gone for quite some time. Where's the coffee?" Ethan asked.

"Oh, they were out," Olivia said, avoiding his gaze.

"They ran out of coffee? At the cafe?" Ethan raised an incredulous eyebrow.

"Uh, yeah. I don't know. We can just make it here," Olivia said, attempting to force a smile that didn't quite reach her eyes.

Ethan and Olivia continuing working for a few more hours, attempting to tackle some of the electromagnetic field equations that had consumed a lot of Olivia's recent focus. They had brewed a pot of coffee in the small break room down the hall from Brittney's office. With the day winding down, Olivia returned to clean the pot.

As she walked down the hallway, she crossed paths with Bradley emerging from Brittney's office. His usual well kempt appearance was in disarray, with his hair tousled and his clothing rumpled. Beads of sweat glistened on his forehead as he attempted to polish his glasses on his shirt.

"See, Olivia. Brittney knows how things work around here," Bradley said with a grin, already halfway down the hall.

Olivia tapped on Brittney's partially open office door, only to find her sitting on the floor. One of her shoulders was exposed because her blouse was pulled down. She struggled to pull her skirt back over her knees and could only get halfway dressed. Her face was flushed, with tears streaming down her cheeks.

"Oh my God, Brittney. What happened? Are you okay?" Olivia asked, as she leaned in closer, her attention darting around the room at papers strewn on the floor and a mug knocked off the desk.

"Go the fuck away, Olivia," Brittney said, her voice cracking as tears continued streaming down her flushed cheeks. She attempted to regain her composure, but her trembling hands and reddened eyes betrayed her distress.

"Brittney, we need to call the police—get you to the hospital," Olivia said, stepping into the room and reaching out to her. But Brittney recoiled, pushing her away.

"I said go away, Olivia. I don't need your help." Brittney's grip tightened on the doorknob as she slammed it shut.

As the door closed, Olivia grasped the weight of what Brittney had just been through—and how close she'd come herself. The realization hit her hard; Bradley was a rapist, exchanging his secrecy for sex. How many other students had he hurt? She understood Bradley would expose the conversation she just had with him and it would ruin her career. It was all her fault; she never should have attempted to change her fate. However, she still contemplated what she could do to stop everyone in that lab.

❖

Olivia spiraled back into a deep, suffocating bout of depression. Her usual energy had drained away, leaving her listless. She spent the rest of the week in bed, with Mulder curled beside her, only slightly irritated by her presence. She'd made the excuse of having the flu to her lab and even roped Ethan into covering for her, all to ward off any suspicion that she might go above Bradley.

Ethan was there constantly, trying to rouse her. He tended to both Olivia and Mulder, cooking for them and offering gentle

nudges toward the outside world. He tried coaxing her into simple outings—a movie, a drive—but even that was too much for
Olivia in her despondent state.

Then, as the weekend crept in, Ethan chipped away at her.
With his steady persistence, he persuaded her to at least think
about returning to the lab.

"You don't have to do anything, Olivia. Just show up. You're
only a few months away from graduating. But if you keep staying
away, they might suspect something."

"What would they suspect? All they know is that I'm sick,"
Olivia said.

But deep down, she understood the truth of Ethan's words.
She needed to return to the lab. The obligation felt like serving
out a prison sentence.

The following week, Olivia mustered the courage to return
to the lab, but no one even noticed she had been gone. Their indifference stung, but it also left her with a peculiar sense of relief.
As she settled back into her daily routine of updating computers,
she contemplated staying home, as no one would notice, anyway.
But she dismissed that tempting thought.

She'd once again accepted her fate, realizing that every effort
she had made up to that point to change her circumstances had
been a massive failure. Her best course of action was to keep her
thoughts and emotions concealed, to grit her teeth and finish her
graduate program in just a few more painstaking months. If she
could make it out, maybe she could find a postdoc opportunity
somewhere, giving her a chance to explore her own research. Or
maybe she should look into teaching positions, a path that seemed
less risky than finding herself trapped in another similar lab.

Every day, as she stepped into the lab, her nerves were still taut. What happened on this particular day left her shaken in a way she hadn't felt before.

In the late morning, Olivia was busy brewing coffee in the breakroom when she overheard a man's escalating voice echoing down the hallway. Entering the hallway, she glanced at Brittney, who had come out of her office, drawn by the commotion.

Together, they ventured down the hallway, where Dr. Collins stood as a gatekeeper, attempting to defuse the situation.

"Who's that?" Olivia asked, leaning closer to Brittney.

"That's Dr. Lynch's husband, Aiden. This is about to get interesting," Brittney said with a grin.

Olivia knew well that Dr. Kingsley had gone upstairs to Dr. Lynch's office about twenty minutes ago, and given their history, she had a pretty good idea of what they were doing, probably with the office door wide open.

"Get out of my way, Dr. Collins! I know she's up there, and I know who's with her. I found the notes from him," Aiden said.

"She's not even here, Aiden. Now, if you don't calm down and leave, I'm going to call campus security," Dr. Collins said, maintaining a remarkable composure.

"Why can't I just go up there, then?" Aiden asked.

"Aiden, she's not here."

"Her car is outside. I know she's up there with *him*," Aiden said, spitting the words like they burned.

"I'm calling security," Dr. Collins said.

Their voices grew louder, and tensions continued to escalate in the lobby as Dr. Collins and Aiden continued to argue. The confrontation turned physical as they shoved each other, and amid the chaos, Dr. Collins shouted to Maya, the administrative assistant, to dial security.

Olivia believed a full-on fist fight was imminent, leaving her torn about whether she should try to step in. Meanwhile, Brittney stood in the hallway, wearing a satisfied smirk, as if the unfolding drama thoroughly entertained her, like she was watching a soap opera.

"Don't bother, Maya!" Aiden said as he delivered one final push to Dr. Collins and stormed out of the building.

"That was close," Dr. Collins said, as he let out a sigh of relief when Aiden exited. He straightened his tie before heading back upstairs to his office.

Brittney strolled back to her office with a sly smile. "Well, that just made my morning. I'd pay to hear that conversation when Dr. Lynch gets home."

Olivia grappled with a mix of emotions. Aiden was aware of his wife's affair with Dr. Kingsley, and he had nearly caught them in the act if it weren't for Dr. Collins' intervention. Olivia realized that part of Dr. Collins' role also involved acting as Dr. Lynch's protector, which, while not entirely surprising, left a sour taste in her mouth.

When Olivia returned to the lab, she recounted the event to Ethan, who remarked that Dr. Lynch might finally get what she deserved. They continued working on Olivia's research throughout the afternoon, but the excitement in the lab was not quite over.

After lunch, Olivia once again overheard an argument in the lobby, assuming that Aiden had returned, hoping to confront his wife if Dr. Collins had gone for the day. However, when Olivia ventured into the lobby, she found a very short, dark-haired man shouting at Maya. He appeared small, dressed in jeans and a button-down shirt beneath a puffy black jacket. Because it had snowed again that morning, snow covered his large boots. Despite his small stature, he exhibited a state of complete hysteria, flailing his arms wildly.

"Maya, she won't answer my calls, so I'm going up there," he said.

"I'm not gonna stop you," Maya said, her hands raised as she slowly backed away.

With determination, he bounded up the stairs. Unfortunately for him, Dr. Lynch had already left for the day, leaving him without the opportunity to speak with her. Disappointed, he descended the stairs, still agitated, and approached Maya.

"Please, don't mention my visit to Dr. Lynch," he said on the way out the door, hoping to catch her off guard on another occasion.

Olivia approached Maya, curious about the commotion.

"What's going on in here today? Is it a full moon? Who was that guy?" Olivia asked.

"That's Dr. Elliot," Maya said. "He had his own lab here before you started. A really great guy, super smart, and an honest researcher."

"That's why he had trouble with *this* lab," Olivia said dryly.

"Just before you started, Dr. Lynch told the dean that she felt threatened by his presence, so they contacted campus security and had him escorted from the property," Maya said.

"That little guy? They actually believed he was threatening?" Olivia raised an eyebrow, a smirk playing on her lips.

"Like I said, he was honest, so he had some... uh... difficulties with Dr. Lynch," Maya said. "Rumor has it Bradley Parker met with him, and shortly afterward, security escorted him away. No one heard from him again... until today."

"Really?" Olivia asked, her voice tight as she recalled her encounter with Bradley. She'd sent him an email confirming she wouldn't proceed—hopefully, that would be enough to keep her safe.

"I don't really know why he was here today, though, but you never know what else Dr. Lynch may have done," Maya said.

As Olivia tried to process the unsettling events that occurred that day, a growing storm of emotions welled up within her. She grew more depressed, and angrier, by the day. The disconcerting discoveries never ceased to amaze her. She couldn't escape the realization that the more time she spent in the lab, and the more she unearthed about her supposed colleagues, the more she would hate them. Revelation by revelation, the lab grew darker—and more dangerous.

CHAPTER 22

"That's it?" Rachel raised an eyebrow, clearly incredulous. "Who the fuck is Dr. Elliot? You've never even mentioned him."

Olivia, sitting across from Rachel, hesitated for a moment before responding. She was still fidgeting with the sleeves of her sweatsuit. Rachel saw beads of sweat on Olivia's forehead and sensed she was too afraid to look up from the table.

"I forgot about him until just now," Olivia said, her voice uneasy, barely above a whisper.

"Olivia, I thought you were heading toward telling me about the explosion," Rachel said, leaning forward.

"I already told you, I know nothing about that. It was just a few days after Aiden and Dr. Elliot barged into the lab, the explosion happened," Olivia said, her voice trembling.

Rachel could feel the underlying anxiety in Olivia's words, the fear of being implicated in something. She doubted that Olivia truly didn't know what had happened.

"You're making this up to protect yourself, piling on suspects like Abbie and Dr. Elliot," Rachel said firmly.

Olivia shook her head, her voice still unsteady. "I'm not 'piling them on.' I'm just telling you what happened in the lab."

Rachel noticed a quiver in Olivia's bottom lip, a sign that she was again struggling to maintain her composure. The fear in Olivia's eyes hinted at deeper emotions threatening to surface once more, perhaps even leading to more tears. Rachel considered softening her approach with Olivia, wanting to avoid causing her to freeze again, but found herself unable to do so.

"We can't confirm anything you've said—Brittney, Aiden, and Ethan are all missing. Now Sofia's not answering her phone or opening her door. And suddenly, there's this Dr. Elliot guy we're not even sure exists." Rachel kept her tone flat.

Tears streamed down Olivia's face, her cheeks flushed. Rachel thought it seemed like she might be on the brink of hyperventilating.

"I didn't do this, I didn't do this," Olivia said.

Then, with a sharper edge, she added, "Isn't it suspicious that *you* can't find Brittney or Aiden, but *I'm* the one here answering questions?"

"You're only here because I grabbed you from the hospital before you vanished. I could say the same about Ethan. Have you even been to his house?" Rachel shot back, her tone sharpening to match Olivia's.

"No, he usually stays with me, and I've told you he has no reason to hurt anyone," Olivia said, shaking her head and trying to steady her breathing.

"I disagree," Rachel said. "The address we have for him is a UPS store. I think either of you could've caused that lab explosion. I don't believe Dr. Elliot exists. And maybe what happened to Brittney actually happened to you."

"Bradley did not rape me," Olivia said, her eyes red and swollen from crying, her features tight with desperation. "I don't know what else I can say to convince you Ethan and I had nothing to do with this."

She reached for a tissue. Rachel noticed her slender fingers trembling as she wiped away the tears streaking her cheeks.

"I'm trying to help you figure out what really happened in that lab. You need to find Brittney and Aiden. My gut says it was one of them. Honestly, I'm leaning toward Brittney. She's always hated me and had every reason to hurt all of us," Olivia continued.

"Olivia, I don't trust you. I'm keeping you in custody until I get more answers," Rachel said, her eyes narrowing.

"Am I under arrest?" Olivia asked, her eyes wide, voice tight with fear.

Rachel watched her body language—every muscle tense, like she was bracing for impact. Rachel wasn't ready to answer that question. Not yet.

"Please, just stay in here while I check in with my partner," Rachel said, rising from her chair to exit the interrogation room. "I'll have the officer bring you some more water while you wait."

Olivia remained silent, her eyes wide and her hands tightly clutching the edge of the table, as Rachel left the room.

CHAPTER 23

Present Day

Wandering the hospital's bustling corridors feels like navigating controlled chaos. The fluorescent lights overhead cast a bright glow on the linoleum floors, and the air carries the powerful scent of disinfectant. It's a busy day, with nurses and doctors rushing by, shouting instructions, the urgent beeping of monitors providing a soundtrack.

I came prepared with a lab coat, but here they're all embroidered with the hospital's name. This won't do. It looks like I'll have to steal one in order to blend in. As I approach a nurses' station, I find a coat rack overflowing with white lab coats. While I take one down, I notice a nearby stethoscope on top of the cluttered counter. I quickly scan the surroundings, ensuring no prying eyes are on me, and snatch the stethoscope. It's the perfect addition to my ensemble, almost guaranteeing I seamlessly blend in with the medical staff. With the lab coat on and the stethoscope hanging around my neck, I set off towards the elevator.

I pass several nurses and other staff members along the way, offering a warm smile, meeting their eyes, letting my charm do the work. They smile back, unaware. I'm just another face in a busy hallway. No one suspects a thing.

But as I round the corner, a doctor blocks my path, his sharp eyes locking onto my face. "Are you new here? I don't recognize you."

"Covering a few shifts for Dr. Harrington. Patient overflow," I reply smoothly, meeting his gaze without a hint of hesitation. Keep it smooth. Keep it casual.

"Where's your ID badge?" His voice hardens, a challenge beneath the question.

My fingers pat my pockets, a mock search. "Uh… I had a temp sticker. Security's machine was down this morning. Must've fallen off."

He studies me, frowning. "Security's machine? It's never down. Let's get this sorted out right now."

His hand reaches for my elbow, an iron grip forming. He knows.

My heart pounds, but I keep my expression calm. Run or play along?

"Doctor!" A nurse rushes up, irritation sharpening her voice. "There you are. They're waiting for you in the procedure room."

"I'll be there in a minute," he says, his grip tightens as he pulls me closer. "I need to get this one to security."

"He's a doctor," the nurse snaps. "He can manage. Your patient can't."

The doctor's hesitation lasts a breath. His grip loosens. "Fine. Go get your badge."

He leaves with the nurse, and I keep walking, forcing my breathing to remain steady. The elevator opens just as I reach them. I step inside, exhale, and stare at the closing doors. No footsteps. No one rushing after me.

Upon reaching the fifth floor, I locate Dr. Lynch's room, guarded by a bored police officer. As I confidently stroll past him and into the room, the officer doesn't even give me a second glance, preoccupied by a message on his phone. I expected this to be harder.

The room is dimly lit, the soft, ambient glow casting long shadows across the light blue walls. Steady, rhythmic humming and intermittent beeping from the monitoring machines fill the air. A privacy curtain, drawn halfway around the bed, obstructs my view. Its presence, however, will prove advantageous for what I'm about to do.

I approach the curtain and begin carefully edging my way around it. On the other side, Dr. Lynch lies still on the hospital bed. Folded crisp, white sheets surround her, and tubes and wires connect her to various monitors. Her face, neck and hands bear many burns, some of which are concealed beneath sterile bandages. The ever-present hiss of the ventilator, breathing for her, punctuates the stillness.

I pause, absorbing the room and Dr. Lynch. The absence of get-well cards or flowers on the bedside table doesn't come as a surprise; it's clear she's not well liked. It's a shame they've kept her in this coma. I had hoped she'd see my face before she died, just to know it was me.

Earlier today, I'd stolen a sizable bottle of potassium chloride powder from the biology lab. To cover all my bases, I swiped syringes and needles as well, unsure if I'd find them easily in the hospital. I dissolved the entire bottle of potassium chloride in water and filled several syringes, preparing for what needed to be done.

The syringes feel cold and slick in my fingers as I carefully withdraw them from my lab coat pocket. I keep my ears sharp for any sound—the police officer outside, a nurse's footsteps. Nothing yet.

The needle slides into Dr. Lynch's IV line, and I press the plunger. Her vitals flicker on the monitor. A slow push—careful.

A voice outside the door grows louder, and I freeze, the syringe half-full in my grip. Footsteps approach, then pause. My pulse quickens, but I force myself to stay still, leaning closer to the privacy curtain.

The doorknob rattles. My body stiffens. My mind races. Pull the syringe? Abandon the plan? No—too late. Hide or act natural? Is it maintenance? A nurse on rounds? I stay where I am. If they enter, I'll nod, feign concern, continue with protocol.

The handle jostles again, then stops. No one enters.

I wait, listening. After a moment, the voice fades, the footsteps retreat. Just a false alarm.

As her heart rate slows, I push the rest of the potassium, then silence the monitors. Her chest rises, shudders, then stills. I wanted Dr. Lynch to suffer. For now, her death will do.

I slide the empty syringes back into my pocket, straighten my lab coat. I leave the room just as confidently as I entered. Another clean exit.

"Have a good night," I say to the officer with a polite smile. He nods, eyes still glued to his phone, oblivious.

As I calmly make my way out of the hospital, I can feel a profound wave of relief. I'm pleased with what I've achieved. I know I have set things straight this time, addressed what needed correction. Anticipation courses through my veins as I walk away from the hospital, determined and ready to confirm my success.

CHAPTER 24

Sweat beaded on Olivia's forehead as she sat in the cold interrogation room, her heart pounding. She'd never been involved in anything like this, the fear of a lengthy prison sentence gripping her like a vice. She'd been trying to show that she didn't do any of this, but her back was up against the wall. The stark reality of her predicament was overwhelming her.

Olivia always felt destined for trouble, a conviction rooted in a childhood scarred by misfortune. She believed the universe ran on predetermined tracks, leaving her helpless against fate's cruel whims. As she struggled to keep her composure, her mind retreated to the echoes of her past. Olivia learned early on that some things in life were beyond her control.

She was born and raised in Clarkston, Georgia. During her childhood, her neighborhood was a small, tight-knit community. A place where everyone seemed to know each other's names and secrets. Olivia's family lived in a simple one-story ranch house painted a cheerful shade of yellow, its tidy lawn maintained.

As an only child, Olivia grew up in a compact family: just her, her mother, and her father. Her father worked as an international sales representative, spending much of his time away from home, traveling extensively. As he crossed continents to meet clients and take part in trade shows, he sold industrial supplies to various countries. Olivia wasn't entirely sure about the details of her father's job, but she knew he focused on selling tools and other materials used in construction.

Olivia's mother worked part-time as an administrative assistant at Clarkston High School. She worked only a few days each week in the principal's office, organizing files and answering the phone. Her mother devoted more time to church activities than to her job, but she only required Olivia to attend church on Sundays.

When Olivia was just eight years old, a fierce thunderstorm tore through Clarkston one summer evening. Rain poured relentlessly, and lightning crackled across the sky. While Olivia lay asleep in bed, lightning struck a nearby tree, causing it to crash through the roof and into her bedroom. Miraculously, no one got hurt, but the event left Olivia shaken, questioning why someone—or something—might have targeted her. Had she done something to deserve an attack by a tree?

"Why did this happen to me?" Olivia's voice cracked, her eyes brimming with tears.

"Sweetheart, God was watching over you," her mother said. "He protected you from harm."

"Oh, come on, Mary," her father said, turning to Olivia. "Things happen we can't control. It's not about what you did or didn't do, Olivia. You have no control over fate."

Both explanations gave Olivia some comfort. At eight, she thought something bigger was always in control: God, fate, or maybe just her parents.

Years later, when Olivia was twelve, her family faced a tough situation when her father lost his job because of an economic downturn. The financial crisis forced his company to downsize because they couldn't predict future sales. As a result, they had to layoff sales agents to save money and keep their business running.

With Olivia's mom's part-time job as their only income, the family battled to make ends meet. They faced the real possibility of having their electricity cut off and often couldn't afford proper meals. Cereal without milk became a common meal, highlighting some of their hardships. The once maintained lawn then bore the marks of neglect, its lush grass now overgrown and choked with weeds. The constant fear of eviction heightened Olivia's worries about what might happen to her family.

Olivia's father didn't blame himself or his boss for losing his job. Instead, he often cursed fate, feeling powerless against the universe and convinced there was nothing he could do.

"It's like we're just pawns in a game, moved around by forces beyond our control," her father said with a shrug, as if he'd given up long ago.

"But why do bad things keep happening to us? Why can't we change things?" Olivia asked.

"It's just fate, honey. We can't change the plan of the universe. Sometimes life just sucks, and there's nothing we can do about it."

By the time Olivia reached high school and took an introductory sociology class, she had fully embraced her father's belief in determinism. She believed fate dictated their lives, leaving them powerless to change anything because everything was already planned.

To help her family financially, Olivia tried to find a part-time job, but she struggled to secure one. Her only option was a job at a local KFC, where she earned far less than $80 per week. Meanwhile, her mother attempted to secure more hours at the high school where she worked, but to no avail. No matter what they did, they couldn't change anything.

Eventually, Olivia's father landed a job at Lowe's after a chance conversation with Olivia's boss at KFC, who happened to be related to the manager at Lowe's. This turn of events provided some relief and kept them from losing their home.

During Olivia's senior year of high school, her mother missed work one day without warning. Olivia usually arrives at school after her mother, so the principal stopped her to inquire about her mother's absence. Olivia, feeling nervous, tried to call her mom, but she didn't answer. At that moment, Olivia's father called both the principal and Olivia to relay news that her mother was in a car accident that morning, which he had just learned about from the hospital. Olivia abruptly hung up on her father, left school, and rushed to Emory University Hospital.

Without access to a car and unwilling to wait for her dad or endure the lengthy trip via public transportation, she opted to spend her KFC-earned money on a taxi ride to the hospital. Olivia's pulse raced as she stepped out of the vehicle. She stumbled slightly; her legs unsteady beneath her as she fought to regain her composure. Her nerves were shot. Before heading towards the hospital's entrance, she steadied herself with a deep breath.

Inside, the ER lobby overwhelmed her senses. Patients shuffled alongside nurses, while security guards kept a vigilant eye on the proceedings. Uncertain of her next move, Olivia's heart hammered against her ribs, her breath shallow and rapid. Olivia's eyes darted frantically, searching for her mom amidst the sea of strangers. With tears threatening to spill from her eyes, she made her way through the crowded lobby, her steps quickening with each passing moment.

"Where's my mom? My mom?" Olivia asked, her voice rising.

The nurse behind the check-in desk tried to calm her down, asking for more information, but her panic proves overwhelming. Despite the nurse's continued efforts to calm her, Olivia struggled to focus.

"What's your mom's name?" the nurse asked.

Olivia's eyes continued to dart around the room wildly, searching for any sign of her mother, her breath coming in ragged gasps, panic clear on her face.

"I need to see my mom!"

A woman then emerged from the automatic doors of the ER and approached Olivia with unexpected gentleness. She wore a casual business suit, her black hair framing her face, but it was her striking blue eyes that caught Olivia's attention.

"Take a breath," the woman said. "Was your mom at the Clarkston Church?"

Olivia blinked, staring at the woman in disbelief.

"What? No, my mom was in a car accident!" Fear and frustration tangled in her voice.

Before the blue-eyed woman could respond, another nurse intervened, guiding Olivia away from the crowded lobby in the opposite direction.

"What's your mom's name?" the nurse asked, her tone gentle but concerned.

Olivia thought she might hyperventilate as she felt her breath quicken. She regained control, taking slow, deep breaths to steady herself.

"Mary Barrett. My dad told me she was in a car accident."

The nurse's expression faltered upon hearing the name and the mention of the accident. Olivia felt a surge of fear, wondering if her mother's condition was worse than she had realized. Was her mother still alive?

They proceeded further into the hospital, making their way up to the neurointensive care unit in silence. Inside the room, her mother lay covered in bandages, her face obscured. Her mother was unconscious and connected to a breathing machine. Olivia's breath caught in her throat as she took in the sight, the reality of the situation hitting her with full force.

A doctor emerged through a set of double doors, his expression grave. Olivia's heart plummeted as she braced herself for the worst. The doctor's voice was gentle but carried the weight of grave news—her mother had suffered severe injuries in the car accident, including brain damage.

As Olivia struggled to absorb the shock of the diagnosis, a whirlwind of questions raced through her mind. How serious was the damage? Would her mother ever wake up? The doctor's response offered little comfort; he admitted they couldn't predict the outcome, but he harbored doubts about her mother ever waking up.

When Olivia's father arrived, the doctor delivered the same grim news, adding that police believed a drunk driver caused the accident but hadn't caught the suspect. The doctor advised further tests and recommended a wait-and-see approach to monitor her mother's condition for any signs of improvement.

Hours dragged into excruciating days as Olivia and her father maintained their vigil at her mother's bedside. Olivia was clinging to the fragile hope of a miracle, given her mother's strong religious beliefs. Each passing moment felt like an eternity as she watched, helpless, but there was no change. It didn't surprise her father. They couldn't change anything.

"Your mother made her wishes clear," her father said. "She didn't want to be kept alive by machines."

He passed Olivia her mother's will, the edges of the paper cool against her fingertips. Olivia had never known this existed until now. Yet there it was, stark and final, outlining her mother's wishes to forego life-sustaining treatments in the event of irreversible brain damage.

"And she wanted to donate her organs. Other people were meant to live according to the universe's plan, not your mom."

In the quiet moments between the rhythmic beeping of machines and the hushed consultations with doctors, Olivia just stared at her mother's still form. She knew no matter what she did, she couldn't change anything.

Olivia and her father stood side by side when the medical team disconnected the life support. Olivia felt numb as she watched the team carry out the procedure with gentle efficiency. With each beep of the machines ceasing, the room fell into a profound silence. As her mother died, Olivia remained numb, her emotions muted in the silent hospital room. Beside her, her father stood motionless, his expression reflecting her own subdued state.

Slowly, Olivia and her father exited the room into the sterile hospital hallway. They stood together, neither looking at the other, their eyes fixed on the floor. Neither spoke, neither shed tears nor reached out to one another. They remained rooted in place, their next steps uncertain.

Olivia lifted her eyes from the floor, feeling lost, only to find a young man staring back at her. She wondered if he was a volunteer, perhaps a candy striper, with his tousled dark brown hair and light hazel eyes. His sad smile, framed by charming dimples, tugged at her heart as he approached. Without a word, he extended a familiar vase with a red ribbon—the type one could easily find in any hospital gift shop—containing a single rose.

CHAPTER 25

As Rachel emerged from the interrogation room, she spotted Mitchell standing just by the two-way mirror, his expression expectant.

"Did you catch any of that bullshit?" Rachel asked.

"So, you definitely think she did it? Everything she says is a lie?" Mitchell asked, his brows lifting, doubt flashing briefly across his face.

"She had something to do with it, but she won't admit it."

"How long do you think it's gonna take for her to admit it?" Mitchell pressed further. "You've already pissed off the Deputy Assistant Director because you're taking too long."

"I don't think it's a good idea to rush; she gets stressed and shuts up," Rachel said.

"Well, the boss might cut her loose. We've got nothing," Mitchell said. He gave a slight smirk, tilting his head, signaling to Rachel that he doubted their current evidence against Olivia.

"Are you fucking kidding me?"

"We got nothing on nobody, and the boss is pissed," Mitchell said, shaking his head.

Rachel pushed her lips together in annoyance, leaning back against the wall. She furrowed her brow, deep in thought, contemplating her next move to coax Olivia into talking.

As they stood in silence, the scene in the police station grew more intense as Rachel noticed a woman sitting at her desk in the bullpen. She wore a long, dark overcoat, and her hair was a tangled mess, as if she had run her fingers through it in distress. Strands of auburn hair fell in disarray across her shoulders as she trembled and tears streaked down her cheeks.

"Right, that's Abbie, Dr. Kingsley's wife," Mitchell said, his eyes following her line of sight. "After we identified Dr. Kingsley's body and notified her, she willingly came in to speak with us."

"Well, that's something," Rachel said, her eyes lighting up.

They crossed the bullpen and introduced themselves to Abbie, who greeted them with a mournful expression.

"I'm sorry," Abbie began, her voice quivering as she fought back tears. "I'm trying to pull myself together for my boys, but I'm just so devastated that he's gone. Who could have done this?"

"So, you don't think it was an accident?" Rachel asked.

Abbie's face registered a hint of understanding.

"Oh, I'm sorry. I just assumed, since you asked me to come down here, that the FBI doesn't investigate accidents."

"Yes, that's correct," Rachel said. "It was not an accident, and we're trying to piece it all together. Did your husband have any enemies? Anyone who would want to hurt him?"

"No, of course not. Everyone loved him." Abbie shook her head with certainty.

"So, you're saying no one in the lab had a reason to hold a grudge?" Mitchell asked.

"Not at all. He worked closely with Dr. Lynch's team, and they were very successful," Abbie said, her response unwavering.

"Do you think he might have been too close with Dr. Lynch?" Rachel asked.

"What do you mean?" Abbie asked, her brow tightening in confusion, missing the implication entirely.

"How was your marriage with Dr. Kingsley?" Rachel asked.

Abbie's voice trembled as she spoke of their relationship.

"It's great. Well, you know, normal. We had some rough patches, but we're no different from any other happy marriage. We have two boys he's devoted to, and he's home every night for dinner and to help with homework." Tears welled up again, and she reached over to gather more tissues.

"I'm sorry for your loss, Abbie, but we need to ask these questions to help us uncover the truth," Mitchell said in a quiet, compassionate tone.

Abbie shook her head while dabbing at her tear-streaked face with the tissues.

"Abbie, did either of you ever have an affair?" Rachel asked.

Mitchell shot her a wide-eyed look, as if to say, *You shouldn't have just come out and asked that.*

"Affairs? Like, was I sleeping with someone else? Of course not! I would never..." Abbie's eyes widened as she leaned forward, her hands fumbling to push her hair from her face.

Rachel paused for a moment. "And what about Dr. Kingsley?"

Abbie's eyes welled with tears as she vehemently defended her husband. "Never. Like I said, he is—was devoted to us and home all the time. When would he even have time to have an affair?" She grabbed more tissues as tears spilled freely down her cheeks.

Rachel exchanged a knowing glance with Mitchell, suspecting that Abbie hadn't considered the possibility that Dr. Kingsley might have been having an affair at work during the day, as Olivia had suggested. It was a detail they couldn't ignore, especially since they couldn't find Dr. Lynch's husband, Aiden.

"Alright, Abbie, we understand. I think we have what we need for now. An officer will take you home," Mitchell said as an officer approached and gently guided her away.

Rachel's glare could have burned a hole through Mitchell. She didn't say a word as Abbie walked away, but the disbelief was written all over her face.

"Rachel, she doesn't know anything. She had no idea about the affair," Mitchell said.

Rachel arched an eyebrow. "And you believe her?"

Mitchell nodded. "Yes. She's hysterical about losing her husband, and now she's left to raise two boys alone. The idea that he was cheating, or involved in anything wrong, is something she just can't fathom. Either she's in deep denial or she completely worships him. Either way, she wasn't involved."

"Fuck," Rachel said flatly.

Mitchell shot her a pointed look, gesturing again toward the swear jar. Rachel let out a sigh, her frustration mounting as she rolled her eyes. She felt like she was spinning her wheels in this investigation, getting nowhere. She and Mitchell just stood in the middle of the bullpen, uncertain of their next move.

Just then, two forensic agents entered the room, specifically seeking Rachel and Mitchell. They approached, smiling, burdened with paperwork, pictures, and yearbooks.

"Did you find something at Olivia's apartment?" Mitchell asked.

"Absolutely," one agent said with a huge grin. "Wait until you see this..."

Their excitement was contagious as they handed over the information directly to Rachel.

Rachel reached for the photos while Mitchell grabbed a few notebooks from the forensic agents. They wasted no time digging through the evidence collected from Olivia's apartment.

As Rachel sifted through the stack of pictures, she felt like she'd seen them before. The teenage girl seemed familiar. Those unruly curls framed her face as she stood beside a stone church with a woman Rachel guessed was her mother.

"Have a look at this yearbook," the forensic agent said, his grin widening again.

Rachel set the stack of photos down on the desk and reached for the yearbook. Its cover, worn with age, revealed it to be from Clarkston High School, dated 2013. Instantly, her mind flashed back to her first FBI case, a memory of the church bombing and the searing sting of pepper spray still fresh in her mind. A knot tightened in her stomach.

Opening the yearbook to a page marked by the forensic agent, Rachel's breath hitched as she saw the senior portrait of Olivia. Shock froze her features, her eyes widening and her mouth falling open in disbelief.

Meanwhile, Mitchell held up a stack of medical records dating back to the very day of the church bombing.

"This says Emory admitted her mother after a car accident on the same day," Mitchell said.

Rachel's head spun. The pieces locked together with a sharp click in her mind. She saw herself again, standing in that hospital hallway, facing a frantic teenage girl—Olivia.

The photograph confirmed it: Olivia, standing in front of the church in a time before the bombing, a snapshot burned into Rachel's memory.

Ten years ago. The day of the explosion. Their paths had crossed long before Rachel ever knew her name.

"Holy shit," Rachel said, her voice barely above a whisper. "We actually met her in Georgia on the day of the church bombing."

"And this..." Mitchell presented her with a yellowed clipping from an old newspaper. "Her mom died from that car accident, and they've never caught the drunk driver responsible."

Rachel's mind raced as she connected the dots in a dizzying blur. "Are you saying she bombed that AA meeting on the same day? How would she even know that soon? And what about the professor?"

Mitchell shrugged, his attention still focused on the stack of items spread out before them, remnants of the thorough search conducted by the forensic team in Olivia's apartment.

"Oh, that's not all," the forensic agent interjected, passing Rachel a collection of notebooks and study materials. Rachel flipped through them until she stumbled upon a printout of a published lab paper originating from Virginia Tech.

"See this," the forensic agent pointed out, directing Rachel's attention to the authors and the school name listed on the front. "Olivia Barrett and Dr. David Hayes published this in 2016..."

"Wait, what?" Rachel said, her eyes darting between Mitchell and the forensic agents.

"We called Virginia Tech," the forensic agent said. "Olivia was a research student there in this lab in 2016 when *someone* blew up that computer lab."

"Are you fucking joking? Olivia did all of this?" Rachel said. "She blew up the computer lab to destroy other people's research?"

"And she was a graduate student here in Boston when a bomb exploded in the subway station," Mitchell said.

"But what about Professor Neil? He's been everywhere and has run from us for years," Rachel said.

"Olivia didn't mention anything about him?" Mitchell asked.

"No," Rachel said. "Olivia never mentioned that she grew up in Georgia, went to school at Virginia Tech, mentioned none of that during her interrogation."

"One more thing, Rachel," the forensic agent said with a smile, pulling a light blue self-adhesive bandage roll from his pocket. "We found this in her bathroom cabinet, but no pipe bomb materials, no suture."

With a decisive motion, Rachel tossed everything onto the desk and strode toward the interrogation room, her frustration and anger radiating off her.

"What are you gonna do, Rachel?" Mitchell asked, reaching out to grab her arm, trying to slow her down before she entered the room.

"I'm going to arrest her. We have enough evidence to show she's involved," Rachel said, gesturing to the items scattered across the desk.

With determination in her steps, Rachel swung open the interrogation room door. The abrupt entrance startled Olivia, who sat across the table, her expression shifting from calm to wary as she registered Rachel's presence.

"Stand up," Rachel said.

"What?" Olivia asked.

"Olivia, stand up. You are under arrest," Rachel said, firm and authoritative.

"What? Why? What's happening?" Olivia said, her eyes wide with fear. Tears welled up as she trembled uncontrollably, shrinking away from Rachel.

Rachel came around behind Olivia and grabbed her under one of her armpits, forcing her to stand. She noticed tears streaming down Olivia's face, but she offered no resistance, her body surrendering to Rachel's will. With Olivia compliant, Rachel guided her out of the room and began reciting her Miranda rights.

Passing through the bullpen, Rachel and Olivia's procession drew a hush over the room with all eyes fixed on them. Olivia remained silent, her eyes lowered to the floor, tears staining her cheeks as she continued to wipe them with the sleeves of her sweatsuit. Rachel thought Olivia might be in the grip of hysterics, her entire world crumbling around her at the decision to arrest her.

Then, breaking the tense silence, Mitchell lowered his cellphone from his ear and called out across the bullpen.

"Hey, guys," he said somberly. "They found Sofia."

CHAPTER 26

The atmosphere grew heavy, time freezing around them. Every person seemed frozen in place, their usual chatter replaced by a tense silence. Rachel and Olivia, caught in the middle of it, halted in their tracks and turned their attention to Mitchell. Rachel recognized the distress in Mitchell's expression and the tension in his voice. She knew that someone had found Sofia injured, or even worse, dead.

Stepping forward, Rachel nudged Olivia, urging her to move away from the bullpen. She didn't want Olivia to overhear any more information.

Olivia broke the silence, her voice shaking. "Wait... where's Sofia?"

Rachel kept moving. "Probably at her apartment."

"Wait... Agent Quinn, please stop," Olivia said. "Please tell me what's going on. I swear I didn't do anything. Why are you arresting me?"

Olivia wiped at her tears, her chin lifting slightly, though her voice still shook.

"Olivia, you never mentioned growing up in Georgia or going to Virginia Tech," Rachel said as they reached the holding cells in the back.

"I'm sorry, I'm sorry," Olivia said, her words tumbling out in a rush. "I'll tell you everything. I was just talking about the lab. What do you want to know about Georgia? I can give you my dad's number. I was born there, grew up there—you have to believe me. I didn't do anything!"

Olivia's face drained of color as her frantic explanation spilled out.

"I was investigating a bomb in Georgia while your mom was in the hospital," Rachel said.

"My mom died in a car accident when I was in high school. She wasn't in a bomb," Olivia said, frowning.

"You were also at Virginia Tech when someone bombed the computer lab," Rachel said, her tone flat as she watched Olivia carefully.

Olivia's face tightened; for a second, she hesitated, then locked eyes with Rachel. Her eyes widened, recognition flashing through them.

"Yeah, I remember that," Olivia said. "You think I did that? I swear, I haven't done anything. A lot of my research was on those servers that got destroyed, but the professor kept everything on his own external hard drive. Everyone did."

Rachel didn't blink. "Light blue self-adhesive bandages—the same kind we found in your bathroom—held together all those bombs."

"What? I've never built a bomb! I don't even remember having bandages," Olivia said, struggling to catch her breath. "Maybe for my dog?"

Rachel sighed and stepped directly in front of Olivia, her mind a battlefield of conflicting thoughts. Rachel's obsession with the professor as the bomber clouded her judgment, undermining her suspicions about Olivia's involvement. Yet, how could she ignore the glaring pattern? Olivia had been present at every single location Rachel had investigated after the explosions. Could it really just be a coincidence?

"What else do you need to know? I swear I did nothing you've accused me of. What can I do to convince you?" Olivia's voice tripped over itself in a panicked rush, her hands trembling.

"Have you ever worked closely with any professors? Or have any close professor friends?" Rachel asked.

Olivia shook her head. "Not really. I mean, I worked with Professor Hayes on my research at Virginia Tech, but I haven't really kept in touch with anyone from Georgia or from school. Why?"

Rachel hesitated, weighing her words carefully. She needed to determine if Olivia had any potential connection with Professor Eric J. Neil, the bomber Rachel had chased for years. However, she was also wary of giving any additional information to Olivia.

"I've been chasing a professor tied to both the Georgia and Virginia Tech bombings," Rachel said. Her voice faltered. "I thought I saw him here too... but now I'm not so sure."

"It wasn't me—it must have been him. What can I do to help you?" Olivia asked. "I'll do anything. I'll tell you anything. I'll go anywhere with you. I'll help you find anyone. I just didn't do this!"

Rachel stood still, arms crossed tightly over her chest, her brow furrowed in deep concentration. She remained silent, wrestling with the weight of her own suspicions and the gnawing uncertainty creeping in.

She exhaled sharply. "Okay, Olivia. Stay here with this officer for a minute while I talk to my partner." Without waiting for a response, Rachel crossed over to where Mitchell stood.

"Where's Sofia?" Rachel whispered to Mitchell, keeping her voice low so Olivia couldn't overhear.

"They found her body at her apartment," Mitchell said, pulling on his jacket. He paused. "It couldn't have been Olivia. She was in the hospital early this morning, then here with you."

Rachel didn't respond—she just slowly shook her head. Had she rushed to judgment about Olivia? Was Olivia working with someone else, maybe the professor? What the hell was going on?

Steeling herself, she walked back to Olivia and the officer.

"My partner and I will check on Sofia. You'll stay here and sit with this officer in the bullpen."

"Okay, okay—good. So, I'm not arrested?" Olivia asked, relief flashing in her eyes.

"Not yet."

"Thank you, thank you, Agent Quinn. I'll help with whatever you need," Olivia said, letting out a shaky breath.

Rachel didn't respond. Instead, she turned to Mitchell, slipping on her own jacket as they fell into step, heading out of the field office, the weight of unanswered questions pressing down on her.

———————————— ❖ ————————————

Rachel and Mitchell pulled up at Sofia's apartment building in record time, courtesy of Rachel's daredevil Boston driving. Bright yellow caution tape cordoned off nearly the entire street, creating an imposing barrier. The street was alive with activity, with police vehicles scattered around, an ambulance parked nearby, and the forensics team going back and forth between their van and the apartment building. The incessant flashing lights from the police vehicles and ambulance had attracted a small crowd of curious onlookers to the scene.

As they approached the entrance, Rachel flashed her badge at the officer guarding the door. Inside the building, officials, completely focused on their work, ignored Rachel and Mitchell. Making their way through the crowd, they reached Sofia's second-floor apartment. Rachel introduced herself, and an official directed her to the head detective overseeing the scene.

"Did you find the body?" Rachel asked.

"No, it was Officer Baker and the landlord, Bill Clairon," the detective said, flipping through his notebook. "Clairon opened the door. Baker told him to wait, but he followed him into the bedroom—and puked when the officer pulled down the comforter."

The landlord's reaction did not surprise Rachel. It wasn't uncommon for the officers to keep civilians out of crime scenes but, despite their efforts, some people simply refused to listen to their warnings.

"They're both waiting outside," the detective went on, his voice steady. "We've interviewed all the neighbors, but unfortunately, no one saw or heard anything."

Mitchell went outside to speak with the landlord, leaving Rachel to move further into the apartment. She donned booties and latex gloves before stepping into the bedroom. The room appeared to be in constant motion as the forensics team methodically collected samples. Sharp clicks of cameras captured the scene, with the occasional flash momentarily bothering Rachel's eyes. Lost in their work, the forensics team paid little attention to anyone else.

Rachel's attention fell upon the lifeless body of Sofia, sprawled in the center of the bed, surrounded by a substantial pool of blood. She couldn't tear her eyes away from the unsettling sight.

"Someone cut her throat efficiently," a forensic tech broke the silence, observing Rachel's fixation. "She probably bled out in less than a minute."

"Do you know when it happened?" Rachel asked.

"The medical examiner estimated sometime between one and three this morning," the tech concluded as he moved away to collect samples.

The head detective walked into the bedroom and carefully handed Rachel an evidence bag, its contents revealing a large, black hardcover book. Silver letters embossed the words *Laboratory Notebook* on the front cover.

"They found her covered by the comforter, with this notebook left open in the center of the bed," the detective said.

Rachel removed the notebook from the evidence bag and thumbed through it. Each page bore the signature of Brittney Turner, the other postdoc, serving as a verifiable record of every experiment she completed. The entire book was a testament to her academic career at the university. Rachel reached the center of the book—and sucked in a breath. Across two pages, scrawled in what appeared to be blood, were the words: *Le temps détruit tout.*

"What the fuck? Is that French?" Rachel asked, staring at the blood-streaked message.

"Yeah, we used Google Translate: 'Time destroys everything,'" the detective said.

Rachel frowned, the phrase tugging at something in her memory. *Le temps détruit tout.* It felt familiar, unsettlingly so, like a whisper from something she'd tried to forget. And then it struck her—*Irreversible.* The brutal, unflinching film she'd seen years ago.

Those words were burned into her mind then, and now they were here—staring back at her in blood.

Mitchell, now wearing his protective booties and gloves, entered the bedroom. Rachel raised the notebook for him to see and relayed her discovery.

"It says 'time destroys everything.' All the pages are signed by Brittney, but anyone could have stolen her lab notebook."

"I already told you—it couldn't have been Olivia. A tech said Sofia died early this morning. Olivia was in the hospital, then with us," Mitchell said.

"Yeah…" Rachel's voice trailed off, but her mind was already racing. The phrase, the film—*Irreversible*—and the brutal inevitability of time's destruction. It was just a movie reference, but here, with a dead body and a bloody message, it felt like something far more sinister. She closed the lab notebook and slipped it into the evidence bag to hand off to a forensic tech.

"The landlord doesn't know anything," Mitchell said. "He doesn't even live in Massachusetts. His caretaker's on vacation, so he had to drive up from New York for the welfare check."

As Rachel and Mitchell stepped out of the bedroom, they peeled off their gloves and booties, their movements slow and deliberate. Rachel's cellphone rang loudly just as they neared the exit.

"This is Agent Quinn."

"It's Dr. Richardson from the hospital. You asked me to call with any developments regarding Dr. Lynch."

Rachel's grip tightened on the phone as her eyes flicked over to Mitchell. "Yes. Is she awake?"

"Uh, no," Dr. Richardson said after a pause. "She passed away about an hour ago."

CHAPTER 27

"I thought you said she was stable?" Rachel asked, her eyes widening as she and Mitchell exited Sofia's apartment building and made their way towards her car.

"She was, but it wasn't a clear-cut case. It's likely she died of complications from her severe burns and internal injuries," Dr. Richardson said, his voice trailing off at the end.

"From where I'm standing, this looks suspicious," Rachel said, her breath forming a small cloud of vapor in the cold air.

Rachel waited in silence, but Dr. Richardson stayed quiet on the other end of the phone, indifferent to Rachel's perspective.

"We'll need to confirm. We should arrange for an autopsy on Dr. Lynch and either have someone come to your location or arrange for her body to be transferred to our medical examiner's office," Rachel said.

"That's fine. I'll inform my boss," Dr. Richardson said tersely before ending the call.

"I think he just hung up on me," Rachel said, as she shot Mitchell a puzzled glance.

"I'll get the autopsy set up," Mitchell said, unfazed by Rachel's comment about the doctor as he reached for his cellphone.

The low, steady drone of the car's defroster provided background noise, helping to clear the frosty windows as Rachel sped away from the apartment building, back toward the FBI field office.

"Oh, I forgot to tell you," Mitchell said, while he waited to speak with the medical examiner. "I talked with Dr. Elliot earlier—the guy Olivia mentioned who yelled in the lab that day. He admitted going there to speak with Dr. Lynch. Since he works in Worcester, he suggested we meet him there later this afternoon."

"Oh, finally we found someone. Do you think he's involved?" Rachel asked.

"I couldn't say for sure over the phone. It'll be easier to gauge when we talk to him in person," Mitchell said.

Rachel nodded in agreement and redirected her attention back to the road ahead. The snowfall had picked up once again, transforming the trip into a frustrating battle against slow-moving traffic.

As they arrived back at the FBI building, Olivia sat quietly at Rachel's desk, a silent officer stationed nearby. Rachel watched her for a few minutes, curious how she behaved when she thought no one was paying attention. Olivia sat straighter now, her hands folded in her lap, the streaks of earlier tears dried on her face. Calm on the surface, but the way she fidgeted with her sleeve gave away the nerves still clinging to her.

Rachel walked over to her desk. Olivia sprang up, eyebrows lifting in alarm.

"Hey, what happened?" Olivia asked.

"Olivia, there's been a development," Rachel said. "We found Sofia at her apartment. Unfortunately, she was dead."

"What?!" Olivia's voice cracked. "I thought you said she wasn't even at the lab when it exploded."

"She wasn't. The explosion didn't injure her. Someone murdered her last night," Rachel said, her eyes narrowing as she watched Olivia closely.

Olivia staggered back a step, her face draining of color.

"Oh my God," she whispered.

Rachel studied Olivia, searching for any sign of deception. But Olivia only sat there rigid, her hands trembling. Her face was so pale she looked ready to be sick.

"You don't think I did this?" she said, voice shaking.

"No, Olivia. You were either at the hospital or with us when it likely happened," Rachel said, then hesitated. "But I'm still not sure I trust you."

Olivia gripped the edge of the desk, knuckles white. She swallowed hard. "I swear—I had nothing to do with it. But if there's anything I can do... I need to clear my name."

Rachel stood silently for a moment as she considered her next move. She still harbored suspicions that Olivia might be involved somehow, and she knew she needed to keep Olivia nearby, at least temporarily. Rachel didn't want Olivia to feel like she was being arrested, so she scrambled to find a plausible excuse to convince Olivia to stay at the FBI field office, or at least remain with her and Mitchell.

"Olivia, we actually have a meeting scheduled with Dr. Elliot this afternoon," Rachel said, keeping her voice even. "You might be able to help. You could have insights into him, or into what he knows about Dr. Lynch and her research."

Olivia shifted her weight, wringing her hands. "I don't really know Dr. Elliot. I mean... I've never met him, but I'll do whatever I can." Her voice wavered, and she dropped her gaze to the floor.

Rachel sensed Olivia was holding something back, her hesitation obvious. The way Olivia's eyes darted away and her fingers nervously tapped against the edge of the desk, as if grappling with the decision to say anything else.

"What is it? Do you know something?" Rachel asked.

Olivia hesitated, letting out a small sigh. Her face scrunched up, and her hands briefly clenched before she finally said, "No... I really don't know him. But I need to go home and feed my dog."

Rachel's disappointment flashed across her face briefly before she let out a laugh. She had expected Olivia to share something more significant, but it appeared Olivia's concern for her dog outweighed her worry about her own situation.

"We can swing by to feed Mulder on our way," Rachel said, still smiling.

"Okay, great," Olivia said, letting out a slow, unsteady breath. "Thank you... for giving me a chance to clear my name. And to help you."

"Absolutely," Rachel said.

Rachel caught herself wavering. She doubted her initial impulse to blame Olivia, finding herself wanting to trust her. But just as quickly, she doubted that trust. Had she jumped to conclusions too fast, letting Olivia's love for her dog sway her judgment? Trusting too much had burned her before.

Nothing entirely convinced her. Still, Rachel felt good about her decision; it would give her the chance to keep a watchful eye on Olivia a while longer.

Together, Rachel, Mitchell, and Olivia walked out to Rachel's car. Snow thickened, large flakes swirling as they drove toward Worcester to meet with Dr. Elliot.

———————◆———————

Rachel gripped the wheel tighter as she sped down I-90, snow hammering the windshield. Worcester lay about forty miles ahead, a destination Rachel thought they needed to reach quickly. In the passenger seat, Mitchell sat in silence, his attention occasionally flicking down to his cell phone. Olivia sat in the back seat, staring out the window at the snowstorm.

They had already stopped at Olivia's apartment to take care of her dog. He again refused to leave his bed for the snowy outdoors. The dog's laziness, albeit amusing, was an unexpected time-saver as well.

Mitchell broke the silence, glancing at Olivia with a small smile. "So, tell us about Ethan. We haven't had any luck getting ahold of him, and Rachel here thinks he's dodging us."

Rachel sighed, shooting Mitchell a dirty look before focusing back on the snow-covered highway.

"I've only known him a few months, since he started as a lab tech. But I really like him. I don't think he could ever do something like this," Olivia said.

"You've only known him a few months. How can you be so sure you know anything about him?" Rachel snapped, shooting a look at Olivia in the rearview mirror. "You didn't even know the address he gave you was a UPS store. Did he tell you anything— where he's from, his family?"

"He told me he lives in Springfield and that he has experience as a physics lab tech, which seems true because he knew a lot about the equipment and experiments in the lab," Olivia said. "He never talked much about his family, but I didn't press him because I don't talk about my family either."

"Have you spoken to him since the explosion?" Rachel asked.

"No, but I think he visited me at the hospital and left me flowers before I woke up," Olivia said.

"He was at the hospital?" Rachel asked, surprised.

"I didn't see him. I just assumed the flowers were from him; there wasn't a card or anything," Olivia said, tapping her fingers against her knee.

"Have you attempted to call him? Can you call him right now?" Rachel asked.

"Oh, yeah, okay," Olivia said, reaching for her cell phone to dial Ethan's number.

Rachel watched as Olivia dialed, no hesitation in her movements—eager, almost relieved to help.

As the call connected, a flat computerized voice echoed through the device: "We're sorry. You have reached a number that is disconnected or is no longer in service..." Olivia pulled the phone away from her ear, staring at it, frowning.

"It says it's disconnected," she said, glancing at Rachel. "Let me try again."

"We're sorry. You have reached..." The same robotic message. Olivia ended the call with a frustrated tap.

"I don't understand," Olivia said, shaking her head.

Rachel shot Mitchell a look—pure *I told you so.* They drove on in silence, snow thickening against the windshield. Mitchell's phone rang, shattering the quiet.

"They found Aiden Lynch," Mitchell said, still tethered to the cell phone pressed against his ear. "The BPD located his car at the Hampton Inn in Natick. The manager told them he's been staying there all week, paying in cash."

"Are you kidding me?" Rachel said.

"They're heading over now," Mitchell said.

Without hesitation, Rachel veered off the next exit and sped up towards Natick, narrowly avoiding a collision on the interstate. She maneuvered the vehicle expertly, a testament to her Boston roots. They arrived at the Hampton Inn ahead of the other officers.

"We should wait for backup just in case he has any explosives with him," Mitchell said.

"No fucking way," Rachel said as she leaped out of the car. Turning to Olivia, she ordered, "Stay here."

"Rachel, wait, we don't even know what room he's in," Mitchell said.

Rachel exhaled hard through her nose. "Fine. We'll go talk to the front desk."

They entered the hotel lobby, clean and bathed in a soft glow from overhead lights and wall sconces. The hotel appeared sophisticated for a Hampton Inn, with rich mahogany furniture and plush, earth-toned upholstery. A solitary figure relaxed on one of the comfortable couches, engrossed in a book. The restaurant, left of the lobby, showed a few patrons chatting at the bar.

Rachel flashed her badge as she leaned in towards the front desk attendant. Her eyes wandered over the artwork on the walls, which depicted picturesque scenes of Natick. "Could you kindly inform us of Aiden Lynch's room number?"

"Uh... let me get my boss." The desk attendant fumbled with a clipboard, then hurried into the back.

As they awaited the manager's arrival, three Boston Police Department vehicles sped into the parking lot, their sirens echoing through the surroundings. Rachel and Mitchell left the lobby and made their way towards the approaching BPD officers.

"He's in room 213," an officer revealed as soon as he got out of his car. "The manager we spoke to mentioned he's been no trouble, prepaid for the entire week in cash, but made the reservation with a credit card under the name Karen Bastarde, his wife's maiden name."

They lined up in a disciplined formation, donning their protective bulletproof vests and gripping their weapons, as they ascended the stairs leading to room 213.

"Aiden Lynch, this is the manager," the lead officer said, rapping on the hotel room door.

Aiden opened the door and the officers immediately stormed into the room, firmly pushing him back onto the bed, their voices commanding, "BPD! Don't move!"

Bewildered, Aiden sat down on the bed, complying with the officers' shouted instructions. Barefoot and clad in sweatpants, a plain gray t-shirt, and a baseball cap, his eyes darted around the room, taking in the unexpected presence of his visitors.

The officers swept through the compact hotel room, shouting, "Clear!" as their eyes scanned every corner.

An unmade king-sized bed with a faded striped bedspread cluttered the room. Beige curtains filtered the daylight, and scattered papers and a half-empty coffee cup littered a small wooden desk. Housekeeping neglected the room for days. Their brief search yielded no other occupants, and no obvious signs of explosives or other weapons.

"What the hell is going on?" Aiden demanded.

"You're Aiden Lynch?" Rachel asked.

"Yes! What's happening?" Aiden said, voice rising.

"Why aren't you answering your phone? Why are you hiding in this hotel?" Rachel shot back.

"Hiding? What are you talking about?" Aiden shook his head, still staring at them, wide-eyed. "What the hell is going on?"

"Aiden, do you know where your wife is?" Mitchell asked, remarkably composed.

"I assume she's at our house with *him*. I left her when I found out she was having an affair with Dr. Kingsley," Aiden said, bitterness creeping into his voice.

"Your wife was in the hospital after the explosion, Aiden," Mitchell said.

"What explosion? What are you talking about?" Aiden said, blinking.

"Don't you watch the news?" Rachel asked.

"No," Aiden said. "I checked myself in here and cut off all access to social media. Turned off my phone. Disconnected from current events—anything to help with my psychological healing. I was anxious and depressed after I found out about the affair. I can't help my patients until I heal myself."

"Oh right, I forgot you were a psychologist," Rachel said, rolling her eyes as she looked over at Mitchell.

"Aiden, someone planted bombs in the lab. They killed several people, including Dr. Kingsley and your wife," Mitchell said.

"Oh, my God. I had no idea," Aiden whispered, his voice cracking as tears welled in his eyes.

"We heard you made quite a scene in the lab just before the explosion," Rachel said, her tone sharper now.

"What?" Aiden said, voice trembling. He swiped at his tears with the back of his hand. "Oh, right. I went there to confront Karen after I found all those *sexy* notes she kept from Dr. Kingsley."

"That must have made you pretty angry..." Rachel said.

Aiden hesitated, then stared hard at Rachel. "Yes, I was mad, but I certainly didn't blow them up, if that's what you're insinuating. I've been here all week, ever since I found those notes."

"Can anyone confirm you've been here and not at the lab?" Rachel asked.

"Ummm... yes! You can ask Brittney," Aiden said, leaning forward on the hotel bed, his eyes wide and voice eager. "It was her idea for me to leave Karen and check into a hotel. She called right after I left the lab that day, told me Karen had been sleeping with Dr. Kingsley in her office for months. Brittney even warned me not to go back to the lab—said Dr. Collins had called security, and if I showed up again, I'd end up banned, just like Dr. Elliot."

"You know Dr. Elliot?" Rachel asked.

"No, not personally, but I know Karen had him banned from the university because she said he threatened her," Aiden said. "So Brittney said Karen would do the same to me, and that I should just leave her. Honestly, that's the healthiest thing to do psychologically, aside from couple's therapy, but Karen would never have agreed to that."

Aiden continued talking about his healing process during his stay at the hotel, focusing on his psychological well-being, but offered little that could help with the investigation. Rachel, clearly uninterested, subtly suggested she and Mitchell should move on.

They exited the hotel room, leaving Aiden in the custody of an officer. As they departed, other officers were gathering CCTV footage and swipe card access data, working to double-check Aiden's alibi.

Once outside, Rachel's phone buzzed. She held it up for Mitchell—the judge had finally approved the search warrants for Brittney's apartment and her boyfriend's. Brittney's boyfriend, a lawyer, had tried to block the approvals, but Massachusetts judges don't look kindly on anyone tied to university lab explosions.

As Mitchell skimmed Rachel's phone, two messages popped up on his own. He showed them to her.

One was from the medical examiner, requesting their presence at Dr. Lynch's autopsy. A junior agent interviewing Dr. Williams in the field office sent the other. According to the agent, Dr. Williams was proving difficult, citing her hectic schedule. She warned that if Rachel and Mitchell didn't arrive within the hour, she would leave.

"How about I head over to the boyfriend's apartment while you and Olivia check with the medical examiner and Dr. Williams at the field office. Afterwards, we can meet and check out Brittney's apartment together. I think Olivia might be more helpful during any interview you have with Dr. Williams," Mitchell said with a grin.

"Sounds like a plan," Rachel said, sliding back into her car with Olivia waiting inside.

"What happened?" Olivia asked.

"I don't think he was involved, but he told us Brittney warned him to stay away from the lab," Rachel said.

Olivia nodded, her expression tightening. "Yeah, I said earlier I thought it might have been Brittney. She hated everyone in that lab and was great at hiding it."

"We just got the warrant to search her apartment," Rachel said. "We're heading there now, after a quick stop at the field office."

As they drove, Rachel glanced back at Olivia, who sat in the rear seat, shaking her head. She thought she saw something—maybe agreement, maybe just frustration. Either way, she felt a small thread of trust forming between them. After all, Olivia had flagged Brittney early on—and she might have been right.

But reaching Ethan was still a problem; his phone remained disconnected.

As they drove, a barrage of lingering questions pressed on Rachel's mind. Where was Brittney? Where was Ethan? Would they find them alive, or were they about to stumble upon a body in Brittney's apartment? The deeper Rachel went into the investigation, the more questions she had.

CHAPTER 28

Rachel stood in the medical examiner's room, her attention fixed on the stainless-steel table that held the body of Dr. Lynch. The chilling temperature of the room sent a shiver down her spine. She had decided again that Olivia should stay in the car.

Dr. Foster, the medical examiner, donned in a white lab coat, a plastic apron, and gloves, was already in the middle of the autopsy when his assistant let Rachel in. His experienced hands held a scalpel as he glanced over at Rachel.

"Hey, Agent Quinn," Dr. Foster said, barely glancing up as he guided his scalpel down Dr. Lynch's charred torso.

The incision was slow, deliberate. Burned tissue curled back under his gloved hands, exposing what remained beneath. The sight hit hard, and Rachel fought the instinct to recoil. She kept her face still, her hands steady at her sides.

Dr. Foster watched her for a moment. His mouth tightened—not with concern, but with something colder. Disappointment, maybe. Rachel guessed he'd hoped to rattle her, and her calm expression had denied him the satisfaction.

"The burns are extensive, covering approximately eighty percent of the victim's body. It's a miracle she survived the explosion, but the internal injuries and infections would have made recovery nearly impossible," Dr. Foster said.

Rachel leaned in closer, her eyes fixed on the doctor's every move. He continued his examination, pointing out various injuries and abnormalities as he went. He described the damage to the victim's lungs, caused by inhaling hot gases during the explosion, and the sepsis that had set in from the burns.

"So, you're saying she died from the explosion?" Rachel asked.

"Agent Quinn," Dr. Foster said, "it's clear that the burns and complications from the explosion likely caused the victim's death. But…"

"But what?" Rachel asked.

"When Special Agent Mitchell arranged for this autopsy, he mentioned your suspicion of foul play during the victim's hospitalization after the explosion," Dr. Foster said, his tone clipped and professional.

"Among healthcare professionals, there's a grim reality: potassium chloride, injected intravenously, is the method of choice for those inclined to kill," Dr. Foster said. "What makes it particularly insidious is how easily it slips past standard toxicology screens."

The examination room, cold and quiet, seemed to hold its breath as everyone fixed their attention on Dr. Foster.

"As soon as we received the body, my assistant drew a cardiac blood sample and sent it for expedited analysis," he continued. "The results showed a significantly elevated potassium level, high enough to suggest an overdose. Possibly fatal. Possibly deliberate."

"Are you saying someone murdered her with potassium chloride?" Rachel asked.

"I can't definitively assert that someone murdered her with potassium chloride, as post-mortem measurements can sometimes be unreliable," Dr. Foster said matter-of-factly. "It's entirely possible the victim naturally succumbed to injuries sustained in the explosion."

"So, what do you think? What's your opinion?" Rachel asked.

"Potassium poisoning is a logical possibility," Dr. Foster said. "Injected potassium chloride causes cardiac arrest and leaves almost no trace—that's what makes it so effective."

Rachel contemplated Dr. Foster's words. Dr. Richardson had assured them that Dr. Lynch was on the mend, showing signs of improvement. Then, out of nowhere, she had died. Dr. Lynch—the burn victim who had survived an explosion—had probably been murdered in her hospital room. Just like Sofia had been murdered in her own apartment.

"Thank you, Dr. Foster. Once you're done, please forward the report to Mitchell," Rachel said, already turning to leave the examination room.

Dr. Foster gave a brief nod and returned to Dr. Lynch's post-mortem.

Stepping out of the medical examiner's room, Rachel emerged into the hallway. The unforgiving glow of the overhead fluorescent lights stressed the clinical surroundings and gave her a persistent headache. Her investigation had taken another turn: she was now hunting a ruthless murderer, someone she suspected was responsible for at least six deaths.

As Rachel walked down the bright hallway and exited the building, a few delicate snowflakes drifted gently from the darkening sky. She headed across the parking lot, where Olivia waited in the car, her expression unreadable. She was trying to trust Olivia, but her gut kept telling her to tread cautiously.

Rachel slid into the driver's seat and turned to Olivia. "Dr. Lynch probably died from the explosion," she said, careful to leave out what she had just learned from the medical examiner. She wanted to see Olivia's reaction.

Olivia stared ahead, silent for a moment, then whispered, "I still can't believe anyone would do this. Why would Brittney do this?"

"We have to go by the field office first. If you want to stay there while I check out Brittney's apartment, that's fine," Rachel said, wanting to avoid involving Olivia in a potential crime scene.

"Okay," Olivia said, turning back to the window, her face pale and withdrawn.

Rachel left the medical examiner's office, navigating the familiar streets towards the FBI field office in Chelsea, just fifteen minutes away. Dr. Williams was already waiting there. Neither she nor Olivia knew they'd be meeting together, and Rachel couldn't help but wonder how it would play out.

Dr. Williams had blamed Olivia; Olivia had claimed Dr. Williams hated Dr. Lynch. Would sparks fly? Would secrets spill?

She was about to find out.

———◈———

Rachel and Olivia stepped through the glass doors of the FBI field office, greeted by a hum of activity. The office buzzed with the constant shuffle of agents and personnel, each engaged in their own tasks. The subtle aroma of freshly brewed coffee lively punctuated the atmosphere.

Navigating through the maze of desks in the bullpen, they reached Rachel's cluttered workstation. Next to the desk sat Dr. Williams, a figure of peculiarity amidst the surroundings. Her attire, a kaleidoscope of vividly colored fabrics, remained as eclectic as ever, albeit lacking her usual lab coat. Across from her sat the junior agent, their expression reflecting impatience.

"Well, it's about time. You had about eight minutes left before I was leaving," Dr. Williams grumbled when she spotted Rachel.

"Hello, Dr. Williams. Thank you for waiting. We just have a few questions for you," Rachel said, keeping her tone polite.

As Rachel addressed Dr. Williams, the junior agent gave her a quick look—one that said *good luck with her*—then quietly excused themselves and crossed the bullpen.

Dr. Williams opened her mouth to retort, but stopped short when she saw Olivia standing beside Rachel. Her expression shifted—a flicker of surprise, quickly masked—and she shut her mouth with a snap. Rachel caught it and offered a sweet smile.

"Oh, Dr. Williams, you know Olivia, right?" Rachel asked.

"Yes," Dr. Williams said, her voice clipped. She didn't look at Olivia.

Rachel pulled over an extra chair and motioned for Olivia to sit beside Dr. Williams, then settled into her own seat behind the desk. Dr. Williams shifted uneasily, her discomfort showing in the small, restless movements of her hands.

Around them, the office was still active with the ringing of phones and muted conversations as agents discussed their cases.

"So, Dr. Williams, when we spoke to you at the scene, you implicated Olivia in the bombing," Rachel said bluntly. She hadn't told Olivia that part—not yet.

"What?!" Olivia said, turning sharply toward Dr. Williams. "You accused me of blowing up the lab?"

"No, I didn't say that," Dr. Williams stammered, her composure slipping.

"In fact, you did, Dr. Williams," Rachel said, retrieving her notebook and flipping through her notes. "You stated, and I quote, 'It has to be Olivia. She's always so quiet, dressed in black with that headbanger music.'"

Olivia stared at her, eyes wide. Her mouth parted, but no words came at first. Then she turned to Dr. Williams, disbelief hardening into disdain.

"I had no idea you felt that way. I actually helped you," she said.

"Oh, right!" Rachel chimed in. "You also told my partner you never worked with Olivia, and you blamed her for the bombing. Again."

"That is such a lie!" Olivia snapped. "I have our emails that show I helped you with your computer program so you could get that five-million-dollar grant."

Dr. Williams said nothing. Her eyes moved between Rachel and Olivia, her jaw tight, her silence stretching just a second too long.

"Did you get that grant, Dr. Williams? Or did Dr. Lynch outshine you, leading you to blow up the lab?" Rachel asked.

"Neither of us got the grant," Dr. Williams said, sounding more exhausted than defensive.

"So, why did you plant those bombs?"

"I didn't plant any bombs!" Dr. Williams shot back, rising from her seat, turning to leave the bullpen.

"We're not finished here, Dr. Williams," Rachel said firmly. "You lied about working with Olivia, and you tried to shift the blame onto her. It's looking like you're deflecting responsibility. You're trying to protect yourself."

Dr. Williams let out a long breath and sank back into her chair.

"Fine. I lied about working with Olivia. I said those things so you wouldn't look into me."

Rachel stayed silent, eyes fixed on her.

"I don't like Dr. Lynch," Dr. Williams continued. "I think she's a reprehensible person who doesn't deserve any grants. They should have fired her a long time ago. But I didn't cause that explosion."

"And why should we believe you after you've lied several times?" Rachel said, leaning forward, her voice cutting through the tension in the room.

"I'm a physicist. I don't know how to make bombs," Dr. Williams said.

"So what?" Rachel shot back. "Anyone can make a bomb—weren't you the one who said you can find anything on the internet?"

Dr. Williams rolled her eyes and let out an exasperated sigh, irritation tightening her expression.

"I can't even get into the building when no one's there," she said. "Dr. Lynch blocked my access years ago."

"She's right," Olivia said. "She and Dr. Lynch haven't gotten along for years. Dr. Lynch even changed all the locks to keep Dr. Williams out of the building."

"I wasn't even home the morning of the explosion," Dr. Williams added. "I was in Connecticut, playing my oboe at a concert. Afterward, I stayed overnight in a hotel and came back later that morning. You can check with anyone who was there."

Rachel motioned for the junior agent to join them, then instructed Dr. Williams to provide the name of the concert hall and the hotel where she'd stayed in Connecticut. The junior agent gave a quick nod and hurried off to verify the alibi. As the agent disappeared, Rachel considered the possibility that Dr. Williams might actually be telling the truth.

"While we're checking to make sure you're not lying about that," Rachel said, "do you think someone else could have done this?"

Olivia hesitated, then blurted out, her voice trembling, "I-I can't believe you're asking her that. She already blamed me. How can you believe anything else she says?"

"I'm sorry, Olivia. I just didn't want them to blame me," Dr. Williams confessed. "Everyone at the university knows Dr. Lynch and I never got along. I thought they'd accuse me immediately... so I blamed you."

"Fantastic," Olivia said, her voice shaking. "That's... difficult to hear. I almost got arrested because of you."

They sat in rigid silence, arms crossed, each pointedly refusing to look at the other. The atmosphere in the room resembled that of a standoff between elementary school students, each unwilling to yield an inch.

The junior agent's return shattered the moment. He reported that the concert hall confirmed Dr. Williams had performed there, and the hotel had verified her stay. The manager even remembered her. Apparently, she'd made an impression with her impatience at the front desk.

The agent added that hotel CCTV footage was on its way. It would likely show Dr. Williams arriving that night, her uninterrupted stay, and her check-out the following morning, confirming that she hadn't left the premises during the night.

"Okay, Dr. Williams, I guess you're in the clear for now," Rachel said. "But don't leave the area. We might have more questions."

"Fine," Dr. Williams said through clenched teeth, rising abruptly. She didn't even glance at Olivia as she strode out.

"Unbelievable," Olivia said, shaking her head.

"Yeah, I get it. Dealing with academics can be a real headache."

Rachel gathered her things and stood to head to Brittney's apartment. "If you want to stay here, I can arrange for the same officer to—"

Her phone rang, sharp and sudden, and she instinctively reached for it mid-sentence.

"This is Agent Quinn."

"This is Detective Johnson. We found some strange lab notebooks at Brittney's apartment. Is Olivia still with you? We could use her help making sense of them," he said.

"Yeah, okay," Rachel said, ending the call. She turned to Olivia. "Never mind about staying here. You said you could help us? Do you think you can take a look at some lab notebooks we found?"

"I can try..." Olivia replied, her voice low as she stood. Rachel noticed the exhaustion on her face. The kind that came from too many long days and not enough sleep.

They set off for Brittney's apartment. With Brittney still missing, and suspicions aimed at her by both Olivia and Dr. Lynch's husband, Rachel wondered what they might find. As they approached the apartment, a heavy silence settled, and Rachel's mind turned to the postdoc at the center of it all.

CHAPTER 29

Olivia kept her gaze fixed on the snow drifting past the car window, her thoughts churning as she and Rachel neared Brittney's apartment. Worry and confusion gnawed at her. Why did she have to be involved in talking to Dr. Williams? Why couldn't she reach Ethan? Was he hurt? Was it true that he didn't live in Springfield? The questions circled relentlessly, refusing to let her mind rest.

According to Rachel, Ethan's address was supposedly a UPS store, which was just an absurd claim. Was she lying? Exaggerating? Trying to bait Olivia into revealing something unpleasant about Ethan? The silence in the car was heavy, thick with unspoken doubts. Rachel clearly didn't trust Olivia, and Olivia was wondering if she trusted Rachel.

Brittney's apartment was on Tremont Street, at the southern edge of the city. Rachel maneuvered the car into a parallel spot with practiced ease, despite the snow-covered street. As she stepped out, Olivia tapped lightly on the window, catching Rachel's attention. Rachel unlocked the back door, and Olivia climbed out. The earlier snowfall had slowed traffic to a crawl, and the flashing red and blue lights of a few BPD cruisers suggested the officers were already inside.

Brittney's apartment was on the fifth floor of a swanky high-rise, its exterior adorned with ornate architectural flourishes and intricate wrought-iron railings. Massive windows spanned much of the building's facade, lending it a striking, almost glamorous look. As Olivia looked up, she couldn't help but wonder how someone on a postdoc's salary could afford such a place. The thought stirred questions about Brittney's finances.

Brittney probably made more than Olivia, whose graduate stipend was barely livable, but rent in a building like this had to be over three thousand dollars a month. Olivia knew Brittney was dating a lawyer, which hinted at the possibility he might help with the bills—rent, at least. Still, she couldn't shake the thought that there might be other, less innocent explanations.

Olivia struggled to keep up as Rachel sprinted down the snowy street toward the apartment building. Inside, the lobby took her breath away—polished marble floors gleamed beneath a glittering chandelier, and the soaring ceilings with intricate crown molding added to the sense of grandeur.

Rachel bypassed the elevator and bolted for the stairs, forgetting Olivia was still behind her. When they emerged on the fifth floor, a hallway lined with rich dark wood paneling and warm light from artful sconces greeted them, the glow spilling onto a plush, deep brown carpet. At the end of the hall, Brittney's apartment door stood wide open, with a uniformed officer posted just outside.

"So?" Rachel asked the guard.

"Empty," he said, face unreadable.

Rachel turned to Olivia. "Alright, you can come in. But stay near the door with the officer. We don't want to contaminate anything."

"Thanks," Olivia said, the edge in her voice sharper than she intended. She'd agreed to be there in the first place to help. But she was tired, and the implication that she might screw something up grated more than it should.

Olivia stayed near the entrance, quietly taking in the scene as Rachel moved deeper into the spacious apartment. A team of officers combed through the space with practiced precision, opening drawers and examining every detail with methodical care.

The apartment was beautiful, impeccably decorated, and spotlessly clean. But what stood out most was Brittney's clear obsession with birds. The curtains were patterned with them, bird-themed paintings hung on the walls, and ceramic figurines of various species were scattered throughout. Somewhere toward the back, a faint, melodic tune played, its source and genre just out of Olivia's reach.

Rachel called out, motioning for Olivia to join her at the back of the apartment. As Olivia made her way through the stylish living room, she glimpsed a lavish bathroom—a spacious glass-enclosed shower and two exquisite, gleaming double sinks illuminated by bright, flattering light. Even here, bird-themed decor was everywhere: prints on the walls, tiny ceramic figurines, even a soap dish shaped like a finch. After a brief pause to take it all in, Olivia continued on toward Brittney's bedroom.

Olivia scanned the room. A queen-sized bed sat between two bedside tables, and across from it stood a desk cluttered with a laptop and scattered notebooks. The apartment's avian theme continued here. Bird motifs decorated the bedspread, curtains, and framed art on the walls. Stacks of books from the National Audubon Society and the Cornell Lab of Ornithology lay on the bedside tables. But what caught her attention was the stack of black hardback books next to the laptop—laboratory notebooks. Olivia recognized them instantly. They weren't supposed to leave the lab.

"Olivia, do you recognize any of these?" Rachel asked, handing her a pair of latex gloves.

Sliding them on, Olivia carefully opened a notebook. Familiarity hit her almost immediately—page after page filled with equations she had devised herself. Olivia's eyes widened as she realized that her research had somehow ended up in Brittney's notebooks—and she hadn't written it. They were the product of the countless hours she and Ethan had spent working on her research into electromagnetic fields in specific geographic regions.

Among the familiar notes, Olivia spotted seSveral far more advanced equations she didn't recognize. But it was the GPS coordinates beside the complex equations that gave her pause: 45°54'30.4"N, 68°54'23.6"W. Written beneath the coordinates were three specific dates: one from four months before the explosion, another matching the day it happened, and the last just two days from now.

As she tried to focus on the notebooks, a soft, looping melody from the open laptop drew her in. Her eyes locked on the serene image of a mourning dove drifting across the screensaver. She couldn't look away.

Rachel stood nearby in silence, watching as Olivia froze mid-page and turned her full attention to the laptop.

"The music's been playing on repeat since we got here," Rachel said. "We haven't dared touch it, not knowing what could happen when you piss off these machines."

Rachel's eyes shifted back to the lab notebooks, a quiet cue for Olivia to do the same. With a slight raise of her eyebrows, she wordlessly urged her: *Focus here, not the laptop.*

"Sorry, no. I don't recognize these," Olivia said, her voice distant, still fixated on the dove gliding across the laptop screen.

"You don't recognize anything in the book?" Rachel asked.

Olivia finally looked away from the laptop.

"I mean, the notebooks aren't mine. They're the kind we use at the lab, and some equations are actually mine," she said. "But others are way more advanced than what I've worked on. And this definitely isn't my handwriting."

"Do you know what they mean?" Rachel asked.

"The equations are designed to alter electromagnetic fields," Olivia said. "But the GPS coordinates... that's not something I've done yet. I'd planned to research geographic areas with anomalies in electromagnetic fields or gravity, but..." Her voice trailed off, uncertainty clouding her expression.

"But...?" Rachel asked.

"I think she might have stolen my work," Olivia said, the weight of realization settling over her as she stared at her own equations sprawled across the notebook—in Brittney's apartment, on Brittney's desk.

"To find that whirlpool you mentioned? To travel through time?" Rachel asked, leaning in to inspect the pages, her voice edged with disbelief and her brows arched high.

"That was the theory..." Olivia said.

"Well, I don't think this is Brittney's handwriting either," Rachel said. "We found one of her notebooks at Sofia's place. It had Brittney's handwriting and signatures all over it."

"If you're thinking it might be Ethan's, trust me, it's not," Olivia said. "I know his writing."

"I just plugged the GPS coordinates into my phone," Rachel said, glancing at the screen. "They lead to Baxter State Park in Maine, near Mt. Katahdin. Does that mean anything to you?"

Olivia shook her head. "I've never even been to Maine."

Olivia racked her brain, trying to make any connection to Maine. Before she could come up with anything, an officer approached Rachel with an update.

"Agent Quinn," he said, "we found no luggage. Several dresser drawers are empty, and a good chunk of clothing is missing from the closet. There's no toothbrush, toothpaste, or shampoo, either. Looks like Brittney might've hit the road."

Rachel nodded, considering. "She stays at her boyfriend's place most nights. I'll call Mitchell. Maybe he can check if she left anything over there."

Rachel put Mitchell on speaker and got straight to the point. "What did you find at the boyfriend's apartment?"

"There's really no sign a woman has ever been here," Mitchell said. "Total bachelor pad—law books, a few suits, nothing suspicious."

"Oh, and you know how we've been tracking cell phones? Ethan's is off or disconnected, but we triangulated Brittney's. Her signal's coming from somewhere in Maine. I've contacted the—"

"Wait," Rachel cut in. "Did you just say Maine?"

"Yeah, why?"

"We just found GPS coordinates in her apartment," Rachel said, a note of triumph in her voice. "So we know exactly where she is."

Before Mitchell could respond, the officer interrupted.

"We also found something over here. It has your name on it," the officer said, handing Rachel a small hourglass.

Despite its size, Olivia could see a snake intricately etched around the wooden frame.

"Holy shit," Rachel said. "How the fuck did this get here?"

"What's happening?" Mitchell's voice crackled through the speaker of her cellphone.

"Brittney's in Maine," Rachel said. "And I think Professor Eric J. Neil may be with her, helping her. I'm going. I'm not letting him slip through my fingers again."

"No way. The director's never going to let you head to Maine without clearing it with the Portland field office, especially if he thinks this is about Neil," Mitchell said.

"I don't care what he says," Rachel snapped. "I'm not losing him again."

"How do you even know he's up there? All you've got is *maybe* Brittney's location. Let the Portland team check it out," Mitchell said.

"Oh, uh... you're breaking up," Rachel said.

"Rachel, I swear to God, if you—" Mitchell began, but she ended the call.

She looked over at Olivia with a hesitant smile. "You up for a road trip?"

———————————— ❖ ————————————

Olivia wasn't entirely sure why she'd agreed to go on a road trip to Maine with Rachel Quinn. She was furious at Brittney for stealing her research—and likely blowing up the lab—and she wanted to see her held accountable. But a quiet fear lingered beneath her resolve. In the past, her efforts to stand up or push for change had often backfired. Still, something was pulling her toward this, something she couldn't quite explain. Part urgency, part self-preservation, and part hope that she could finally clear her name.

As they left Brittney's apartment building, the snowfall had tapered off, but traffic was worsening with the approach of rush hour and the slow creep of dusk. Olivia was worried about Ethan. A few minutes earlier, she'd called her landlord to confirm he could take care of Mulder for the night, then tried once more to reach Ethan. The result was the same: his number was disconnected.

Rachel had stepped away to make a private call, but as she returned to her car, Olivia caught the soft murmur of *"I love you, too"* just before she hung up.

"I'm riding in the front this time," Olivia said, offering a slight smile in an attempt to lighten the mood.

"Alright," Rachel said, nodding as she unlocked the car.

Olivia wasted no time fastening her seatbelt, as Rachel's reputation as a wild driver preceded her. The car's defroster rattled in the background as Rachel navigated the thickening traffic. She merged smoothly onto Route 1 and, after several miles, seamlessly transitioned onto I-95. Outside, light snow flurried against the windshield; inside, a quiet tension settled between them.

Rachel stayed silent, her knuckles whitening as she gripped the steering wheel. The hourglass they'd found in Brittney's apartment sat conspicuously on the center console, its wooden base engraved with one word: *Rachel*.

Olivia had always felt a certain level of apprehension around Rachel, recognizing her as a intense individual, tightly wound. Now, with the hourglass sitting between them, Rachel's agitation seemed to deepen. The silence stretched unbearably, and Olivia found herself too nervous to break it.

But after what felt like an eternity, curiosity won out.

"So, who gave you that hourglass?" she asked.

Rachel turned toward Olivia, her blue eyes locking on with an intensity that seemed endless. She glanced down at the hourglass on the center console, let out a subtle, irritated sigh and then focused back to the road.

"Professor Eric J. Neil," Rachel said.

An awkward silence settled over the car as Olivia waited for Rachel to continue—but she didn't. Rachel's eyes stayed fixed on the darkening road, the world outside now fully swallowed by night. Though the snowfall had stopped, the air inside felt colder. Rachel seemed different. Not just frustrated, but burdened by something heavier. Olivia considered asking another question but chose instead to sit quietly.

The tension thickened until Olivia's cellphone suddenly rang, its screen flashing *unknown number*. She usually ignored those. But this time, desperate to break the silence, she answered.

"Hey, it's me." Ethan's voice came through the phone, and Olivia's heart leaped with relief.

"Oh my God, Ethan! Where are you? Are you okay?" Olivia asked, her words catching Rachel's attention.

"I'm fine. I'm at your apartment. Where are you?" Ethan asked.

"I'm on my way to Maine with Agent Quinn... It's a long story," Olivia said.

"Where is he, and where has he been?" Rachel asked, her impatience unmistakable.

"Agent Quinn has some questions. Do you mind if I put you on speaker so you can talk to her since she's driving?" Olivia asked.

"No problem, anything I can do to help," Ethan said as Olivia activated the speakerphone.

"Ethan, I'm Special Agent Rachel Quinn with the FBI. We've been trying to get in contact with you about the lab explosion where you work," Rachel said, not bothering to hide her irritation.

"Yeah, I dropped and broke my phone the other day. I didn't really have the money for a new one, so I grabbed this throwaway when I got back and heard about the explosion," Ethan said.

"Back from where?" Rachel asked.

"Olivia didn't tell you? I left her apartment early that morning to go to the laboratory sciences conference at UMass Amherst."

Olivia closed her eyes and slowly shook her head. "I'm so sorry. I must've been so worked up about my committee meeting that I completely forgot you were in Amherst."

"Can anyone verify you were in Amherst?" Rachel asked.

"Sure, pretty much everyone at the conference."

"And can you just verify your home address for me?" Rachel asked.

"I rent a room from a student at 86 Rochelle Street in Springfield. Why?" Ethan asked.

"When we were trying to find you, we discovered your address was listed as a UPS store."

"Oh," Ethan said, clearly embarrassed. "I've been staying with Olivia, and I didn't want to be presumptuous by forwarding my mail to her place."

"Where are you now, Ethan?" Rachel asked.

"I'm at Olivia's apartment. She wasn't here when I got here, so I called right away. I was worried."

"Stay there. I'll have an officer come by to confirm," Rachel said.

"Okaaaayy..." Ethan said, unsure how to respond.

"Don't worry about it, Ethan," Olivia said. "Agent Quinn doesn't trust anyone. I'm just glad you're okay."

"Me too," Ethan said, letting out a relieved sigh.

"Don't let Mulder bite you. I'll check in once we get to Maine," Olivia said, a warm smile spreading across her face at the thought of her grumpy old terrier.

"Be careful, Olivia. I love you," Ethan said—then abruptly ended the call.

Olivia blinked, startled. *I love you*—Ethan had never said that before. His voice had dipped slightly, almost as if something was weighing on him. Worry, maybe. The weight of his words lingered, stirring something deep within her. She kept replaying the moment in her mind. Did he truly mean it? Or was he just anxious about her going to Maine?

The only other person who had ever said those words to her was her high school sweetheart, who had left after senior year to attend college in California. They'd lost touch soon after, never exchanging another word.

A warmth spread through Olivia's chest, her cheeks flushing as she instinctively placed a hand on her forehead and looked down at her lap. Ethan's voice, usually so steady, had carried a subtle tremor, a vulnerability that struck something within her. Despite herself, a faint smile tugged at her lips. She couldn't deny it anymore—she loved him, too. Unequivocally.

Olivia slid her phone into her pocket, fidgeting with her fingers in an unconscious attempt to hide her nervous energy.

Rachel's attention had returned to the road, the passing landscape a blur beyond the windshield.

"So, I hope you believe me now. Ethan and I had nothing to do with this," Olivia said. "Do you think it's that professor who's helping Brittney?"

CHAPTER 30

Rachel remained silent behind the wheel, her eyes fixed on the darkness slipping past the window as they headed toward Maine. Her fingers tapped out a nervous rhythm on the steering wheel, occasionally tightening their grip. Trusting Olivia didn't come easily—suspicion gnawed at her mind like a persistent itch.

She had a gut feeling the professor was connected to the bombings, but she wasn't ready to reveal more than necessary about him.

Despite lacking solid proof, Rachel couldn't shake her doubts about Olivia. The coincidence of her being present at every bombing site—from Georgia to Virginia to Massachusetts—was too much to ignore.

"Professor Eric J. Neil," Rachel repeated quietly.

She took what felt like forever to gather her thoughts, weighing her words with care. Surprisingly, Olivia remained patient, saying nothing as she waited.

"When I started at the FBI, my first case brought me to Georgia," Rachel began. "I was investigating Professor Eric J. Neil, a faculty member at Emory. I believed he was responsible for bombing an AA meeting at St. Michael's Church in Clarkston—where you just happened to live, Olivia."

She glanced over. Olivia's face was unreadable.

"We didn't have solid evidence," Rachel said, "but my gut said he was involved. So I confronted him—alone, stupidly. That's when he threw what was basically pepper spray in my face and took off."

"Pepper spray?" Olivia asked.

"Yeah," Rachel said. "I took a risk going solo, and it landed me in hot water with the FBI. After that, I spent years trying to track him down, but came up empty."

She fell silent, her mind drifting back to those early days with the professor. The weight of the memories pressed in, heavy and vivid, lingering in the dark confines of the car. Even after all this time, they felt sharp—each moment etched into her mind as if they had happened just yesterday.

"Next, we went to Virginia Tech, where he detonated a bomb in the computer lab. He was going by the name Professor Lucas then," Rachel said. "He seemed more jittery, more on edge than when I saw him in Georgia. He was running from us across campus and disappeared near one of the churches. Funny you were at both places."

She shot a brief glance in Olivia's direction.

"I really had nothing to do with any of that," Olivia said. "Yeah, I went to that church in Georgia, and I was at Virginia Tech, but... I mean, it's just a coincidence. It has to be."

Rachel tried to study Olivia's face, hoping to read the truth in her expression, but the darkness inside the car offered only a vague silhouette. The road ahead demanded her focus; she couldn't afford to look away for long.

"After that," Rachel said with a sigh, "I kept searching for him for years. I was sure I saw him everywhere, but none of the leads ever panned out. Eventually, it got me into trouble again with the FBI. They said I was neglecting other cases."

"You saw him everywhere?"

"Yeah. In every case I worked, I was convinced he was behind it. I kept spotting him everywhere. In the press crowd, on street corners, anywhere," Rachel said.

"Wow. I can't imagine how frustrating that must have been."

"Then there was the Massachusetts bombing in the subway. That's when he resurfaced, this time as Dr. Aron at MIT," Rachel said. "But he was different. Visibly nervous, much thinner, sweating. Something was off, but I couldn't quite put my finger on it."

Rachel caught a shift in Olivia's expression, as if something in her story had struck a nerve. It seemed tied to the professor's change in appearance, but Olivia stayed silent, still waiting for Rachel to go on.

"We didn't have a face-to-face encounter. Just subway CCTV footage," Rachel said. "We tracked him to MIT, but he was already gone. He left an address behind. We went there, but once again, he'd vanished. All he left was this hourglass."

She glanced at the hourglass on the console between them, its shape barely visible in the dark car.

"Did he look older each time you saw him? Or was it more like he was nervous, scared?" Olivia asked.

Rachel narrowed her eyes. "What do you mean?"

"Nothing. I'm just wondering why you think his appearance changed for you," Olivia said, tucking a strand of hair behind her ear. Her tone was a little too casual. "I've never set foot on the MIT campus."

Rachel caught the subtle shift—Olivia trying to steer the conversation elsewhere—but she let it go. For now.

"But you were in Massachusetts in 2019, right?" Rachel asked.

"Yeah. I started my PhD program up here in 2018, but I don't have any connections to MIT. I swear I wasn't there," Olivia said. "Was that the last time you saw him?"

Rachel paused before answering. "Not exactly…"

CHAPTER 31

July 2021

Rachel had dedicated another two years to her secret pursuit of Professor Eric J. Neil, carefully refining her ability to investigate without drawing attention. That was especially important after her previous trouble with the FBI. No matter how hard she tried, her success stayed just out of reach. Still, after eight years in the profession, both she and Mitchell had become widely known as top investigators.

And yet, Neil continued to linger in her thoughts. She couldn't stop thinking about him. She suspected him of every bombing they were assigned to, even when there was no real reason to. Rachel had chased the professor for years, her obsession never fading. But her attention had begun to turn elsewhere—toward her family.

After returning to Massachusetts from Quantico in 2013, Rachel married her high school sweetheart, Alex, in a quiet courthouse ceremony with two witnesses she barely knew. Alex, a plumber from Southie, shared Rachel's roots—they had both grown up in the same neighborhood. Eight years later, she discovered she was pregnant.

With so much of her career devoted to pursuing criminals, most notably the professor, Rachel was looking forward to a well-earned break. The long maternity leave ahead felt like a rare gift: time to spend with her loving family.

Rachel felt utterly drained after enduring a grueling 35-hour labor. A marathon that ended with the birth of her twin daughters. Madison and Morgan arrived just thirteen minutes apart. Throughout the ordeal, the doctors had warned that a C-section might be necessary, but fate took a different course. Rachel delivered the girls naturally. The delivery had taken everything out of her; even lifting her head felt impossible. And to think she once believed chasing bombers was hard.

Her husband had left her alone in the hospital room, saying he was giving her a chance to rest. In truth, he and the rest of his close-knit family were gathered at the nursery, unable to look away from the beautiful, healthy newborn girls. They'd agreed that Rachel deserved a little time to rest and recover before the twins were brought to her room.

Rachel was exhausted. Her limbs felt like stone. Even blinking took effort, yet real sleep eluded her. She didn't want to move. She was warm and comfortable in her hospital bed. The blankets hugged her body, and the quiet hum of machines soothed her nerves. Caught between wakefulness and a hazy doze, she drifted in and out of awareness.

A nurse entered the room, carrying a small vase tied with a red ribbon, a single rose inside. She smiled warmly as she approached Rachel's bedside and placed the vase on the table.

"Congratulations, Agent Quinn," she said. "Your twins are absolutely beautiful."

Rachel gave a tired nod and a grateful smile, murmured a thank-you, and watched as the nurse left. Alone again, she turned her attention to the unexpected flower. Roses weren't something her family usually sent. The simple gesture felt strange.

Then she noticed the card.

When she picked it up, her heart skipped a beat. A chill crept over her as she saw the image on the front: an hourglass, its sands slipping away.

She knew instantly who had sent it.

She opened the card slowly, her breath catching in her throat. Inside was a simple message, written in neat, deliberate handwriting:

Congratulations on your new arrivals, Rachel. Stay rooted. The north wind may carry secrets better left undiscovered.

Rachel's heart raced as she clutched the card. Adrenaline surged through her. She threw off the covers and leaped from the bed, shouting for the nurse.

"Who gave you this vase? Is he still here?" she asked, her voice echoing down the hospital corridor as she limped toward the door.

"I didn't see him. It came up from the gift shop," the nurse said, her expression tightening. "What's wrong? Are you okay?"

Ignoring the nurse's concern, Rachel continued her determined hobble toward the elevator. Before she could reach it, her husband, Alex, appeared at her side.

"Rachel, what are you doing?"

"Professor Eric J. Neil was here. He sent me flowers." Rachel's lip curled as if the words themselves were sour.

"Okay. Come back to the room and sit down," Alex said. "I'll call your partner. You're in no shape to be chasing anyone around the hospital."

He guided her back toward the room, steady and calm. Reluctantly, Rachel followed, her exhaustion plain as she sank into the hospital bed.

Rachel wasn't surprised when Mitchell showed up at the hospital. She knew he was worried—he always was when it came to the professor. She could see it in the way he looked at her, like he was waiting for her to break again. He arrived ready to offer support, but Rachel wasn't in the mood for reassurance.

"Relax, Rachel. I'll check out the gift shop. You just focus on resting," he said, trying to calm her.

Mitchell had gone straight to the hospital's security office to review the CCTV footage from the gift shop. He'd later told Rachel that he was genuinely surprised by what he saw. On the screen was a man who looked strikingly similar to the figure they'd seen in the subway footage years ago. Like before, the man—short and slight—kept his face hidden beneath the hood of a sweatshirt, making a full identification impossible.

He'd watched as the man purchased a vase with a single red rose, pulled a card from his pocket, scribbled something on it, and attached it to the vase. Then, without hesitation, the man left the hospital.

Mitchell had tried to track him on the parking lot cameras, but the man simply walked out of the lot and headed toward the nearby subway station. His face never appeared clearly on any of the footage. By the time Mitchell had reviewed it all, nearly a full day had passed. The trail had already gone cold.

When he told Rachel what he'd found, she immediately insisted on returning to work and reopening the Professor Eric J. Neil case.

"You're on maternity leave," Mitchell said. "And you can't be sure that the man on the security footage was Neil. Let me handle this while you focus on your family."

"No way. He was just here, sending me flowers. I know it was him." Rachel clenched the card in her hand, the corners bending under the pressure.

"Rachel, you can barely walk across this hospital room. I'll take care of it."

Predictably, Mitchell's investigation turned up no substantial leads. The gift shop offered no usable evidence—no fingerprints on the vase or the card, and no witnesses who could describe the man. None of the CCTV footage revealed a clear image of his face. But Rachel knew it was him.

What struck her this time was the tone of the message. It didn't mock her, not obviously. So why had he reached out now? What did he want?

Rachel embraced every moment of her well-earned 12-week maternity leave, soaking in the precious time with her newborn twins. But even during diaper changes and sleepless nights, her thoughts kept drifting back to the professor. The note had taken root in her mind and wouldn't let go.

Alex and his family were always nearby, giving her breaks when they could, offering support. Still, the message lingered.

Upon returning to the FBI, Rachel pleaded with the director to reopen the investigation into Professor Eric J. Neil. But the response was the same as Mitchell's: there was no new evidence, and the case had been closed for years. It was now with the cold case department. It was time to move on.

Rachel and Mitchell settled back into their usual routine, finding comfort in the familiar rhythm of their work. But Rachel's suspicions about the professor never faded. With every bombing they investigated, her doubts resurfaced, a steady undercurrent throughout her career. Her conviction only grew: she was certain he was behind the deaths of more college professors.

Still, one question haunted her. Why had he come to the hospital? Was it simply harassment—or was he trying to tell her something?

CHAPTER 32

"Why do you think the professor contacted you?" Olivia asked.

"I don't know. To rub it in that I can't catch him?" Rachel shrugged.

"But the message... it sounded more like a warning. About the 'north winds.' You know—Maine? Where we're headed?"

"Exactly. So I don't find him *there*." Rachel almost laughed, the bitterness catching in her throat.

Olivia hesitated. "It's just... weird. I've gotten a rose in a vase with a red ribbon every time I've been in the hospital. When my mom died in high school. And now, after the bomb."

"Seriously? From the professor?" Rachel's eyebrows shot up.

"No," Olivia said, shaking her head. "I got it from a volunteer when I was a teenager. And like I said, I don't know who left it this time. There was no card."

Olivia paused, frowning. "It's just... strange. Maybe it's just a common thing from the gift shop. Maybe everyone gets one."

The weight of her ten-year investigation was wearing Rachel down. "You're not helping. I'm already questioning everything, and you're just piling it on," Rachel said, sarcasm covering the exhaustion in her voice.

"I'm sorry," Olivia said, offering a small, sincere smile.

The car fell into a heavy silence as Rachel stared out the windshield, her thoughts miles away. Olivia stayed quiet, probably unsure of what to say.

"I thought I saw him in the press crowd on the first day I started investigating the lab bombing," Rachel said at last. "But he disappeared right away. Just like always."

"Do you think he's connected to Brittney?" Olivia asked.

"I don't know…" Rachel shook her head, her attention drifting back to the blur of passing scenery.

"Maybe he's helping Brittney with the research they stole from me," Olivia said.

Rachel scoffed. "You seriously think they're trying to travel through time?"

"Yeah, I do. Honestly…" Olivia's voice trailed off as she sank into thought, replaying fragments of her research.

"What?" Rachel said, staring at Olivia like she'd just spoken another language.

"Well, some strange things have happened lately. And parts of your story reflect the more negative aspects of time travel I came across in my research," Olivia said.

"Like what?" Rachel snapped, still unconvinced. Time travel wasn't real. It just didn't exist.

"When we were in the FBI office," Olivia began, her voice carrying a hint of conviction, "I swear I saw traces of old brick walls—like something that had been there years ago. And remember how you said you didn't go up the stairs at my apartment? You just appeared at the front door?"

"So?" Rachel snorted, her tone thick with sarcasm, like Olivia was pitching a sci-fi movie instead of explaining real life.

"To travel through a whirlpool," Olivia went on, her voice steady now, "you have to change the environment—gravity, electromagnetic fields, something. It's not random. No one's falling through time by accident."

Rachel stared out the windshield, silent. A small sigh escaped her, and she finally glanced at Olivia, skeptical disbelief written all over her face.

"So this could be the source of the time slips—and the changes you noticed in the professor. Thin, sweating, nervous... basically unraveling," Olivia said. "You can't just walk from the present into the past without consequences. It fractures the laws of physics. When the environment's altered, it creates a rip in space-time—and those rips come with fallout. This is what I kept worrying about when I read those theories, wondering what could actually go wrong."

Rachel raised an eyebrow. "You're saying that's why I keep seeing him—more frantic every time—until he just vanishes?"

"Yeah," Olivia said. "Based on everything you've described, and what we've both seen, I think it's possible. And if the electromagnetic changes continue, it won't stop at time slips. We could be looking at real-world disasters: earthquakes, floods... people could get hurt."

Rachel's brow furrowed, her thoughts tangled with doubt. She'd firmly rejected the idea of time travel. But now, curiosity pressed in, threatening to crack her certainty.

"That hourglass we found in Brittney's apartment has been locked in the FBI evidence room. I have no idea how it ended up there," Rachel said.

"Could he have made another one? Or maybe Brittney's messing with you?"

237

"No one outside the FBI knew about that hourglass. I guess he could've made another one, but I don't think so," Rachel said.

"Can't you check with someone in evidence? See if it's still there?" Olivia asked.

"Well… I'm kind of off the grid right now," Rachel said.

"Off the grid?" Olivia frowned. "What does that mean?"

"I mean, I'm not exactly cleared to be driving up to Maine with you," Rachel said.

"Is this a joke? What happens when we get there?" Olivia asked, her voice rising as the weight of it all seemed to hit her. "You're not planning to catch this guy on your own, are you? Didn't he pepper-spray you the last time you tried that?"

"Only that one time…" Rachel said, a faint flush creeping into her cheeks. "Honestly, I haven't thought that far ahead. I just know I have to do this. I have to stop him."

"Stop a crazy bomber you haven't been able to catch in almost ten years? On your own?" Olivia shot her a look. "Doesn't he always disappear?"

Rachel fell silent, her knuckles whitening as she gripped the steering wheel. Eyes locked on the road, she squinted at the approaching exit sign, her brow furrowed, thoughts elsewhere.

"What if he's not even there? What if it's just Brittney?" Olivia asked, tension creeping into her voice. "Did you really risk your job just to keep chasing him?"

Rachel didn't answer. Her eyes stayed on the road, jaw tight, narrowing at another exit sign like it wasn't making sense. The edge in Olivia's voice caught her attention, and she glanced over briefly. No need to ask—Olivia was second-guessing this entire trip. Ever since Rachel had mentioned Eric J. Neil, it was clear Olivia thought she'd lost her grip.

"You know, no matter what you do, you can't change any-thing. We've had this conversation before, too," Olivia said, eyes dropping to her lap. She fidgeted with the ends of her sleeves, her voice unsteady.

"Fuck off, Olivia. I *can* change things," Rachel snapped, veering onto the highway's shoulder before correcting the wheel. "I made the decision to come up here without permission. I made the decision to bring you. There's no fate forcing my hand."

Out of the corner of her eye, Rachel saw Olivia's fingers clamp around the door handle. She said nothing, but her wide eyes and rigid posture said enough. For a moment, Rachel wondered if Olivia actually thought she'd crash the car just to prove a point.

"Did you see that last exit sign?" Rachel asked, frowning.

"No, I wasn't really paying attention," Olivia said.

Rachel closed her eyes for a second and shook her head, trying to clear it. Something felt off.

"I think we need to stop for the night. I'm exhausted, and I could swear I've passed the same motel exit four times."

As they continued down the dark, seemingly endless high-way and took the exit, the landscape outside seemed eerily famil-iar. Like the world was looping in on itself.

CHAPTER 33

Olivia extended her hand through the swirling mist, reaching for the stone wall to touch the roses—then woke to the soft cooing of mourning doves. She blinked, disoriented. For a fleeting moment, she thought she was back home, tucked in bed with her grumpy terrier curled beside her.

But the illusion dissolved quickly. Faint motel light filtered through unfamiliar curtains, and the hum of the heater built into the window AC unit reminded her where she really was: a cheap roadside motel in Maine. She and Rachel had checked in late last night, but everything after that was a blur. Olivia couldn't remember anything after they entered the room. They must've crashed the moment they hit the beds.

The room was on the dingy side, but it had its comforts. Two spacious queen beds, a bulky television, a compact mini fridge, and a modest one-cup coffee maker. Her eyes drifted to the window. The doves, she guessed, must be nesting on the old window unit. They'd done the same back home.

Across the room, Rachel lay sound asleep in the other bed. Olivia eased herself out from under the covers, her shoes sinking into the worn carpet. Moving carefully, she filled the small coffee maker, its peculiar design making her pause. Soon, the rich aroma of brewing coffee filled the room.

Her stomach growled. Had they eaten last night? She couldn't remember.

The soft clatter of the coffee pot stirred Rachel. She sat up slowly, rubbing sleep from her eyes, and looked at Olivia with a puzzled expression.

"Do you remember how we got in here?" Rachel asked.

Olivia shook her head, her memory foggy. "Not really. I remember checking in, opening the room door... and then waking up just now."

"Huh." Rachel glanced around the room, brow furrowed, as if seeing it for the first time.

Olivia settled back onto the bed, still in yesterday's clothes, cradling the warm coffee cup in both hands. Across the room, Rachel disappeared into the bathroom. Olivia glanced around and noticed her bag was missing. A prickle of unease crept in—hopefully, it was still in the car.

Rachel emerged a few minutes later, drying her hands. "Okay, let's get going. We're only about two hours from the GPS coordinates."

Olivia's stomach growled loud enough to betray her. "Rachel, I'm starving. Can we stop at the diner next door first? Just something quick."

Rachel looked ready to argue, irritation flashing in her expression. But then her face shifted, softening.

"Yeah," she said, almost surprised. "I guess I'm hungry too."

"Did you bring anything in from the car?" Olivia asked as they were about to leave.

Rachel glanced around, then ducked into the bathroom for a quick check. When she returned, she was frowning, clearly trying to remember.

"No. I guess I didn't."

Once they stepped outside, they headed straight for the car. Their duffel bags, Rachel's FBI credentials, and her gun were all still inside. Olivia caught the surprise on Rachel's face as she realized she'd left her weapon behind. But she said nothing about her oversight, and they crossed the dusty parking lot in silence, heading toward the diner.

Halfway there, Olivia stopped, frozen by a strange, over-whelming sensation.

Rachel turned to her. "What's wrong?"

"I don't know," Olivia said. "I feel like I've been here before. Everything looks... familiar."

Olivia scanned the surroundings, unsettled. The hazy gap in her memory since arriving at the motel gnawed at her. Her heart fluttered with unease, as if her instincts were warning her of something just out of reach.

"I thought you said you'd never been to Maine," Rachel said, watching her closely.

"I haven't." Olivia's fingers drifted over the sleeve of her coat, tracing idle patterns as she tried to steady herself. "Maybe it's just déjà vu."

Olivia focused on her breathing—deep inhales to fill her lungs, slow exhales to release the tension coiled in her stomach.

"Seriously? Déjà vu strikes again?" Rachel asked, her voice faltering as she nodded toward the diner. "Do you still want to grab some food?"

Olivia paused, eyes closed for a moment. Then she offered a faint smile and gave a slow nod. With measured steps, she started toward the diner, letting hunger momentarily outweigh her unease.

Still, each step felt just a little heavier.

The diner was a classic, old-fashioned spot, housed in what looked like the elongated body of an antique train car or trailer. Its chrome-trimmed exterior gleamed beneath a neon sign that read "Diner," with a plate and silverware icon glowing behind the letters.

Retro memorabilia—framed black-and-white photos and faded advertisements for long-forgotten products—lined the walls inside. The checkerboard tile floor, worn and scuffed by years of foot traffic, added to the place's well-worn charm.

Olivia glanced around as they stepped inside, unsure whether to wait or seat themselves. Most of the counter stools were occupied, but a few booths along the windows remained open. She was surprised to see the place so busy, especially with only a handful of cars in the motel and diner parking lots.

Behind the counter stood a striking young waitress with fiery red hair and vibrant neon-green eyes. Her white apron marked her as staff, but it was her warm smile that stood out, lighting up her entire face.

She looked up and greeted them, her voice cutting through the steady clink of silverware and low hum of conversation.

"Hey, Rachel! Nice to see you again! You guys want your usual?" the waitress called out cheerfully.

Rachel and Olivia exchanged a glance, both clearly caught off guard. They turned back to the waitress.

"We've never been here before," Rachel said, her voice cautious as her gaze swept the diner, trying to make sense of it.

The waitress waved her off with a grin. "Yeah, yeah. You say that every time. Just sit anywhere. I'll bring you some coffee."

They looked at each other again. Rachel mouthed, *What the fuck?* Olivia only shrugged, just as lost, and they made their way to one of the open booths.

The waitress, now practically buzzing with energy, hurried over with a steaming coffee pot. She flipped the upside-down mugs on the table and filled them with generous pours.

"Your usuals are already on their way," she said, then flashed a quick smile and darted off to the crowded counter.

Rachel and Olivia sat across from each other in silence, their eyes drifting around the diner. After a moment, Rachel broke the quiet, her tone laced with dry amusement.

"She's definitely got us mixed up with someone else. Let's just hope those people like what we like for breakfast," she said, reaching for the newspaper on the table.

Olivia didn't answer. Her brow remained furrowed, thoughts tangled. How could the waitress have recognized them?

"This is yesterday's paper," Rachel said, annoyed she couldn't catch up on today's news.

The waitress returned, setting down two plates with practiced ease. In front of Rachel: a warm, toasted cinnamon raisin bagel with a side of cream cheese. Olivia's plate held a fluffy omelet—just cheddar and tomatoes—alongside whole wheat toast.

They stared at their meals, confusion settling into something closer to dread.

"Is something wrong?" the waitress asked, pausing at the edge of their table.

"Uh… no?" Rachel said, her voice trailing off with a rising intonation, as if trying to convince herself.

"Great!" the waitress beamed, then spun away to refill coffees down the line.

Rachel leaned in, voice low and urgent. "What the fuck is going on here? This is what I eat. Every. Fucking. Day. In Boston."

"I know," Olivia said. "How did they know I only put tomatoes and cheese in my omelets?"

Her voice trembled. She fidgeted with the edge of her plate, eyes scanning the diner, searching the faces around them for something—anything—that made sense.

Rachel was doing the same. "I think we should get out of here."

Olivia hesitated, her eyes fixed on the omelet. Apprehension pulsed through her, but the hunger twisting in her stomach was stronger.

"I'm really starving, though," she said, her voice unsteady. "If I don't eat soon, I might pass out."

Olivia picked up her fork with caution, but one bite was all it took—warm, rich, exactly how she liked it. Hunger took over. She devoured the omelet, matching Rachel's own voracious appetite as they both cleared their plates.

The waitress returned, scooping up the empty dishes and leaving the check. As she turned to leave, Rachel stopped her with a quick gesture.

"Could you bring us today's paper?"

"This *is* today's paper," the waitress said with a playful roll of her eyes.

"No, it's yesterday's," Rachel said, flipping the front page and pointing to the date.

"You always try to mess with me," the waitress said, still smiling as she turned away with their empty plates. "Today's Friday, February 8th."

Rachel angled her iPhone toward Olivia, her voice dropping to a whisper. "Today is *Saturday*, February 9th," she said, the screen clearly displaying the date.

Without another word, she tossed cash on the table to cover the bill and tip. They slid out of the booth and made for the exit, the bell over the door chiming as they left.

Behind them, the waitress called out brightly, "Have a fantastic day, you two! Don't stay away so long next time!"

———◆———

Olivia burst out of the diner, her footsteps crunching over the icy gravel lot. Rachel followed close behind, and they reached the car in seconds. Inside, they slumped into their seats, breath shallow, bodies trembling.

Rachel, ever the professional, was the first to steady herself, fingers closing around the grip of her holstered gun.

"Wait—are you gonna shoot someone?" Olivia asked, recoiling against the passenger door, hands instinctively raised in alarm.

"No," Rachel said, glancing at Olivia, her eyes sharp but composed. "I just don't know what's going on. And I want to be ready."

Olivia closed her eyes and drew in deep, steadying breaths, trying to calm her racing heart. When she opened them again, Rachel was leaning forward, tapping the GPS screen to confirm it was still guiding them to the coordinates they'd found in Brittney's apartment.

246

Without a word, Rachel shifted into reverse, sending dirt and gravel spraying as they peeled out of the lot and back onto the winding road. Minutes passed. Olivia's pulse gradually steadied, but the silence in the car lingered—Rachel's grip on the wheel was as tight as ever, her face unreadable.

Olivia turned to look out the window, expecting to see the highway by now. She could've sworn the motel and diner were just a quick turn off the exit.

"What do you think we'll find at those coordinates?" Rachel asked, breaking the silence that had settled over the car like a heavy fog.

"I have no idea," Olivia said, her voice still trembling. Deep down, she hoped they'd find nothing. Just another dead end in a trail of cryptic clues from Brittney or the professor. A wild goose chase. Another waste of Rachel's valuable FBI time.

Though Rachel sat composed behind the wheel, Olivia could see the cracks—tension in her jaw, the tight grip on the steering wheel. Rachel was trying to stay calm, but Olivia sensed the unease beneath it. Rachel doubted her, kept her at arm's length. But now, for the first time, it felt like she trusted her.

Lost in thought, Olivia continued to stare out of the window. It wasn't until they passed a familiar-looking gas station that something clicked—and then, just ahead on the right, she spotted it. The motel. The diner.

"Is that the diner?" she asked, her voice tinged with panic as she squinted through the windshield. A sinking feeling twisted in her gut, and a wave of anxiety muddled her thoughts.

Rachel's eyes narrowed. "No way. I've been driving straight, looking for the highway. There were no turnoffs. No side roads. Nothing."

247

Olivia spotted the neon sign: "Diner," with a plate and silverware glowing behind the letters. She turned toward the motel. Every window air conditioner had a bird's nest perched on top.

"We must've turned around somehow." Olivia was thinking of the same gas station, the same diner, the same snowy landscape they had just left behind.

Rachel pressed harder on the gas, eyes scanning the road ahead, searching for any sign of an alternate route—a turnoff, a side street, anything. But just minutes later, Olivia's heart sank.

The gas station reappeared. And there, on the right, was the diner. "Oh my God."

Rachel tried everything—driving faster, slower, turning around, even reversing—but nothing worked. No matter what she did, the diner reappeared, and each time, it seemed to happen faster than before.

Olivia's breathing quickened. Panic clawed at her chest as the realization sank in: they couldn't escape. Her eyes darted across the snow-covered landscape, searching for an exit, a side road, *something*. Sweat beaded on her forehead. Her hands trembled in her lap, her body taut with dread.

Rachel brought the car to a stop outside the motel.

"Is this one of your whirlpools? How do we get out of here?" Rachel's voice held less fear than Olivia expected—and far more anger.

"I don't know. I don't know," Olivia said, her voice shaking. Her thoughts spun, wild and fragmented, as she shook her head.

With a sudden burst of fury, Rachel slammed both palms against the steering wheel and let out a furious yell while blaring the horn in one long, jarring note. The sound shattered the stillness, sending a shockwave through the motel's quiet.

Startled, the birds scattered from the window air conditioners. Dozens—no, hundreds—of mourning doves burst into the sky, veering sharply in the opposite direction from where Rachel had been driving.

Olivia stared after them, her mind suddenly clear, the pieces aligning.

Birds navigate using electromagnetic fields. They knew where to go.

"Follow those doves," Olivia said, her voice still trembling as she pointed after them.

"Are you *fucking* kidding me?" Rachel snapped, disbelief flaring in her voice. Her brows knit into a deep scowl as she stared at Olivia, hands clenched tight on the steering wheel.

"No. They use electromagnetic fields," Olivia said, trying to sound steadier than she felt.

Rachel rolled her eyes and sighed. "Fine. Anything's better than looping past that goddamn diner again."

Rachel turned the car around and tried to follow the birds. They flew in loose formation, some veering off in erratic directions, breaking from the main flock. With no roads or side paths in sight, Rachel stuck to the ones flying closest to the roadside.

But even going the opposite direction, the landscape refused to change—the same endless road, the same snow-covered fields, repeating over and over.

When the gas station came into view again, Olivia's stomach churned. She thought she might be sick. Then the dashboard lights flickered. The engine sputtered. Panic surged. Her heart pounded. Dizziness swept over her like a wave. She closed her eyes, took a shaky breath, and tried to steady herself.

When she opened them, the world tilted—colors bleeding at the edges, shapes distorting, the horizon rippling like heat off pavement. Her vision faded. Her thoughts scattered.

And then everything went black.

CHAPTER 34

Olivia slowly opened her eyes, her head lolling back against the seat as the dimly lit ceiling of Rachel's car came into view. The air was still. Her body felt heavy, her thoughts slow to gather. Outside the windows, darkness pressed in. It was a bright morning when she lost consciousness while trying to escape the diner. Now darkness enveloped their surroundings.

The car sat motionless in the stillness, its engine silent. But the headlights remained on, casting a pale, steady glow ahead. The beams illuminated a weathered stone wall, overgrown with crimson roses, their petals dusted in a delicate flurry of snowflakes.

Olivia sat in disbelief, half convinced she'd slipped into another dream. Her eyes locked on the wall—*the* wall. It had haunted her dreams for years. Night after night, she'd reached for those roses, only to wake before her fingers ever brushed a single petal.

She tore her eyes away and turned to Rachel, still slumped in the driver's seat, unconscious.

Olivia reached out, shaking her shoulder—gently at first, then with growing urgency. "Rachel," she said, the name rising in volume each time. Rachel stirred, startled, her hand flying instinctively to the sidearm in her holster.

"It's me, it's me," Olivia said, her voice low but firm, stopping Rachel from drawing the weapon.

"How did we get here?" Rachel blinked hard, groggy, her confusion rippling through the quiet.

"I don't remember," Olivia said. She glanced out the window, back to the stone wall, then met Rachel's eyes again. "But I'm guessing these are the coordinates we were looking for."

Rachel looked at the GPS. Its dull glow confirmed it—this was the place.

They stepped out into the night. Frigid air bit at their skin, their breath visible in the cold. Snowflakes drifted around them, creating a gentle flurry that painted the scene in a thin layer of white.

The stone wall before them, covered in roses blooming in shades of red and pink, wasn't just a wall, but the weathered facade of a small, one-room building. It looked like the remnants of an ancient stone church, or maybe a schoolhouse. Nearby, a congregation of trees stood, their bare branches dusted with snow. Olivia strained her ears, catching the distant cooing of mourning doves hidden within the leafless boughs.

Rachel stepped closer, drawn to the impossible sight of roses thriving in the dead of a Maine winter. She reached out and touched one of the delicate blooms.

"How are roses blooming in the winter in Maine?" Rachel wondered aloud.

"I've mentioned before that there are places where the usual rules don't always apply," Olivia said absently, eyes scanning the branches above as she tried to spot the hidden mourning doves, narrowing her gaze against the dark sky.

Rachel retrieved her flashlight. Its beam cut through the darkness as she swept it across the area, searching for a door, a path—any sign of movement. The light fell upon a compact sedan parked in the shadows. Snow blanketed the roof and windshield. No lights, no sign of life.

"There's a car," Rachel said, drawing her gun. She tucked the flashlight beneath it, steadying the beam on the driver's side.

"I think that's Brittney's car," Olivia said, her voice tight with recognition—and fear.

"Stay back," Rachel warned, advancing toward the car.

Rachel's flashlight pierced the darkness, landing first on the empty driver's seat. Olivia watched as she shifted the beam to the passenger side—and froze. A figure sat motionless, eyes wide open, glassy and vacant. The corpse stared out into nothing, its body rigid, a dead cell phone clutched in one hand, the screen dark.

Rachel swept the light across the rest of the interior. No movement. Nothing stirred. Just the hollow stillness that follows death.

But Olivia's heart hammered in her chest, fear and curiosity warring inside her. Despite Rachel's warning, her feet moved forward, slow and uncertain. Each step felt like pushing against gravity, against reason. The urge to see firsthand eclipsed her impulse to flee.

Olivia's breath hitched. The distinctive blonde pixie cut. The buck teeth. It was Brittney—no question. She sat slumped in the passenger seat of her own car, stiff and silent, her face contorted into a grotesque mask of death. Olivia couldn't look away. That blank, frozen expression—caught mid-breath—would be seared into her memory forever.

Panic surged. Olivia's chest clenched as her breaths came faster, sharp and shallow, like the air itself had turned hostile. Sweat beaded on her forehead; her hands trembled, slick with fear. The world narrowed, the sound muffled by the roar in her ears.

"I told you to stay back," Rachel said.

"That's Brittney," Olivia said, each word catching in her throat.

"It looks like she's been dead for days," Rachel said. "I'm going to call the Maine field office to get help, maybe an ambulance." She turned and headed back to the car to use the radio.

Olivia didn't move. She kept staring at Brittney, questions tumbling through her mind. How could this be happening? Did Brittney orchestrate all of this, then just kill herself? But is that possible if she's been dead for days? And what of Professor Eric J. Neil, the main reason Rachel had come here in the first place?

"Fuck. No cell service. And the radio's dead," Rachel said. Her voice jolted Olivia from her thoughts, yanking her back into the moment.

Olivia's hand trembled as she pulled out her phone, fingers fumbling in a desperate search for a signal. Her stomach sank like a stone when she saw it—no bars. Nothing. The horrifying realization gripped her: they were cut off. No contact. No help. Just the two of them… and a corpse.

But what if Brittney didn't take her own life? What if someone had killed her? Were they *really* alone out here?

Olivia turned her attention back to the ruined stone building. Beyond it, there was nothing but the vast snow-covered field, silent and empty, framed by a scatter of ancient trees. As she squinted into the darkness, Olivia thought she saw a faint movement. Only a ripple across the snow. A silhouette of something, maybe an animal? But the darkness concealed its identity from her.

She stood frozen, her breath clouding the cold air, mirroring Rachel's stillness.

A few moments later, Olivia spotted what looked like the same animal moving along the same path. She blinked, then shook her head, convinced her terrified mind was playing tricks on her. But when she focused again, there it was—the same creature, tracing the same path across the snow.

"Did you just see that bobcat, or whatever it was, run across the field?" Olivia asked, her voice still trembling with panic and confusion.

"What?" Rachel asked, turning toward her.

Olivia's heart pounded. What was going on? She thought she saw bobcats crossing the field in single file. Why did three of them walk in such a neat row?

Before Olivia could answer, a voice echoed from the stone building. It sounded like a heated argument, growing louder with each second. Olivia and Rachel turned toward the building in unison.

In a swift, calculated motion, Rachel crouched low, gun raised, and snapped off her flashlight. She shot Olivia a look and pressed a finger to her lips—*stay quiet.*

Rachel moved forward, slow and deliberate, every step measured. Olivia followed. Rachel tried to wave her back, but Olivia had no intention of staying behind with Brittney's body, especially with Rachel having the only weapon. The prospect of utter isolation in the dark was terrifying. Her mind was already conjuring up prowling animals waiting just beyond the reach of the car's dying headlights.

Olivia shook her head, hard. "I'm coming with you."

Rachel gave her a sharp, exasperated look and raised her finger to her lips again, urging silence.

Rachel pressed her back against the stone wall, the roses rustling against her shoulders as she crept toward the corner. Moving with care, she leaned out and peered around it.

More roses clung to this side of the building, but at the far end, tucked amid the flowers, stood an open door. Light spilled from within, casting long shadows across the snow. The voice continued, sharp and agitated, but the words were still impossible to make out.

Olivia followed closely as they tiptoed around the corner. The crunch of snow underfoot punctuated their every step. The closer they came to the open doorway, the slower they moved, straining for silence.

Then the voice stopped. Both froze. Had they been heard? In the hush that followed, neither dared to breathe. The silence was complete—too complete.

Rachel stayed frozen for what felt like an eternity, Olivia close behind her, struggling to keep her rising panic in check. At last, Rachel moved—one slow, step, then another, inching toward the door with even greater care, every motion calibrated for silence. The last thing they needed was to tip off whoever was inside.

As Rachel neared the open doorway and cautiously looked inside, Olivia felt her pulse spike. She watched Rachel's eyes widen. She pivoted around the corner, gun raised.

"Drop it, Professor Neil!" Rachel commanded.

As Olivia looked around the corner, she heard a man's voice, pleading, "Rachel, you don't understand."

Her eyes locked onto a very short, dark-haired man standing in the center of the cramped stone room. Her heart raced. She braced herself to see a weapon—but instead, he clutched a small, square black box, with a single red button stark at its center.

Rachel had called him Professor Neil, but Olivia recognized him immediately. The short stature, the puffy black jacket—it was Dr. Elliot. The same man who frantically barged into the lab, demanding to see Dr. Lynch.

Olivia's apprehension deepened as she scanned the room, her eyes darting from corner to corner. On the far wall, a second exterior door stood shut. Off to the side, a table held a collection of materials, including tightly wound wires, an array of electronic components, and containers filled with ominous-looking powders and liquids. Along the base of two walls, a series of cylindrical pipes lay arranged in a careful pattern, their surfaces bristling with wires and strange attachments.

It all connected in an instant, icy dread crashing over her. This man was holding a detonator.

And he was about to blow the building to pieces.

CHAPTER 35

" I said, drop it!" Rachel's voice cracked like thunder.

"No, Rachel. You don't understand. I have to destroy it," the professor said.

"Professor Neil, we can talk about this. You don't have to destroy anything." Her voice stayed calm, almost gentle—steady in a way that didn't match the gun in her hand.

Her grip on the gun eased, just slightly. The muzzle lowered, but hovered close enough to snap back in less than a second. Every nerve in her body thrummed. She scanned the room, taking in every detail, cataloging corners, shadows, and exits. Pivoting a half-step, she angled herself just inside the doorway— close enough to act, far enough to see.

And then she spotted Olivia, frozen at the threshold, eyes locked on Professor Eric J. Neil.

"Olivia, please go back out to the car. Professor Neil and I are just going to have a conversation," Rachel said, her voice slow, calm, and measured.

"Olivia? Olivia's here?" The professor's brow knit tight.

"No, Professor. She's heading back to the car... Wait... how do you know Olivia?" Rachel's voice sharpened.

"She can't be here! She shouldn't be here!" The professor's voice spiked.

Rachel kept her tone steady, almost hypnotic. "Alright, alright, Professor. She's leaving now. It's okay."

"That's Dr. Elliot," Olivia said.

"What?" Rachel asked, eyes flicking toward her.

"Dr. Elliiot. The guy who caused a scene in the lab that day and tried to get to Dr. Lynch," Olivia said, her eyes wide.

Rachel turned back to the professor, her mind racing, unsure how to proceed.

She hovered at a fragile crossroads, instinct tugging in opposite directions. A direct confrontation felt risky considering his agitation. His grip on the detonator was too tight, his mind too far gone. She couldn't afford to push him further; the detonator in his hand was a ticking time bomb, both figuratively and literally.

He paced, muttering under his breath, the device clenched in his fist like a lifeline. The tension coiled tighter around the room, and Rachel knew she had to tread carefully.

After summoning her courage, she took a deep breath and adjusted her grip on the gun. With quiet precision, she angled the barrel upward, toward the ceiling—a deliberate signal: not an immediate threat… not yet.

"Professor, please. Let's just put the detonator down and talk."

"I can't," he said, eyes darting. "How did you get here? How did you know where we were?"

"We found the coordinates in Brittney's apartment."

His expression changed—confusion, then something sharper. His thoughts seemed to rush, but then he paused. Rachel watched the realization dawn in his eyes like a switch flipping in the dark. He'd connected something. She could see it.

"Rachel, you have to get out of here. I have to destroy it," the professor said again, desperation thick in his voice.

"Professor, you can stop this. There's no reason for you to hurt anyone else," Rachel said, unwavering.

"I haven't hurt anyone!" His voice cracked, echoing hard off the walls. His hands shook with the effort of holding on—whether to the detonator or his fraying control, Rachel couldn't tell. Sweat clung to his brow, his flushed face twitching as his eyes searched the room, wild and uncertain.

"Okay. Breathe," Rachel said gently. She kept her voice low, steady. "Maybe people were hurt, maybe not—but you can choose a different path today. You can put the detonator down. That's your choice. You have the power to stop this."

The professor's anxiety climbed with every second. He paced back and forth. The detonator clenched tighter with each pass. His movements were jittery, his eyes darting across the room like a trapped animal searching for a way out.

"I tried to stop it! I was always too late! But I thought... I thought I could warn Dr. Lynch. I tried to stop it!" His voice raw with panic.

Rachel lowered her gun until the barrel lined up with his chest again. Her arms were steady, but inside, she churned. She didn't want to shoot him. She wanted him held accountable, to answer for the destruction and all the lives lost.

The weight of it pressed down on her, but clarity held firm. This man was responsible for eight confirmed deaths. Maybe more. If it came to it—if it meant protecting Olivia, protecting anyone—she wouldn't hesitate to take the shot.

"Professor, drop the detonator," Rachel said again, her voice steady. As she spoke, she took a step back, guiding Olivia farther from the looming danger.

The professor's muttering didn't stop—"I have to, I have to"—a broken mantra cycling endlessly through the air. But then, without warning, he froze. The pacing ceased. The tremors stilled.

He stood still, head bowed, eyes shut. The panic seemed to drain from him, replaced by something quieter. Acceptance, maybe. Resignation.

He nodded slowly.

"It's the only way," he said, calm now—eerily so—as he raised the detonator, arm steady, like the gesture itself was inevitable.

Rachel pulled the trigger. The gunshots cracked through the room as two bullets found their mark on the professor's chest. Olivia screamed as the professor staggered, then collapsed.

He hit the floor hard. The detonator slipped from his hand and skittered across the floor, landing near the doorway. Blood pooled fast beneath him. He gasped, a soft, broken "no" escaping his lips before his eyes went vacant, locked on the ceiling.

Rachel moved toward him. She crouched beside him and checked for signs of life—there were none. Confirming the detonator was out of reach near the closed door, she stood up.

Her pulse gradually slowed as she closed her eyes for a moment and released a deep breath. When she turned, she saw Olivia in the doorway, knees buckled beneath her, hands shaking, tears streaming down her face.

"It's okay, Olivia. We're safe now," Rachel said, reassuring Olivia, and maybe herself.

Just as the words left her lips, the door across the room creaked open.

A man stepped in, a dimpled smile graced his face as he began a slow, mocking clap. His eyes locked on Rachel as he strolled forward and casually bent to pick up the detonator.

"Thanks for that, Rachel. You handle him for me about eighty percent of the time," he said, smiling wide—too wide.

Rachel froze, her mind reeling. Who the hell is this?

Until now, she believed Professor Eric J. Neil was solely responsible for everything. The assumption had always been that he acted alone, that madness had driven the bombings. She'd thought he was the villain, delusional, dangerous, maybe suicidal. But now?

Rachel surged to her feet, gun snapping into place, aimed squarely at the newcomer. She hadn't even found her voice, but Olivia did—quiet, laced with recognition.

"Ethan," she whispered. The name lingered, heavy in the air.

———————————————— ❖ ————————————————

Olivia couldn't believe her eyes when she saw Ethan standing inside the stone building. The confusion built up inside her. Her mind scrambled to make sense of it. Just earlier, on the phone, he'd told her he was at her apartment. He'd even warned her to be careful.

Now, realization broke over her like a wave—he *knew*. He'd known exactly where she was going. He'd known she would end up here, that she would find him at these precise coordinates.

"Ethan?" Rachel asked, shock unmistakable in her voice. "The lab tech?"

"That's me," Ethan said, still wearing his trademark dimpled smile. Only now, he was holding the detonator.

"What's going on, Ethan? You told me you were at home, at my apartment," Olivia said, her voice a quiet, scratchy whisper that betrayed the turmoil and confusion churning inside her.

"Everything is for you, Olivia. All of this, everything I've done. It's all for you," Ethan said, glancing toward her with unsettling calm.

Olivia's heart pounded as she tried to make sense of his words. She had fallen in love with Ethan, and for a moment, seeing him here had brought a sense of relief. But now, that comfort gave way to doubt. Familiar and creeping, it mingled with the warmth she still felt, even as he stood before her with a detonator in his hand.

"What do you mean? What have you done, Ethan?" she asked, her voice unsteady. Her breaths came faster, shallower, as panic threatening to pull her under. The room seemed to spin around her, the walls inching closer.

Ethan said nothing, just stared at Olivia.

Rachel hadn't moved. She stood firm beside the professor's body, gun still trained on Ethan.

"Ethan, drop that detonator," Rachel commanded, her voice sharp.

"Oh, right." Ethan complied, moving toward the table and set it down gently. "I didn't want to blow this place up, anyway. That's always Eric's thing."

"Professor Eric J. Neil?" Rachel asked, nodding toward the lifeless body on the floor.

"Actually, it's Dr. Eric J. *Delano*," Ethan corrected, his tone casual. "He's been chasing me. I've been chasing him. Round and round we go." He turned and gave Olivia another of those dimpled, reassuring smiles.

Olivia stood frozen, mouth slightly open, struggling to process what she'd just heard. Her eyes darted between Ethan and Rachel, trying to make sense of the bizarre exchange. Nothing added up. No words came.

"What are you talking about, Ethan? How do you know Professor Neil?" Rachel asked.

"Again—it's Dr. Eric J. Delano," Ethan said. "He's a physicist. I used to be a doctor myself, too. Didn't finish my psychiatry residency, though." He gave a short laugh. "He always said I chose psychiatry because I was a little obsessive."

As he spoke, Olivia watched as Rachel was edging away from the professor's body, while Ethan was moving slowly forward. Olivia took a few hesitant steps deeper into the room. Fear pressed in on her, but something else tugged at her—some strange pull she couldn't explain.

Ethan's gaze drifted, his smile fading. For a moment, he looked almost reflective. Then he sighed.

"Anyway, he'll be back."

"Ethan, why don't we leave this building and head out to my car?" Rachel suggested. "We can keep talking when we're not surrounded by bombs."

"It never happens that way," Ethan said.

Olivia frowned, her thoughts spinning as she mulled over Ethan's words. *He'll be back. It never happens that way.* The words echoed in her head. Fragments of her research on Einstein's whirlpools and timelines flared to life. As erratic as he was now, Ethan had propelled her work forward in ways she never could have imagined alone.

Olivia could see that Rachel hadn't lowered her gun. She held it steady, but her eyes betrayed her confusion.

"What do you mean, Ethan?" Olivia asked. "When you say *it never happens that way*?"

"We don't leave the building at this point," he said, voice weary. "I've seen it so many times."

"How many times have you seen it?" Olivia asked.

"More than I can count," Ethan said, eyes dropping to the floor. "But one of these times, I'll get it right."

Rachel and Olivia said nothing, just stared at Ethan.

Olivia's mind reeled. She understood the physics, the whirl-pools. But even with everything she'd studied, even knowing how far Ethan had helped push her research, part of her refused to believe him. Theories were one thing. But the human body was just ill-equipped to handle time travel. She thought it was impossible. And yet... she loved him. However, as Ethan spoke, that love began to tangle with doubt.

Rachel hadn't lowered her weapon. Her posture remained tight with tension, and when she turned slightly to meet Olivia's eyes, the look they exchanged said everything—*Is he just crazy?*

Ethan cleared his throat. When he spoke, his voice held the weight of confession.

"When I first went back, Olivia," he said, his attention fixed on her, "I tried to save your mom."

"What?" Olivia's breath hitched in her throat. Her voice was barely audible, her eyes wide.

"I thought if I took out the drunk who hit her, it might change your career path," Ethan continued, his tone almost gentle. "But of course, that piece of shit didn't even show up to the AA meeting like he was supposed to..."

Disbelief swept across Rachel's face.

"You blew up that church in Georgia?" she asked.

"Yeah, but it didn't work," Ethan said with a solemn nod. "So I tried to sabotage her career at Virginia Tech—again, so she wouldn't come up here, to Massachusetts, and keep going with physics."

A heavy silence settled over the room. The weight of his words hung thick in the air. Olivia and Rachel exchanged a bewildered glance, both struggling to process the depth of what Ethan was confessing. Questions flooded Olivia's mind. How did Ethan know all this? How could he have known she'd end up in Massachusetts after Virginia Tech?

Ethan's arms moved with idle restlessness, like someone sitting through a story he'd told a hundred times. He sighed, not out of regret—but from the sheer fatigue of repetition.

"Nothing was working," he said flatly. "So I planted the bomb at the MIT subway station. I figured if I took out those professors early on, it might save Olivia."

"Jesus Christ, Ethan—*you* killed all those people?" Rachel's voice cracked, her eyes wide with shock and disbelief.

Ethan only shrugged, a casual gesture that said everything—he felt cornered, out of options, like this had made sense to him.

"Eric tried to stop me. He's told me over and over—you can't change anything," Ethan said with a nod. His attention shifted to Olivia, and he offered a small, bittersweet smile. "He's a determinist. Like you."

Olivia didn't move. Her hands trembled at her sides, her wide eyes locked on Ethan. No words came. The weight of it—all of it—crashed down in silence.

"He's tried to leave you clues, Rachel, like the hourglass, or that card he left at the hospital," Ethan said. "Why do you think he always knew where you were? When you were watching him? We've already seen it happen."

"Then why did he run from me?" Rachel asked. "Why not just tell me what was going on?"

"He wanted to stop me," Ethan said, "but he couldn't bring himself to turn me in to the FBI. Brothers are like that."

"*He's your brother?*" Rachel asked, the revelation catching her off guard.

Ethan nodded.

Olivia didn't react. Couldn't. Months of conversation, affection, and trust growing between them. It all collapsed under the weight of the truth. Everything felt like a lie now. She had misjudged him completely, and the realization hit her like a blow to the chest.

"He tried again with Dr. Lynch," Ethan said. "She ruined his career back when he was still Dr. Eric J. Elliot, but he still tried to warn her. He knew I wouldn't stop—not until I saved Olivia."

"Saved me from *what?*" Olivia asked, her voice edged with frustration, the feeling of being left behind growing stronger by the second.

Ethan ignored her question, his focus firmly on Rachel, absorbed in his own explanation.

"When he couldn't protect the lab, he tried to draw you out to Worcester. He thought if you stayed there, you wouldn't end up here. But it only works... maybe seventy, seventy-five percent of the time."

Rachel drew in a sharp breath. "You did all of this? You killed all those people—Dr. Lynch? Sofia? And Brittney?"

"I had to," Ethan said without hesitation. "They were terrible people. And I couldn't save Olivia. Not the way things were. I had to save her, and I think... I think the changes I made this time worked."

Olivia stared at him, the truth settling like a stone in her stomach—Ethan was a murderer.

Guilt rose sharply in her throat as she remembered all the times she had vented to him about her lab colleagues, half-joking about how she wished they'd just disappear. Now they were gone. And she couldn't shake the feeling that, somehow, it was her fault.

"Ethan, they didn't deserve to die. I never wanted this," Olivia choked out, her voice breaking between sobs, tears falling freely. The love she felt for him was still there—undeniable—but it twisted with anger and shame. She had never imagined he would go this far, would cross so many lines, just to save her from that toxic lab.

"Olivia, you don't get it," Ethan said, his voice desperate. "You don't know what happens to you in that future."

Silence fell over the room.

From somewhere beyond the stone walls, the soft cooing of mourning doves drifted through the open doorway. Olivia's breath caught. In the quiet, something shifted—barely perceptible. A whisper of another future brushed against her, light and cold. A glimpse. A shadow of what Ethan had seen.

A future filled with tragedy.

CHAPTER 36

Future

As I walk through the sterile hallways of the inpatient psychiatric unit at Massachusetts General Hospital, I can't help but wish for gentler surroundings. Fluorescent lights cast a harsh glow on the off-white walls, draining warmth from the space, leaving it cold and clinical. I've always thought this place could try harder to develop a softer, more empathetic environment for the patients in our care. The familiar backdrop of low conversations and the occasional squeak of a gurney accompanies me—sounds I've grown used to during my years here as a psychiatry resident.

At the nurses' station, two nurses huddle together, reviewing the day's cases. One, a middle-aged woman with kind eyes and a steady smile, looks up as I approach.

"Dr. Delano," she greets me with a nod. "You're the resident on tonight?"

"Yes, ma'am," I answer, matching her smile.

"We have a new admission for you from the ER," she says.

"Oh yeah? Who's the patient?"

She glances down at the clipboard in front of her.

"Room 214. Olivia Barrett," she says, her voice gentle. "She's a young woman, late twenties. Admitted after an attempted suicide. Her landlord found her in the bathtub when her dog wouldn't stop barking." She hands me the patient file.

"How is she doing now?" I ask.

"She's physically stable, but emotionally... fragile. She hasn't said much since being transferred to the ward."

"Got it. Thanks, Theresa. I'll go introduce myself."

I find Room 214 tucked at the far end of the corridor. I take a deep breath, bracing against the familiar irritation at the unforgiving glare of the harsh lights and the sterile chill of the walls. It's always harder to reach patients who are acutely aware of just how unwelcoming this place can be. After a gentle knock, I step inside.

The room is sparse—a narrow bed against one wall, a plain wooden chair and desk by the window. Sturdy bars line the glass, an unmistakable reminder of the institutional setting.

A young woman lies on the bed, her wrists wrapped in clean bandages, her arms secured to the bedframe by padded restraints. Her hospital gown mirrors the dull gray of my scrubs beneath the white coat. Her curly brown hair spills messily around her face, her gaze fixed on the ceiling. She's still, the restraints holding her in place, though she shows no inclination to move. Her eyes, faintly glazed, suggest sedation, yet there's something else—a flatness, a quiet surrender.

"Olivia?" I ask, my voice barely above a whisper.

Her head turns slowly, and her eyes find mine—deep brown, intelligent, and guarded. Something stirs in my stomach, an unfamiliar flutter I can't quite name. She nods, her lips quivering.

"I'm Dr. Delano," I say, stepping a little closer. "I'm the doctor assigned to your case. I'm here to help."

Silence. Her stare doesn't waver, pinning me with a steady, unreadable intensity. A faint discomfort settles over me, a sensation I'm not used to. I've spoken to countless patients, but something about her unsettles me. Have I seen her before?

"Olivia, do you want to talk about what happened?" I ask, easing into the chair beside her bed.

After a long, heavy silence, she finally speaks, her voice so faint I have to lean in to hear.

"I... I just couldn't take it anymore. I didn't have a choice," Olivia whispers.

Tears pool in her eyes, and instinctively, I reach into my coat pocket and offer her a tissue—only to freeze, realizing she's still restrained to the bed. Embarrassment flares in my chest, and I fumble, the tissue clutched uselessly in my hand. Her quiet presence has me more rattled than I'd like to admit.

"Sorry," I mutter, my fingers trembling as I struggle with the keys. I unlock the restraints, and she sits up slowly, takes the tissue, and dabs at her eyes with a delicate, almost careful touch.

"You always have a choice," I tell her, trying to keep my voice steady.

Olivia scoffs, shaking her head as she offers me a sad smile.

"Yeah, sure. *Choice*," she says, bitterness lacing her voice.

I stay quiet, letting the silence do its work, giving her room to speak at her own pace. But she doesn't. Her eyes stay locked on the floor, occasionally flicking up to meet mine, then darting away. As the minutes stretch, an inexplicable pull tugs at me—an unsettling, magnetic sense of connection I can't shake. It feels irrational, inappropriate, but undeniably real.

I remind myself of my role. She's my patient—depressed, suicidal. My duty is to help, not to entertain personal feelings or exploit hers, not to mistake my concern for something more. But what is this? What is happening to me? Why is she affecting me like this?

After a prolonged silence that seems to stretch on endlessly, I clear my throat and force myself to remain steady.

"Olivia," I ask, my voice low, careful. "Have we met before?"

Olivia stays silent, shaking her head. There was something familiar about her, a nagging sense of recognition, but I can't quite place it.

"Olivia, please know you can talk whenever you're ready. I'm here to help, to support you however I can. Our treatment team will work closely with you to ensure you get the care you need."

Silence stretches between us again, a quiet that seems to press down on the room. She offers a faint, fragile smile.

"Thank you, Dr. Delano," she says, her eyes meeting mine, holding just a second longer than expected.

"One step at a time," I say. "Take your time, and when you're ready, you can share your story with me."

As I rise to leave, an inexplicable attraction to Olivia lingers, a subtle, disquieting warmth that leaves me questioning my professionalism. Stepping into the sterile, fluorescent-lit corridor, I draw a deep breath, grounding myself—reminding myself who I am here. A doctor. A psychiatry resident. Her doctor.

I lock the door to Olivia's room and force myself down the hallway, moving from patient to patient, but no matter how hard I try to focus, her face, her voice, her guarded eyes refuse to leave my mind. I can't get Olivia out of my head.

Five long days passed in the inpatient unit before Olivia broke her silence. During our one-on-one sessions, she sat across from me, staring at me, but her lips were sealed. In group therapy, she remained silent, but there was a subtle shift—she seemed to listen, absorbing the stories of the other patients. A faint, almost imperceptible glimmer of engagement. Beneath her withdrawn exterior, Olivia wasn't entirely disconnected.

Gradually, as our conversations continued, I learned about fragments of Olivia's life. She spoke of losing her mother at seventeen, and then—like a bolt of lightning—it hit me: I knew her. The memory crashed over me with a shocking intensity. Years ago, during my undergrad years volunteering at Emory in Georgia, I had met her. I had given her a single rose.

I couldn't tear my eyes away from her, couldn't bring myself to speak. Olivia continued, undeterred by my silence, her voice a steady thread. I traced the contours of her face, the unexpected connection between us settling in, sharp and undeniable.

She painted a vivid picture of her academic world, a chaotic ecosystem of ambition and betrayal. She described the lab where she studied physics, the affair between her so-called mentor and the chair of her PhD committee, the drunken plagiarist who stumbled through her research group, and the professor—clearly not the sharpest tool in the shed—who guarded her mentor for grant money bribes like a corrupt sentinel.

"Olivia, I've worked with many patients who've faced similar situations in academic settings—ethical breaches, corruption. These things, unfortunately, are more common than they should be. But what makes you believe they were directly harmful to you?" I asked, trying to keep my tone gentle.

She paused, drawing a slow, shaky breath. "The ombudsman," she began, her voice barely above a whisper. "He crossed every line imaginable. Tried to trade sexual favors for his silence. He even assaulted one of my colleagues. And when I refused... when I wouldn't give in to his demands... he exposed me. Told my corrupt PhD committee that I was planning to report them."

It was the ruthless retaliation that shattered Olivia's dreams. They didn't just strip away her chance to complete her PhD—they blacklisted her, shutting every academic door she tried to open, turning her once-bright future into a dead end. That relentless campaign against her wasn't just a setback—it was a crushing blow, one that plunged her into despair. A despair so deep it led to her suicide attempt.

I carefully documented her history, noting the sequence of betrayals and the depth of her emotional wounds. As I considered her treatment plan, I leaned toward cognitive-behavioral therapy with me, an approach that felt more promising for her recovery than relying solely on antidepressants.

While I understood antidepressants could be life-saving for many, I worried they might worsen Olivia's suicidal thoughts. More than that, I believed I was the one who could truly help her. I had known her years ago—our paths crossing again felt almost like fate.

She was on Lexapro, prescribed in the emergency room, and I hesitated to make sudden changes. But in the long run, I wanted to be the one guiding her toward healing—through therapy, not just medication.

By the eighth day of Olivia's hospitalization, something shifted. She seemed calmer, less agitated, though the shadow of her depression still lingered. But there was a subtle difference—a faint spark in her eyes, a quiet recognition that maybe, just maybe, she deserved another chance at life. Group therapy seemed to be part of it. Listening to others share their struggles seemed to make her feel less alone.

In our one-on-one sessions, I felt her warming to me. Her gaze would linger a second too long, a shy smile playing at her lips before she looked away, her cheeks flushed. It wasn't just progress—it was a connection. I had to help her, to save her from herself.

Normally, hospital protocol didn't keep inpatients from the ER for over ten days, especially when they showed signs of improvement, like Olivia. They arranged for her landlord to pick her up and help her settle back into her apartment. But during one of our final inpatient sessions in my office, I couldn't help myself—I got personally involved. I knew it was crossing a line, knew it was wrong, but the pull was becoming impossible to resist.

"Olivia, I know this is going to be a long road, but I think I can help you after you're discharged," I said, leaning forward.

"Yes, Dr. Delano. I know I have to come back twice a week for outpatient therapy," Olivia said, brushing her unruly curls out of her face.

"No, I mean... I think I can help with your career," I hesitated, then pushed forward. "My brother is a physics professor."

Her reaction was immediate—she shook her head, her expression tightening. "No. I can't risk it again. I tried, and the universe just... just kept shitting on me. You can't change things. I'm not meant to be a physicist."

275

"Olivia, just consider this—maybe it's fate that brought you here, that brought us together. Maybe it's a chance to finish your research," I tried to keep my voice steady, my hope clear, desperate to convince her.

"I don't know…" she said, her voice trailing off, her eyes fixed on the floor, her head still shaking.

"My brother's name is Eric. He's a genuinely good person, with strong ethical values. In fact, he's on the ethics committee at the university where he teaches," I said, working to control the shake in my voice. "He's got an impressive track record—published many articles, secured multiple research grants."

Olivia stayed quiet, her eyes still locked on the floor, her fingers tracing the edge of her sleeve. I couldn't tell if she was listening or just trying to escape the conversation.

"I'm sure he'd be willing to meet with you, hear your story, and discuss your research. I could set it up, and I could even go with you." My voice softened, a quiet urgency threading through my words. I needed her to say yes. I needed to save her.

"I'll think about it," Olivia said, her eyes never leaving the tiles. A small step—but it felt like a move in the right direction.

On the day of her discharge, it felt like I might have finally reached her. Tuesday morning arrived, and Olivia had carefully arranged a month's worth of outpatient sessions with me, starting as soon as Thursday. Her condition had improved, but I could still see the weight of her depression clinging to her. Yet I was confident—as long as she kept coming to see me, she wouldn't be a danger to herself.

"Thank you again, Dr. Delano, for everything," Olivia said, her eyes meeting mine as she shook my hand.

The touch lingered a heartbeat too long, a warmth that edged beyond mere professional courtesy. In her deep brown eyes, I saw the shadow of sadness that hadn't yet released her. Slowly, she withdrew her hand, her steps unhurried as she walked toward the hospital exit. I watched her climb into her landlord's truck. Just before they pulled away, her eyes met mine one last time and something sharp twisted in my chest.

I was consumed by this girl. I had to save her. She was so lost, so resigned, convinced her fate was sealed. But I could save her. I would change her fate.

CHAPTER 37

Future

I've always prided myself on maintaining composure and professionalism, a cool detachment that comes naturally in my line of work. Boundaries and ethical principles aren't just guidelines; they're essentials in my role as a training psychiatrist. But the past two weeks have been different. Now, as I stand by the window in my cramped resident's office, a knot tightens in my chest.

My office sits at the far end of the inpatient psychiatric unit, a tranquil space with walls in calming shades of cream. My desk, small but functional, anchors the room. A single bookshelf beside it is lined with my psychiatry textbooks. A comfortable armchair faces me, reserved for patients, and a discreet filing cabinet melds into the desk's side. The old-fashioned wall clock ticks steadily, each second cutting into the quiet. Through the window, I catch a view of the garden, a glimpse of greenery beyond the glass. The leaves sway gently, their shadows shifting with the breeze. Sunlight pools on the grass, tracing patterns across the manicured lawn.

Olivia was supposed to be here. My first outpatient session with her, and she isn't here. A heavy burden settles on me in her absence. I was the one who treated her after her suicide attempt, and now she's missing. Did I make the right decision to discharge her? Did she deceive me? Was I fooled by her apparent progress?

My fingers drum against the windowsill as I glance at the phone, willing it to ring—hoping it's her, apologizing for being late. But the minutes crawl by, and my pulse quickens. I can't just sit here. I grab my phone and dial her number. It rings once, twice, then straight to voicemail.

No response. My heart pounds faster, a dull, insistent pressure in my chest. I try her landlord next. After a few rings, he answers.

"Dr. Delano, what can I do for you?"

"I'm sorry to bother you. Have you seen or heard from Olivia today?"

A brief pause. "No, I haven't seen her since I left for work a few hours ago. Why?"

"She missed her appointment with me, and I'm concerned." My mind races, grasping for a rational explanation.

"She's had car trouble before—maybe she's just running late," the landlord says.

"I tried calling, but she didn't answer. I'm worried. I'm going to contact the police for a welfare check." My anxiety sharpens, and before he can respond, I hang up and dial 911.

Sitting alone in my office, I contemplate my next move. The patients here today are my responsibility—I have a duty to them. The police will handle the situation, and I should stay put. They'll call and let me know Olivia is fine. That's how this should work. But with each passing minute, my unease intensifies, the worry twisting tighter. I can't shake the image of Olivia, nor the gnawing sense that something is terribly wrong.

My fingers tremble as I grab my phone, pulling up her address on the maps app. I know I shouldn't leave, that I'm crossing a line. But my fear for her safety drowns out any concern for professional boundaries. Before I can second-guess myself, I'm already moving, rushing out of the hospital without a backward glance.

As I drive, Olivia consumes my thoughts. I'm desperate to find her, desperate to help. Her home is a two-family house on Huntsman Drive, just fifteen minutes from the hospital. The neighborhood is eerily quiet as I turn onto her street, my heart hammers against my ribs. But as I approach, flashing red and blue lights pulse against the house. My stomach drops. Dread clenches tight.

The police are already here, knocking on the doors—first the downstairs unit where the landlord lives, then the upstairs apartment, Olivia's.

I barely register parking before I'm out of the car, rushing up the stairs to join them. I knock urgently on her door, the officers beside me doing the same. A dog barks from within, sharp and insistent. But there's no answer. Panic thrums through my veins. Her car is missing from the driveway, but as I look around from the top of the stairs, something catches my eye—an old garage, half-hidden at the back of the property.

I race down the stairs toward the garage, my footsteps striking hard against the steps. The structure is old and weathered, its paint peeling, the metal door streaked with rust. I grab the handle—locked. But through the grimy window, I see her. Olivia slumped over in the driver's seat of her car, the engine still running.

A surge of terror crashes over me. "Help! Over here!" I scream, my voice raw with desperation. Frantically, I claw at the ground, searching for anything to break the window. My trembling fingers close around a rock. Without hesitation, I hurl it at the glass, and the shatter echoes through the garage like a gunshot.

The police rush over, and with a collective effort, they kick in the side door of the garage. I stumble inside, my legs weak beneath me. Olivia is unconscious, her skin ashen. She's not breathing. The deadly exhaust from the running car must have been filling the small space for hours—carbon monoxide poisoning.

A panicked scream tears from my throat as I lunge toward her, reaching for the ignition, for Olivia herself. But the officers grab me, pulling me back, their firm hands a barrier between me and my desperation. They drag me out of the garage as I struggle, helpless.

The ambulance, already on-site for the welfare check, springs into action. Paramedics rush in. One of them shouts for additional support while the others haul Olivia from the car, laying her on a gurney. CPR begins immediately—compressions, breaths—mechanical yet desperate. They wheel her out, continuing CPR even as they load her into the ambulance.

But even from where I stand, I can see it—it's too late. There's no response, no sign of life. She's been gone for hours. The ambulance speeds away, siren wailing, fading into the distance. An officer steps forward, leans into the car, and turns off the engine.

With the bright sun high in the New England sky, I sat on the dirt driveway, leaning against the garage, tears streaming down my face. The events of the past few weeks had taken their toll. Police officers brought out the contents of Olivia's car, and each item they carried seemed to magnify my grief.

On the passenger seat, they found an envelope stuffed with cash, labeled simply "Mulder." A small, heartbreaking smile tugged at my lips, even through the tears. At least she had thought about her dog in her final moments.

Beneath the envelope lay a thick three-ring binder—Olivia's research. It overflowed with pages of equations and hypotheses exploring Einstein's river of time theory. Scattered among the sheets were journal articles and notes on the work of other scientists studying altered electromagnetic fields and gravity. But streaks of red marker slashed across the pages, brutal and unforgiving. Even worse were the words scrawled in the margins—self-deprecating comments woven into her notes. Olivia had harshly criticized herself, branding her work as worthless and labeling herself as useless.

On impulse, I grabbed the binder when no one was watching and tucked it into my car. I couldn't bear the thought of others discovering her vicious self-judgment. For a few more minutes, I lingered at the scene, clinging to an irrational hope—maybe the paramedics had revived her on the way to the hospital. But deep down, I knew she was gone. I blamed myself for believing she was getting better, for missing the signs, for failing to save her.

The police called me to the station to provide a statement, but they didn't suspect me of any wrongdoing. After giving my account, I took it upon myself to arrange and finance Olivia's funeral. We couldn't locate her father, not even to inform him of her death.

The funeral took place in a modest chapel nestled within a peaceful cemetery. Only a small gathering of mourners—some friends and colleagues—came to pay their respects. Olivia's casket, a simple but elegant mahogany, held a spray of white lilies and delicate baby's breath. I had placed a portrait of a happy, smiling Olivia amidst a setting of flickering candles and flowers. The scene was both beautiful and unbearably sad. I stood at the back, struggling to hold back tears while the minister spoke gentle words of remembrance and comfort.

I never returned to my job at the hospital after the funeral. The walls of the inpatient unit felt suffocating, a constant reminder of everything I had lost. Unable to bear it, I took a leave of absence from the psychiatry residency program. My mentors had their reservations and tried, again and again, to convince me to stay.

"Ethan, are you sure about this?" Dr. Anderson, one of the senior psychiatrists, asked me. "I understand this has hit you hard, but leaving the program might not be the right move. You have a promising future in this field."

"We all lose patients, Ethan," Dr. Lindberg, another senior doctor, added, his voice calm but firm. "You're a brilliant doctor, but loss is part of our job. It's an unfortunate reality."

Despite their persistence, I couldn't stay. I had lost patients before, but Olivia's death struck me differently—an ache that refused to fade. I felt like a failure, the weight of guilt pressing down on me. I hadn't saved her, and trying to continue in the field felt like a betrayal, a hypocrisy I couldn't live with.

After leaving the program, I drifted into a monotonous routine, mostly confined to my home. Days blurred together, each one fading into the next, as I let guilt consume me. But a quiet knock on the door interrupted my isolation—a welcome disruption. It was my brother, Eric. He had always been there for me, and that hadn't changed. Like the doctors at the hospital, he tried to convince me not to abandon my residency.

"What will you do with your life now?" Eric asked.

"I don't know," I said, feeling tears welling up in my eyes.

"Maybe you should see a psychiatrist," Eric said with a faint smile.

I couldn't help but laugh at the irony of his suggestion, given my profession. A brief silence stretched between us as I considered his words.

"Maybe I'll become a physicist," I said, and I showed him Olivia's research, explaining how I had taken the notebook from her car.

Eric, a physicist himself, joined me in the living room. If anyone could make sense of Olivia's research, it was him. I watched as he flipped through her notes—complex equations and intricate diagrams covering the pages. At first, he skimmed them with an air of detached curiosity. But then, something in those dense sheets caught his attention. I saw the shift in his expression, the subtle spark of genuine interest, his scientific curiosity fully engaged.

In a hesitant voice, I asked him the unthinkable, my words coming out slowly, each one carefully measured as I gathered the courage to broach the subject.

"Could we use her research to find the supposed whirlpools in time and space—to go back and save her?" I asked, my voice quivering, a faint echo of the tremors that had once characterized Olivia's own.

"Absolutely not," Eric said. "That's sheer madness, Ethan. Maybe you really do need to see a psychiatrist."

I sighed heavily, the weight of his words pressing down on me like a ton of bricks, suffocating what little hope I had left. A sense of defeat settled over me as I grappled with the emptiness of his response.

"Look, I'll go through her notebook," Eric said as he turned to leave, "but I'm not promising anything."

And with that, he left, Olivia's notebook clutched tightly in his grasp. I stayed where I was, slumped on the couch, swallowed by darkness and silence, the weight of depression pressing down on me. But that same evening, my phone rang, and Eric's voice buzzed with excitement on the other end.

"Ethan, I might have stumbled upon a scientific breakthrough."

"What do you mean?" I asked, trying to shake off the fog of despair.

"After going through Olivia's notebook," Eric said, his eagerness unmistakable, "I uncovered a set of coordinates in Maine where the laws of gravity and electromagnetic fields are... abnormal."

"Okay...?" I said, feeling a mix of confusion and disbelief, struggling to keep up with his excitement.

"With Olivia's equations and this device I've been tinkering with," Eric said, his excitement building, "I think we might be able to manipulate those fields and witness something truly extraordinary."

"Extraordinary? Like we can save her?" I asked, a glimmer of hope surfacing as I tried to grasp his words.

"Well, no," Eric clarified, his tone shifting. "These are just theoretical concepts on paper. Time travel isn't possible, especially since the human body couldn't handle any significant changes in the surrounding environment."

"But you said something extraordinary."

"Even if it were possible—which I highly doubt," Eric said, "changing the past is impossible. Every life follows a predetermined path. You can't change what's already happened."

"But you still want to go to Maine? See something extraordinary?" I asked.

I would have done anything to save Olivia. With his device in tow, we set out on a road trip to Maine the very next day. With each passing mile, a deepening sense of purpose settled over me, even as Eric remained openly skeptical. Against all odds, I believed—desperately—that we could change the course of time. I would save Olivia.

———◆———

Eric and I have been driving to Maine for hours. The sun dips below the horizon, plunging the world into darkness. The steady hum of the tires on the asphalt becomes a constant background noise, filling the silence between us. Neither of us has spoken for a while. We had made a pit stop earlier to refuel and grab some snacks. Now, we are navigating a desolate back road, surrounded by emptiness. We're getting close to the coordinates Eric found.

After just a few minutes of driving down the barren road, our headlights catch sight of what looks like the remains of an ancient stone building. Red and pink roses cover its weathered walls. There is nothing else around, except for a small cluster of trees nearby.

As we pull up and open our car doors, countless birds perched in the trees fill the quiet surroundings with their soft cooing. It's as if the birds have been waiting for our arrival. I climb out of the car, my boots crunching on the gravel beneath my feet.

I lean closer to the wall, feeling an irresistible urge to reach out and touch one rose, but I stop myself.

"This is super weird, right?" I ask, my voice caught between excitement and disbelief.

Eric joins me, his eyes scanning our surroundings as he nods in agreement. Together, we move toward the entrance of the stone building. Strangely, there's no door, just an open passage inviting us inside. Crossing the threshold, we're met with air dense with the scent of aged wood and the lingering fragrance of roses. The room is bare, except for an ancient oak table standing against one wall.

As we move further into the room, a wave of dizziness washes over me, and my vision blurs. A quick glance at Eric confirms he's experiencing the same unsettling disorientation. But he stays calm, reaching into his bag and pulling out two small devices. The first is an electromagnetic field radiation detector—an EMF meter. The second is the prototype he developed, based on Olivia's research. He entered her equations into the device and made a few alterations of his own. He believes this device has the potential to manipulate electromagnetic fields and, if we're in an area tied to one of Einstein's supposed whirlpools, it might even affect the fabric of time.

With trembling hands, Eric activates the EMF meter. The screen flickers to life, displaying a digital readout of numbers.

"Whoa," Eric says, studying the readings. "This number is off the charts."

"What do you mean?" I ask, leaning closer.

"The electromagnetic fields here are extremely abnormal," he says, a hint of nervousness slipping into his voice. "I'm not sure what will happen when I turn on my prototype."

"Are you afraid to try it? You can go outside, and I'll turn it on. I have to try it," I say, determination tightening in my chest.

"No," he says, meeting my eyes. "We'll do it together."

Eric stands still for a few minutes, meticulously recording the EMF readings in his pocket notebook. He adjusts a few dials on his prototype, then looks up at me, his hand hovering over the on/off switch. I meet his gaze and nod, signaling that I'm ready—whatever happens next.

With a determined expression, Eric flips the switch, and the room transforms instantly. The air seems to thicken, a subtle, swirling blur of colors rippling across the room. My earlier dizziness disappears, replaced by an inexplicable sense of strangeness—something I can't quite name.

The quiet outside shatters. A flurry of wings erupts as the birds take flight, their chaotic, frenzied rustling filling the air as they scatter into the sky.

Without a moment's hesitation, we rush out of the ancient building. The lingering scent of roses clings to the cool night air, mingling with the fading calls of the birds as their wings slice through the darkness. We emerge into the open and immediately sense something is wrong. The atmosphere around us shimmers with an indefinable energy.

Already airborne, the flock sweeps away from the building before wheeling around, executing a graceful turn and circling back toward us. As they draw closer, their distinctive cooing becomes unmistakable—mourning doves, their calls haunting the night.

My attention locks onto an area just beyond the structure, where the air looks thicker, almost vibrating with an unusual resonance. The birds seem instinctively drawn to it. I point it out to Eric, and together, we walk toward the strange, shimmering space.

As we draw closer, another wave of dizziness sweeps over me, my attention fixed on the birds as they soar into the denser, shimmering section of the air. I reach out, trying to touch it, but there's nothing there—just empty space. The air remains the same, intangible and impossible to grasp.

Eric and I press forward, our pace steady, but the thickened patch of air seems to slip away from us, drifting further and further ahead. It's like we're caught in a maddening game of cat and mouse, a sense of futility growing with each step. I can't shake the feeling that we may never reach it.

Then, without warning—like a switch being flipped—everything snaps back into sharp focus. The shimmering, the blurriness, the thickened air—all of it vanishes in an instant. I glance around, realizing that we've somehow wandered a little farther down the desolate road. The birds are returning, settling back into the small cluster of trees beside the building.

I shake my head, trying to clear the lingering disorientation. Beside me, Eric stands motionless, staring down at the EMF meter and his prototype, his expression clouded with disappointment.

"The readings on the EMF meter are back to normal," Eric says, his shoulders sagging.

"You saw it too, right?" I ask.

He nods. "At first, I thought my prototype had triggered something. But now I'm wondering if our reactions were just a natural response to the electromagnetic field."

We make our way back to the car in silence. I feel utterly devastated. My hopes had soared, convinced that with Olivia's research, we could rewrite history. But now that hope feels like smoke slipping through my fingers.

Eric packs away his devices, then places a reassuring hand on my shoulder, trying to offer some comfort. "We did everything we could," he says, but his words feel hollow.

"Remember, these were just theories," Eric reminds me. "We found nothing tangible, couldn't prove anything definitively. But it was worth a shot."

I pause, letting his words sink in. My eyes sweep across our surroundings, searching for any lingering signs of something unusual. But everything looks normal—no trace of the strange shimmering in the air.

"We should start heading back now. We can find a motel for the night, grab a bite to eat," Eric says, already making his way to the car.

I slide into the passenger seat, sinking into the silence. My heart feels unbearably heavy, and I stare out the window, watching the landscape blur by as we leave the old stone building behind. Deep down, I know our goal was always a long shot. But the guilt over losing Olivia still gnaws at me, twisting into an irrational hope that somehow we could have done the impossible.

Soon, we come across a run-down motel beside an old-fashioned diner with shiny chrome accents along its exterior. A neon sign reads "Diner," with an image of a plate and silverware behind the words.

We walk inside and take seats at the worn counter, both of us feeling the weight of an empty stomach after a day without food. We place our orders—coffee to clear our minds and a meal to quiet our hunger. Then we just sit there, lost in contemplative silence.

Eric's eyes widen. He reaches for an abandoned newspaper lying on the counter, his fingers trembling. He stares at the headline, a jolt of recognition flashing across his face. The headline is about the Boston Marathon Bombing.

"Ethan, that happened in 2013—over ten years ago," Eric says, his voice trembling as he points to the newspaper.

I stare down at the headline, then glance around the diner's interior. Realization claws at me, a cold rush of disbelief. I wave the waitress over, trying to keep my voice steady, even managing a warm, dimpled smile.

"Excuse me, miss," I begin politely. "We've been on a road trip for days, and I think we've lost track of time. What's today's date?"

"April 17th," she says, casually refilling my coffee cup.

"And the year?" I ask, my pulse racing.

"2013," she answers, frowning. "You haven't been in the car for years, have you?" She moves down the counter, refilling other patrons' cups without looking back.

"Holy shit," I whisper.

CHAPTER 38

"You expect me to believe you've traveled through time?" Rachel's voice was steady, her aim unwavering as the gun remained trained on Ethan's chest.

Ethan sighed, frustration sharpening his tone. "Yes, I've done it countless times. I've already explained."

The tension in the room thickened. Olivia edged closer, closing the gap between herself and Ethan. He had already stepped back, acutely aware of the gun pointed at him. His gaze darted nervously to the small detonator on the table. Rachel retreated, inching toward the open door, her glare lingering on Olivia.

Olivia moved further in, her position nearly between Rachel and Ethan, her shadow falling over the professor's lifeless body sprawled across the floor.

"That doesn't make any sense, Ethan. Time travel? It's not real," Rachel said, her usual caution slipping. Olivia recognized the look—Rachel saw Ethan as unhinged, yet she handled him with none of the care she'd shown the professor.

"I've ridden this whirlpool so many times," Ethan said, leaning forward, urgency edging his voice. "It flows both ways, you know? I go back, change events, jump forward, then back again—fixing things."

"Ethan, please, stop." Olivia's voice wavered, her worry clear. "You're lucky to be alive. Messing with electromagnetic fields, trying to alter the past—it's reckless." She shook her head, slow and steady. "You could destroy lives, Ethan. You could end the world."

Ethan stood silent, his eyes locked on Olivia. After a slow, steady breath, he shook his head with quiet resolve. "No, Olivia. You're wrong. This time will be different. This will save you."

"We've experienced time slips and time displacement back home in Boston," Olivia said, urgency threading through her voice. "But here, it's worse. We couldn't escape from that town. We drove in circles, lost time, experienced black outs. You're tearing holes in space-time, Ethan. You're endangering lives—people you've never even met."

Rachel shot Olivia a bewildered look—her disbelief clear. Olivia could almost feel Rachel's judgment, the same as she'd shown the professor now directed at Ethan. But there was something else in Rachel's glare—disdain, as if she couldn't grasp why Olivia would take Ethan's wild claims seriously.

"I've never seen anything like that," Ethan said, frustration tightening his voice. "Except for those damn birds that keep following me."

"Those birds rely on electromagnetic fields for navigation, Ethan," Olivia said, a slight tremor betraying her attempt to stay calm. She tried to steady herself, but the faint shake in her voice and the tension in her body gave her away.

"It's fine, Olivia," Ethan said as he rolled his eyes, sighing, his fingers tapping impatiently near the detonator. "I'll keep traveling back—reliving the past over and over until I save you. I don't care about the consequences for the universe, the town, or even myself."

"Ethan, come on. Let's go out to the car. You can tell us all about your travels there," Rachel said, trying to steer everyone away from the explosives.

But Ethan ignored her, leaning against the table, his hand hovering dangerously close to the detonator. His gaze drifted to the closed door at the back of the room, his focus slipping somewhere beyond the present.

"No. It doesn't happen that way," he said, almost to himself. "But this time... this time feels different. I think I've changed things."

"You can't change anything." Olivia's voice trembled, her eyes welling with tears. She begged him to understand, her gaze pleading silently.

"That's what Eric always said. But I do make changes. Every time, something changes."

"Yeah, little things. But the future is already determined. You can't change anything substantial, can you?" Olivia's voice broke, tears now streaking down her cheeks.

Silence settled over the room, thick and heavy. Olivia stepped closer, shortening the space between herself and Ethan until she stood within arm's reach. She could see the unyielding resolve etched in his expression. She wasn't sure she could change his mind.

"Not true. We fall in love," Ethan said, a bittersweet smile touching his lips as he stared at Olivia.

"Ethan, you tricked me into falling for you. You knew what I wanted, because in the future, you were my therapist."

"No. We've always been in love," Ethan said, his eyes never leaving hers. Slowly, his fingers closed around the detonator on the table.

Rachel's body tensed, her voice sharp. "Drop the detonator, Ethan! Don't make me shoot you! I thought you wanted to save Olivia?"

"I will save her. Olivia, please," Ethan pleaded.

"Ethan..." Rachel began, but Olivia stepped forward, cutting her off.

"It's alright. Everything's alright," Olivia said, raising a hand to silence Rachel. She moved directly in front of Ethan, blocking Rachel's line of sight.

"Olivia, we all need to go outside," Rachel said through clenched teeth, her patience fraying.

Olivia stood firm and gently clasped Ethan's wrists. Her hands traced a slow, deliberate path up his arms, settling on his shoulders before she pulled him into a tight embrace.

"You did change things," she said, her voice unsteady as she struggled against her tears. "I do love you."

In that charged moment, Olivia leaned in, her lips meeting his—tentative at first, then deepening with growing intensity. Her fingers traced a slow path down his arms as they kissed, their breaths mingling. When Ethan pulled back, his eyes remained closed, a visible calm settling over him.

"This has never happened before," he said, a quiet awe in his voice. "I love you, Olivia. So much. I told you I changed it this time."

"I know," she whispered, her hands still continuing their descent down his arms. "It's alright, Rachel. You can go. Ethan and I will slip out the back."

Ethan stood motionless, eyes closed, a calm serenity washing over him, wholly absorbed in Olivia. Rachel hesitated, the urgency of the situation gnawing at her, her gaze darting between them. Olivia cast a brief, pleading glance over her shoulder, a silent message meant only for Rachel.

Her grip tightened on Ethan's hands. Her thumb positioned over the bright red button on the detonator.

"Olivia..." Rachel's voice faltered, but her words died on her lips.

Olivia pressed the button.

———————————————❖———————————————

Realization struck Rachel in a rush of clarity. Paralyzed by the sheer intensity of the situation, she hadn't grasped Olivia's intentions until it was too late.

Olivia had positioned herself squarely between Rachel and Ethan, a living barrier that cut off any chance of Rachel intervening without hurting her. Just before Olivia pressed the button, their eyes met—a fleeting, wordless exchange. But Rachel's mind was still racing, tangled in confusion, her body frozen.

Then instinct took over. Adrenaline surged, and she threw herself toward the open door. The milliseconds stretched unbearably as a deafening explosion ripped through the stone structure just as she hurled herself into the air.

As Rachel dove through the doorway, searing heat lashed at her back. Flames caught the fabric of her jacket. Instinctively, she hit the ground, rolling violently, desperate to smother the fire. Her uneven, erratic crawl carried her farther from the blazing wreckage, each breath thick with acrid smoke.

Her ears rang, the world reduced to muffled noise and frantic motion. Ash and debris swirled, her vision a disorienting blur. But she kept crawling, her body propelled by pure survival.

When she felt distant enough from the inferno, Rachel rolled onto her back, propping herself up on shaking elbows. What she saw was surreal, like a distorted mirage in the explosion's aftermath. Shimmering, ethereal swirls of color danced in the air, shifting like fractured light around the remains of the once-solid stone structure. She blinked, dazed, struggling to make sense of the otherworldly sight.

The wind howled around her, relentless, tearing through the smoke and swirling colors. Faint cooing echoed from unseen birds, their cries lost within the shifting chaos. Then, just as suddenly as it had begun, the phenomenon vanished—colors fading, smoke thinning—leaving only a desolate expanse of embers. Where there had once been an old stone building surrounded by scattered trees, nothing remained but smoldering emptiness.

Rachel slowly surveyed the scene, a tight, sinking feeling coiling in her chest. Only two cars remained—hers and Brittney's. Brittney's body was still inside. No trace of the building's ruins. No sign of anyone else. Just glowing cinders.

The distant wail of sirens shattered the silence as she struggled to her feet. Police cars, ambulances, and fire trucks raced down the snowy road, their lights painting the gray landscape in red and blue flashes. She had thought escape might be impossible—her phone had no signal, and neither car would start. But relief washed over her at the sound of the approaching sirens.

Mitchell had contacted the Portland office when he couldn't reach Rachel. Worried for her safety, he'd driven up to Maine, following the coordinates they'd found in Brittney's apartment. Rachel was grateful she'd told him where she was going, even if she'd left without permission.

Disoriented and covered in ash, Rachel struggled to find her voice. "It's all gone," she said, her eyes fixed on the empty, scorched landscape.

"What's gone?" Mitchell asked, his eyes sweeping over the barren scene.

"Everything." Her voice was thick with disbelief. "The building, Professor Eric J. Neil, Ethan, Olivia… We were all inside when Olivia blew it up. It's all gone."

Her words hung in the air, heavy and unreal. Mitchell's shock reflected her own as he continued to take in the devastation. Paramedics, their faces grim, carefully removed Brittney's lifeless body from her car. Mitchell turned to Rachel, his eyes silently searching for answers.

"Brittney Turner," Rachel said. "She was already dead when we got here."

Nearby, firefighters sifted through the charred remains, searching for any trace of the collapsed structure or its occupants. But their efforts turned up nothing.

After tending to Brittney, the paramedics turned to Rachel. Despite her protests, Mitchell insisted she go to the nearest hospital for a full evaluation. As they carefully guided her toward the waiting ambulance, Rachel's attention remained fixed on the desolate scene, dread tightening around her thoughts.

She climbed reluctantly into the ambulance, her mind still reeling. Mitchell followed, staying close. Once inside, Rachel settled onto a stretcher, and Mitchell draped a blanket over her shoulders. One paramedic checked her vitals while another prepared an IV.

Mitchell sat beside her, a quiet, steady presence. Rachel struggled to piece together what had happened. A massive, burly paramedic, who seemed to possess years of experience, surprised her with a soft, comforting voice.

"We're taking you to the hospital to make sure you're okay," the paramedic said gently. "Can you tell me your name and the date?"

Rachel nodded slowly, her voice unsteady. "Rachel Quinn. I'm not sure of the date. I... I think it's February 9th?"

"Good. You're doing great, Rachel," the paramedic said with an encouraging smile.

Rachel leaned back against the stretcher's cushion, her eyes drifting shut as the ambulance sped toward the hospital. Mitchell reached over, his hand finding hers, his grip firm and reassuring.

"How you holding up, kiddo?" Mitchell asked.

"I... I don't know. I can't make sense of what happened."

Rachel recounted everything to Mitchell—how Professor Eric J. Neil had rigged the building to explode, how she'd been forced to shoot him, Ethan's arrival with his impossible stories, and finally, how Olivia had pressed the button. The explosion. The sudden nothingness. Her memories swirled, disjointed and fragmented. What the fuck was going on?

Mitchell listened without interrupting, absorbing every word. But suddenly, Rachel's pulse quickened. Panic flared, and she tried to sit up.

"Where are we? Can we get away?" she asked, her voice rising.

"Calm down, Rachel. We're on our way to the hospital. You're safe now," Mitchell assured her, his grip on her hand steady.

"No, I don't think we can leave," she said, trying to lean forward, straining to look out of the windshield.

The burly paramedic gently but firmly eased her back onto the stretcher, speaking in his uncharacteristically soft voice.

"It's okay, Rachel. We're off the back road now. We're on the highway. Just a few more minutes to the hospital."

Rachel took a slow, deep breath, her body sinking into the steady rhythm of the ambulance as it pressed toward the hospital. Exhaustion washed over her—bone-deep, both physical and emotional. But fear lingered beneath it, an icy knot in her chest. The last time she'd blacked out, she'd woken up at the stone building with the roses.

She tried to fight it, forcing her eyes to stay open, but the weight was too much. With one last look at Mitchell, her eyelids fluttered, then closed—overwhelmed, unable to fight it any longer. The relentless tension gave way to darkness. The sounds of the ambulance, the paramedics' hushed voices, and the pulsing anxiety all melted away as she slipped into the depths of unconsciousness.

CHAPTER 39

The FBI combed through the aftermath of the explosion, their trained eyes sweeping every inch of the scorched ground. But despite their exhaustive search, they found nothing. Not a shard of debris from the old stone building. Not a splinter of the sturdy wooden table that had once stood within. Even the rose bushes had vanished without a trace.

The agents scoured the area, hunting for any sign of explosives or the suspects Rachel had described—Professor Eric J. Neil, Ethan, and Olivia. But there was no evidence of the pipe bombs, no trace of a detonator. No bodies, no bones, not even teeth. It was as if no one else had ever been there.

Everything was gone. Even the birds that had once circled overhead were nowhere to be seen. Only a solitary tree remained, its twisted branches reaching toward the gray sky.

The FBI meticulously searched Ethan's rented room in Springfield and Olivia's apartment in Boston, leaving no drawer unopened, no corner unchecked. But there was nothing. They also swept through Dr. Eric J. Elliot's apartment in Worcester—or was it Eric J. Neil? Or maybe Eric J. Delano? Regardless of the name, the result was the same: nothing.

Rachel recovered quickly from the explosion—but what she saw still left her shaken. What had she really witnessed? How could an entire building just disappear like that? And where were the bodies?

Reluctantly, she complied with the FBI's insistence on seeing the department psychologist to assess her readiness to return to duty. The psychologist was clear—she wasn't even close to being ready for fieldwork. But if her career was on hold, what was she supposed to do?

"Spend more time with your family. Your twins," the psychologist said.

She considered it, but her thoughts kept drifting back to Olivia.

Rachel had asked about Olivia's dog during the FBI's search of her apartment. They told her the dog was still there, with the landlord stopping by to feed him. But the landlord wasn't thrilled about it, describing the dog as a "little menace." The idea of the dog essentially living alone didn't sit right with Rachel, so she decided to take him in herself. She remembered the dog as grumpy and prone to nip, but Olivia had once joked that he didn't have any teeth left anyway.

A sense of obligation to Olivia lingered, a thread connecting Rachel to a mystery she couldn't solve. The psychologist had even said that taking care of the dog could be a positive step in her healing process—maybe even a step toward returning to duty with the FBI.

After another therapy session, Rachel swung by Olivia's apartment to get the dog. She'd called the landlord, but he hadn't answered. Undeterred, she parked in the driveway, noticing the absence of any other cars. She made her way around the house and climbed the back stairs to Olivia's apartment.

Rachel reached out and knocked on the door. A brief hesitation followed—why knock when she knew Olivia wasn't there? Still, she leaned in, pressing her ear against the door, listening for the familiar bark of Olivia's dog. Instead, faint strains of music seeped through the cracks, catching her attention.

She knocked again, louder this time, calling out the landlord's name, half-expecting a response. Maybe he was inside, cleaning out the apartment or handling maintenance. But the only reply was the steady, muffled music.

Rachel's FBI training had left her more than capable of handling locked doors. She retrieved her lock-picking tools from her pocket and set to work. It took longer than she expected, but soon enough, the lock clicked, and she cautiously pushed the door open.

"Hello? It's Agent Rachel Quinn!" she called, her voice echoing through the empty apartment.

There was no response—only the music, growing louder, drifting from somewhere deeper in the apartment. Probably the bedroom. Rachel stepped through the kitchen and living room, her gaze sweeping over the unusually clean space. Gone were the textbooks, papers, and scattered research materials that had once cluttered every surface. Everything was neatly arranged, almost sterile.

Pushing open the bedroom door, she found Mulder—Olivia's grumpy terrier—stretched out comfortably across the bed, as though he owned the place. He barely spared her a glance, his previous bark and growl replaced by lazy indifference.

The soft melody that had drawn her attention flowed from an open laptop on the desk in the corner. Rachel recognized the tune, though the name escaped her. The lyrics whispered from the speakers, stirring a strange sense of familiarity she couldn't quite place.

Rachel knew better than to tamper with electronic devices, but she couldn't shake her doubts about the thoroughness of the FBI investigation. Had they missed the laptop? Or was someone else deliberately playing this song? Maybe the landlord had left it on by mistake while cleaning.

As the song's last notes trailed off, it immediately restarted—looping endlessly. Rachel noted the detail, deciding to ask Mitchell about it later. For now, her focus was on the immediate task: convincing Mulder to come with her.

Spotting Olivia's dog leash on the bedside table, she grabbed it and approached Mulder, her voice adopting a sugary, coaxing tone. But the terrier responded with a low growl, his dark eyes fixed warily on her.

Unfazed and determined, Rachel reached to clip the leash onto his collar, only to recoil as Mulder snapped at her with a menacing bark.

Startled, Rachel stepped back, uncertainty knotting in her chest. Should she just leave the dog behind? No. She couldn't just walk away—not when she felt she owed it to Olivia.

Rachel went into the bathroom and noticed a towel hanging by the shower. Grabbing it, she returned to Mulder. With a quick toss, she draped the towel over him, then tried to lift him. But the terrier twisted and thrashed beneath the fabric, growling and snapping. Realizing she couldn't keep hold of him, Rachel carefully lowered him down to the floor before she accidentally dropped him.

Still wrestling to secure the leash around his collar, her attention shifted. From beneath the bed, a well-worn three-ring binder peeked out, its edge just visible.

As the song looped again from the laptop speakers, a spark of recognition struck her—Pink Floyd. "Your Possible Pasts." The familiar melody pulled at her memory, taking her back to the road trip to Maine. Olivia had mentioned how Ethan's obsession with the band had rubbed off on her, shaping her own taste in music.

With cautious fingers, Rachel slid the binder from its hiding place. An envelope, with her name scrawled across it, was taped to the front. She hesitated. Should she open it? Should she involve the FBI? A surge of anger flared—how had they missed this during their search? And yet they had sidelined *her* from fieldwork.

Carefully, she opened the envelope, pushing aside her frustration. Inside was a card featuring an hourglass on the cover. Her breath caught as she read the message within:

Do you still think you have the choice to change your fate, Rachel?

Stunned, Rachel's mind raced. Who had left this for her? How had they done it? She'd seen them die—watched them vanish. Had the FBI truly missed this, or had someone placed it here afterward? Doubt clawed at her, echoing the psychologist's warnings about her mental state. Was she losing her grip? Maybe she wasn't fit for field duty after all, especially after this case.

Rachel flipped open the worn binder. Page after page listed coordinates spanning the country—Maine, Virginia, Louisiana, Wyoming—dozens of states, including a nearby location in Woonsocket, Rhode Island. Each entry detailed the city and state, accompanied by complex equations she couldn't begin to decipher.

Her fingers trembled as she turned the pages, and suddenly, she froze. Photographs were arranged alongside the coordinates—each one showing stone walls or buildings, all covered in climbing roses of various colors. A shock rippled through her, tightening her chest, her breath catching, a wave of nausea threatening to rise.

No. This couldn't be real. Someone must have doctored these photos, making them look different from the building she'd watched explode and disappear in Maine. But how had this binder remained hidden during the FBI's search of Olivia's apartment?

She wanted to call Mitchell, to demand how they could have missed such crucial evidence. But another thought gnawed at her—Woonsocket, Rhode Island. It was close. Less than an hour's drive, especially with the way she drove.

Determined, Rachel made up her mind. With steady hands, she finally managed to secure Mulder's leash, a small victory. To her surprise, he grudgingly complied, walking beside her to the car. She lifted him into the front seat, ignoring his grumbles and low growls. Despite his protests, a sense of relief washed over her as she shut the door behind him.

Sliding behind the wheel, Rachel paused, her fingers gripping the leather-wrapped rim. Apprehension tightened around her thoughts. Memories of the stone wall covered in roses rushed back, vivid and unsettling. But she forced them aside, dismissing them as tricks of her imagination—a conclusion the department psychologist had reinforced. Years of trauma exposure at the FBI, they'd told her, could easily warp perceptions.

Still, caution won out. Rachel tapped out a quick text to Mitchell, letting him know she was making an impromptu trip to Woonsocket, Rhode Island, with Olivia's dog in tow. She assured him everything was fine and promised to update him on her way back. Now she was covered. If Mitchell didn't hear from her, she knew he'd come looking.

Glancing over, she saw Mulder curled up on the front seat, his head resting on the cushion, watching her with a mix of curiosity and quiet judgment.

Rachel didn't waste any time. Backing out of the driveway, she eased onto the road, her foot pressing a bit harder on the accelerator. Within minutes, she merged onto the Mass Pike, heading south without a second thought.

───────◆───────

Rachel's trip to Woonsocket, Rhode Island, passed in a blur, a mix of anxious anticipation and a nagging sense of dread. With each passing mile, memories of Maine replayed in her mind—endlessly driving past that same diner, lost in a loop. She tried steadying her breathing, but the tightness in her chest refused to ease.

She glanced at Mulder, curled up in the passenger seat, blissfully asleep. She envied his obliviousness.

Following the coordinates, the scenery shifted, the highway giving way to the desolate countryside. When she arrived in Woonsocket, the GPS led her down winding dirt roads, flanked by snow-capped fields and skeletal trees. Her tires crunched over frostbitten ground, the empty, frozen landscape pressing against her nerves, stirring echoes of what had happened in Maine.

And then she saw it. The old stone building loomed against the winter landscape, its weathered exterior stark and cold. It looked eerily like the one in Maine—an abandoned church or a forgotten one-room schoolhouse. Nearby, a cluster of trees swayed in the frigid breeze, their bare branches stirring with the soft cooing of mourning doves.

Rachel parked, stepping onto the frozen ground. Her boots crunched against the snow, her breath misting in the icy air. Mulder remained undisturbed, curled in a peaceful slumber on the front seat.

As Rachel approached the decaying stone building, she saw climbing roses snaking along its walls—white ones, unlike the red and pink blooms she remembered from Maine. Reaching out, she gently brushed the delicate petals.

A flicker of movement tugged at her peripheral vision. Her heart jolted, pounding against her ribs. Rachel turned sharply—only to find him standing there.

Ethan's dark-brown hair hung long and tangled, a wild, un-kempt mass whipped by the wind. His scruffy beard had grown into a thick, untamed mess, neglected and uneven. The sharp angles of his jawline had softened, fatigue etched into every line of his face.

"Hello, Rachel," Ethan greeted her, his voice slow and sad. He tried to smile, but the familiar dimples were gone—or perhaps they had faded along with everything else about him.

Rachel's hand darted toward her holster, muscle memory reaching for her FBI-issued gun. But her fingers grasped only empty air, the cold realization settling over her: she wasn't on duty, and she wasn't armed. Heat rushed to her cheeks, a flush of embarrassment tightening her chest as she withdrew her hand.

"I'm glad you came," Ethan said.

Rachel hesitated, studying him. Ethan's posture had changed—slouched, hunched, every movement labored, as though even standing had become a struggle. His eyes were dull and heavy-lidded, dark circles beneath them, as if staying awake required immense effort.

"How are you here? I watched you die in Maine," Rachel said.

"I've tried so many times," Ethan's voice cracked, raw with emotion. "So many times. I can't save Olivia. She's always there when I go back, but no matter what I do... she always dies."

His words hung between them, heavy with despair, the weight of endless failure pressing down on him, his desperation teetering on the edge of madness.

"Ethan, please... come with me. Stop hurting yourself," Rachel said.

"I need your help," he pleaded, a wild light in his eyes. "How can I save her? What should we do?"

"Just get in the car with me," Rachel said, her voice firm but gentle. "Maybe my doctor can help you."

"Rachel, we can go back—both of us. We can save Olivia. You can help save her," Ethan said, his voice rising, his movements growing frantic. His eyes darted around, scanning the area as though expecting threats to emerge from the shadows.

Despite his unraveling composure, Rachel caught a hint of resilience buried in his tired eyes, a stubborn refusal to surrender beneath the crushing weight of his failures.

"No, Ethan. Olivia's gone. I don't think you can save her. I think you need help," Rachel said, taking a step closer to him.

Ethan's face flushed red with anger, his hands trembling. Tears threatened, but he fought them back, his voice fierce and strained as he shouted, "I will save her!"

Ethan's hand shot into his pocket, pulling out a small device. He pressed a button before Rachel could react. On pure reflex, she dropped to the ground, bracing for an explosion, her mind screaming *detonator.*

But there was no blast. Instead, swirling colors erupted around her, twisting through the air in violent gusts, a surreal, chaotic storm.

Ethan sprang into motion, darting around the corner of the crumbling stone building. Rachel remained crouched, frozen by the distorted, swirling world, her mind reeling.

"Stop, Ethan!" she cried out, her voice swallowed by the wind. She couldn't see him—couldn't hear him.

Despite the wild, whipping gusts of color, Rachel struggled to her feet and stumbled toward the building's corner. But the swirling storm pushed back, turning every step into a battle.

Then, just as before, the chaos vanished as suddenly as it had begun. Silence and stillness settled around her, a heavy, un-natural calm.

With the whirling storm gone, Rachel could move freely, unhindered by any strange forces. She searched tirelessly, circling the weathered building, peering through the door, and scanning the empty surroundings. But Ethan had disappeared—slipped away again, chasing his hopeless quest to save Olivia, like a gam-bler taking one last desperate spin of the wheel.

Rachel had always believed in free will. But now, she ques-tioned herself. Did she truly have any control? Was everything predetermined—an inescapable twist of fate? Would Ethan's relentless attempts to rewrite the past eventually erase her from existence? And would it be because she refused to help him save Olivia?

A chill settled over her. Maybe there was nothing she could do—maybe even her helplessness was part of a predetermined plan she couldn't escape.

Rachel finally turned away, walking slowly back to the car where Mulder waited, his grumpy eyes barely lifting to acknowledge her. She tried to accept the truth—she couldn't catch Ethan. She found herself trapped in the same maddening cycle that had consumed the last ten years.

As she settled behind the wheel, a bleak understanding gripped her. This pursuit of Ethan would never truly end. As long as Ethan didn't erase this version of her, she would keep chasing him, just as she had spent a decade chasing his brother.

It was a fate she could neither control nor change, a burden tethered to Ethan, shaping every breath of her existence. The engine roared to life, its steady hum blending with the dull ache of resignation in her chest.

As she pulled away, the road stretched endlessly before her, a grim reflection of the never-ending pursuit waiting ahead. And Rachel understood, with a hollow certainty, that no matter how hard she fought, nothing would ever change.

ACKNOWLEDGEMENTS

It turns out that showing up to write every day really does work—thanks to the habit-building advice that got me started. Thanks as well to those who offered encouragement and guidance in the early stages—especially Amanda Reynolds, whose coaching sessions gave me a few much-needed nudges forward.

Huge thanks to Jericho Writers, and especially to Richard Blandford, whose thoughtful, thorough, clear-eyed, and generous manuscript assessment helped bring this story into sharper focus and made it a stronger novel.

To my dad—thank you for always asking if I was still writing, for cheering me on day after day, and for believing I would finish. I miss you more than words can say.

ABOUT THE AUTHOR

Lynn M. Kristopher writes genre-bending thrillers that explore obsession, identity, and the eerie space between what is and what could be. Her debut novel, *Fixed Point*, blends psychological suspense with speculative twists, challenging the boundaries of fate and free will.

With layered characters, mounting tension, and a taste for the uncanny, Kristopher's work lingers long after the final page. When she's not writing, she's usually found chasing strange questions, hoarding notebooks, or rewatching *The X-Files* in the shadowy corners of Central Florida—far from the beachgoers and sunshine.

Connect with Lynn:

Website: www.lynnmkristopher.com

Facebook: facebook.com/profile.php?id=61576516245566

Instagram: https://www.instagram.com/lynnm.kristopher

Subscribe for bonus stories and book updates:
https://lynn-m-kristopher.kit.com/6d003e9d3b

ALSO BY LYNN M. KRISTOPHER

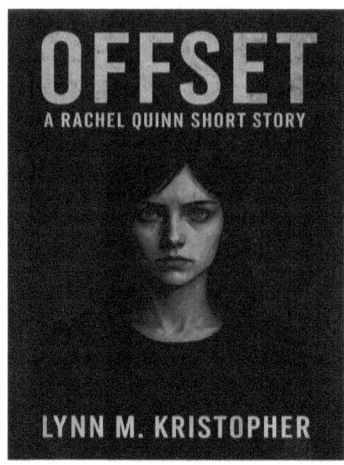

OFFSET: A RACHEL QUINN SHORT STORY

Read the chilling prequel to Fixed Point.

Sixteen-year-old Rachel Quinn just wants to disappear for the summer. Keep her head down. Stay unnoticed. But then she sees him. Same man. Same café. Same time.

Every. Single. Day.

When she takes his usual seat, the world shifts—just slightly. A memory misplaced. A moment misaligned. Reality is cracking at the edges.

And Rachel is the only one who sees it.

Get it FREE at www.lynnmkristopher.com

Coming Soon: *The Conference Conundrum*

Rachel Quinn returns in a speculative crime thriller set at a veterinary conference, where unexplained deaths and strange phenomena hint at something far more unsettling.

www.ingramcontent.com/pod-product-compliance
Lightning Source LLC
Chambersburg PA
CBHW050010120726
47903CB00006B/1712